KING
OF
Devon

Book 4 of the Kings of the Castle Series

Book 1 is the Introduction

Books 2-9 are standalones

Naleighna Kai

Macro Publishing Group
Chicago, Illinois

King of Devon by Naleighna Kai Copyright ©2019
ISBN: [Ebook] 978-1-7331782-2-8
ISBN: [Trade Paperback] 978-1-7331782-3-5

Macro Publishing Group
1507 E. 53rd Street, #858
Chicago, IL 60615

Cover Designed by: J.L Woodson: www.woodsoncreativestudio.com
Interior Designed by: Lissa Woodson: www.naleighnakai.com
Editor: Lissa Woodson: www.naleighnakai.com

KING

OF

Devon

Book 4 of the Kings of the Castle Series

Book 1 is the Introduction

Books 2-9 are standalones

Naleighna Kai

◆ DEDICATION ◆

Jean Woodson, Eric Harold Spears, LaKecia Janise Woodson, Mildred E. Williams, Anthony Johnson, Tanishia Pearson Jones, Priscilla Jackson.

♦ ACKNOWLEDGEMENTS ♦

All praises to the Creator for all lessons and blessings.

Sesvalah, Debra J. Mitchell, J. L. Woodson (for the awesome cover design for King of Devon and the entire series), Kelly Peterson, Bobby Kim, LaVerne Thomspon, Kassanna Dwight, Olivia Gaines, Vikkas Bhardwaj, Betty Clawson, Amanda McCoy, Christine Pauls, Ellen Kiley Goeckler, the Kings of the Castle Ambassadors, Members of Naleighna Kai's Literary Cafe, the member of NK Tribe Called Success: J. D. Mason, Terri Ann Johnson, Anita L. Roseboro, Siera Kay, Michelle D. Rayford, Shanna Harper, Shakir Rashaan, Pat G'Orge-Walker, Siera London, Mo Sytsma, and my fellow KOC writing queens: J. L. Campbel, Janice Allen, Karen Bradley, Lisa Watson, London St. Charles, MarZe Scott, martha Kennerson, and S. L. Jennings.

One Love,

Naleighna Kai

CHAPTER 1

"What do you mean she's in labor? Jai gripped the edge of the desk, with the phone pressed to his ear. "That's … well, that's impossible."

His heart slammed in his chest when Kelly Peterson didn't retract her statement.

Everything was happening much faster than he expected. A patient, who fell into a coma after a tragic car accident, had been in his health center for a year. Her circumstances took a downward and unfortunate turn because she had not been pregnant when she arrived. He, along with all of his male employees, were now under intense investigation. Didn't help matters any that almost all of the employees were ex-felons who were aiming for a second chance in life. Even worse, his holistic practices at Chetan had drawn the ire of the medical industry because of the substantial success rate. The Health Bureau had been trying to find any reason to shut him down. Temple Devaughn's newborn baby would provide a direct avenue for that to happen.

The media was abuzz over the situation and their actions were being fueled by Donald Amos, a former high-level member of The Castle who was itching to regain his seat on the board. Not going to happen with Jai and his eight fellow Kings at the helm. Dr. Taylor had said Temple would carry to term. Seven, almost eight months in and evidently, nature had other plans. His life was about to hit the porcelain goddess and circle the bowl for a few rounds before the royal flush. "In labor, right now?"

"Yes," Kelly whispered. "Right now."

He rounded the glass desk and grabbed a leather briefcase, then jammed the meeting notes he'd been scanning inside. "Are the paramedics on their way?"

"They're about twenty minutes out," she replied, and he steeled himself for even more bad news. "Dr. Taylor is in Africa on a health mission, and isn't expected back until next week. So, no one from her team is at the hospital right now. That means whoever is going to be part of the delivery hasn't been briefed on the delicacy of this particular situation. Overall, things are about to be pretty damn interesting."

And that would present a problem within itself. Jai had chosen Dr. Julie Taylor because she was not afraid of the challenges Temple's pregnancy presented. Every other doctor had taken a hard pass. Their careers were on the line, and the potential failure could damage their reputations and their licenses. Julie had been a family practitioner who changed her discipline once she realized how few OB/GYNs were in Africa, and how desperately they were needed.

"I'm on my way," he said to Kelly as he made it to the front door of his home. "Thanks for all you do."

"It's always a pleasure, Jai."

Twelve minutes later, he arrived at the glass-and-steel building that housed the Chetan Healing Center and parked in his reserved spot near the entrance. This frantic pace wasn't a good way to start the morning, but the situation called for him to be on high alert.

The moment the smoke-tinted doors slid open and he set foot across the threshold—all while balancing his phone, tablet, and briefcase—Kelly rushed toward him. Her ivory skin was flushed to crimson and her reddish-brown hair plastered to the side of her face as though she'd sprinted an entire marathon. Not a good sign.

"We can't reach Temple's mother or fiancé," she said, gasping for breath. "The center has power of attorney for health care. You'll have to act on our patient's behalf."

A chill passed through Jai, rendering him almost numb. He handed off his briefcase and accepted the documents she held as he tried to come to terms with what her words meant. "Power of attorney for an issue that happened at Chetan, yes. This is something entirely different."

"No, it isn't," she countered, hooking her arm under his and directing him to where the paramedics were wheeling a gurney across the threshold toward the waiting ambulance. "Go with her to the hospital."

"Hey, be gentle," he warned the crew navigating the concrete. "She's not a piece of meat."

The men didn't stop or bat an eye. "She's comatose," the slimmer one of the pair said. "She can't feel it anyway."

"That is *not* acceptable," Jai roared, and Kelly held his arm in a vice-like grip to keep him in place. "What if she was your mother . . . or sister? Treat. Her. Gently."

Kelly relaxed her hold on him, and Jai threw her a glance, expressing his thanks without speaking. She nodded in response and gave him a slight smile.

The men halted a few feet from the vehicle, shared a speaking glance that revealed their irritation, but they complied by significantly slowing their movements.

Jai stepped into the back of the ambulance and perched on a silver bench, watching as they situated the IV, then strapped the patient in before the burly one ran to the front and sped away from the sidewalk.

The fifteen-minute drive was tense and silent, except for the blare of the siren and the furtive glances the two-member crew sent his way— one from the rearview mirror. The ambulance pulled into the emergency bay of Meridian Hospital. A team of nurses and a salt-and-pepper haired doctor with a dour expression swept out of the doors and scurried toward the vehicle.

He extended a hand to Jai. "I'm Dr. Christian."

When the two nurses gripped the silver railings, the shorter of the paramedics said, "Treat her like glass or this guy will have a conniption."

His partner nodded in Jai's direction and scowled.

"That was uncalled for," Dr. Christian said, his tone sharp and forbidding, matching the frown that appeared on his face.

"We don't have the time to belabor the point that comatose doesn't mean deceased," Jai shot back, glaring at the two men who were ignoring the warning looks from the nurses.

Dr. Christian flinched, then his head whipped around to Jai. "Wait a minute. Did you say comatose?"

Jai kept his gaze on the men and didn't bother to answer the question.

The doctor recovered his composure and gave the two emergency personnel a stern look as he warned, "You'll hear about this later."

"Whatever, man." The stockier one waved him off.

Jai made a mental note to address the entire situation when things calmed down. No telling what other process those two had let slide. While he understood that most of their fellow paramedics had been on strike for a while, their attitude was out of order.

The preparation for the baby's arrival soon became a synchronicity of nurses pulling together all needed materials, equipment, and getting Jai in place. The fact that the doctor had been thrown for a loop became evident in the furrowed brow, anxious expression, and solemn bearing.

"You're the father?" Dr. Christian asked, suiting up and gesturing for Nurse Jennifer to outfit Jai in the same manner.

"No, I have power of attorney to see to Temple's well-being."

Dr. Christian lowered his mask to ask, "So, she was pregnant when she arrived at your center?"

"The notes are all here, doctor," Jai said, passing him a set of documents Kelly had the presence of mind to compile and place in a manila folder.

The doctor slipped off his gloves, scanned the pages, then blinked several times before focusing on Jai. "She's *that* woman? From the news?"

"Yes," Jai answered through his teeth and offered nothing more since the rest of the nursing staff had turned curious gazes in their direction.

Dr. Christian held up a hand to keep Jai from moving forward. "So, we're going to do a C-section to get this over and done with."

"Dr. Taylor already had a plan in place to induce a semi-natural labor," Jai said, flipping the page and putting an index finger on the summary paragraph of the health plan he'd worked out with Dr. Taylor. Her method would be best for Temple's overall health."

"That might be true," he countered, switching out his gloves. "But I'm not Dr. Taylor and what I say in this hospital goes."

"I get that," Jai shot back, moving until only a few feet stood between them. "And I'm still saying, do not cut her unless it's absolutely necessary. You haven't even assessed her to see what the best course should be."

Jai had researched several cases that were similar to Temple's in that the women were also pregnant and in a coma. The difference had been in the fact that in the information he came across, the women were already pregnant before going into the coma. Temple's pregnancy occurred several months *after* she arrived at Chetan. The plan Dr. Taylor put in place meant a possible chance for Temple to fully recover after the birth and resume treatment at Chetan. She'd need special care, and he along with his staff, were well prepared for that contingency.

The nurses were now tending to Temple, but moving at such a slow pace Jai was certain they were listening intently to the exchange.

"Dr. Taylor is willing to take chances that I am not," he admitted. "It's my license and practice that would be at stake, not hers. The patient isn't having a normal delivery process and that bears a great deal of consideration. It's possible she would not survive. Be more merciful that way."

"And your attitude is the very thing I'd hoped to avoid. She's been through enough," Jai said, giving the people gathered around them a cursory glance. "Having to go through a C-Section would be unnecessarily traumatic."

"No more traumatic than what happened to put her in this condition," Dr. Christian shot back, gesturing to Temple's belly. "And it happened in your special little facility. I don't even know why you're here. Aren't you under investigation as one of the men who might have impregnated her?"

Jaidev Maharaj saw red.

CHAPTER 2

"What the hell is going on here?!" Snatched Hiram Fosten from a sound sleep. Actually, sleep was more a dream where he was inside Marilyn and the heat was driving him to a rip-roaring orgasm. His eyes flew open in time to witness a strange, half-naked woman—unfortunately, not *his* woman—running from the bedroom.

Hiram yanked up a robe from the end of the bed. Never mind that it was Marilyn's floral print silk. He tossed it on and struggled to keep his massive chest covered.

"Who was that woman?" he whispered, as a pang of anxiousness whipped through him while his feet hit the carpet in a rhythm that matched his heart rate. *This cannot be good.* No, he hadn't been in a drunken stupor and brought a random woman home. He didn't drink, nor did he have the inclination to cheat on the woman he loved.

His thoughts cleared as he rushed through his personal space that had been turned into an impromptu stage for this incredible drama unfolding before him. The cathedral windows let in brilliant sunlight, which confirmed that Hiram was up a creek without a paddle or a boat for that matter. The two antagonists faced off as if he wasn't in the room.

"So, what are you going to do, Mom," the stranger said to Marilyn, whose expression was nothing short of thunderous. "You're going to stay with him after I slept with him?"

Hiram did a mental flip through his memories from last night until now. Work at Chetan, home for a meal, back to Chetan, then home for an early-morning slide into heaven when he curled his body around Marilyn, closed his eyes, and embraced the luscious and sensual woman who had become the best thing that ever happened to him.

"I never touched her," Hiram protested, leaning against the living room wall to brace himself. *Wait. Did she say mom?* This was one of Marilyn's daughters?

The May-December relationship between them was fairly new. They were giving it some time before they brought family members into the equation. Somehow, someone figured out enough about their interactions to create this fiasco. "I didn't even know she was here. I was trying to get some shut-eye before I have to meet up with Jai." He flickered his gaze to the face of the naked woman with honey skin, but quickly averted his eyes to the leather sofa. "I don't know who she is or where she came from. Or what kind of game she's playing. I. Don't. Know. Her."

The front door burst open and yet another woman entered his condo, gasping for breath as she gripped the knob for balance. At least this one still had on all of her clothes. The other female proudly displayed her birthday suit as though the place had suddenly become a Vegas brothel and a client was going to mosey on through the door at any moment.

The newcomer, who resembled the jaybird, splayed a hand across her heaving chest, saying, "I tried to get up here as fast as I could."

"What is going on here," Marilyn screamed, hands balling into fists so tight a fingernail was trying to make an exit stage left.

Hiram wished he could scream, too. Everything he was building with a woman who had embraced him, even with his past, was crumbling on a lie. And he didn't understand why it was being directed his way. "And put some damn clothes on," she roared. Marilyn's creamy skin flushed to pink and her hazel-green eyes flashed fire.

The naked one didn't budge from where she stood between the sofa and the center table. Instead, she inched her red-manicured hands to her hips. All sass and no class.

Oh, that one has a pair of balls that could rattle someone's cage. Hopefully her lies don't rattle mine.

"Daddy promised her some money if she managed to seduce him." The other female folded both arms and nodded in Hiram's direction.

Daddy? The delicate features of the newcomer indicated she was Marilyn's oldest daughter.

The naked one stiffened and glared at her sister, who didn't back down. Whoever she was, Hiram was grateful for the truth coming to light. Now maybe they could make sense of these shenanigans and get the bold one into some clothes and out of his house. This scenario also explained how Marilyn's key to his place had come up missing a few days ago. Then it mysteriously reappeared in his mailbox last night which neither of them could figure out.

Marilyn blinked several times to clear her vision. "What did you say, Crystal?"

"Daddy orchestrated this mess," she clarified before turning her attention to Hiram, giving him a not-quite-disdainful once-over that sent a shiver of unease up his spine. "He can't live with the fact that you've moved on."

Evidently, Marilyn's daughters couldn't either, if the oldest one's expression told the story.

"And he did this?" Marilyn asked. Her eyes cut to the youngest, who folded her arms across a pair of breasts that were obviously the work of a surgeon's knife. She was so enthralled with her own body, she still didn't feel the need to cover up. Or maybe she'd bought so far into this charade that she wanted to make the lie more believable—a woman who had just slept with a man and wasn't nearly as embarrassed by being caught in a compromising position as she should be.

Suddenly, it would mean a six-foot-three-inch, muscle-bound male wearing a floral silk robe wasn't quite the picture that was presented when he first emerged from his bedroom.

"It's not because he wants me back," Marilyn mused. "It's because he doesn't want me to be happy." She crossed the distance from the entryway, passing the easel and tattoo bench situated near the window until she stood directly in front of the liar of the family. "What the hell did you do?"

Head lowered, she stuttered, "I—I … I."

"Tell the truth, Wanda," Marilyn snapped, causing her to flinch.

Wanda inched back and squeaked like a petulant child. "I need that money." Then her bravado returned and she glowered at her mother as though she was the reason her bank account was coming up snake eyes and she had crapped out. "You wouldn't help me, so I had to help myself."

Though he was certain those words hurt Marilyn, they didn't give him a sense of relief. An entire theater-style drama had played out in no time. The lie was laid and had been disputed, all in a span of—he checked his watch—five minutes. Last thought in his mind was the way Marilyn had put it on him before he passed out for a good spell of sleep. Now he considered how much more her ex would impact their lives. If he was willing to use his daughter in such a blatant way, it meant the man had some deep issues. Had Victor done something to his daughter that Marilyn wasn't aware of or wasn't admitting?

"So, you would help a man, who hasn't loved me from day one, to break up my new relationship because you couldn't figure out your life without his money?" She jabbed an index finger in her daughter's chest. "How selfish of you."

Marilyn snatched up a throw from the sofa and tossed it to Wanda before turning a sorrowful gaze toward Hiram. "I'm sorry there was even room for doubt in my mind. The one thing he ..." She gestured to Hiram. "hasn't done, is hurt me. But you have this unhealthy attachment to Victor, Wanda, and God forbid, he checks out of here. What's going to happen when you actually have to do the adult thing and get a life?"

"You don't care about me," Wanda sobbed into the soft material bunched in her hands. "You let those people almost put me out of my house, the lights and gas got turned—"

"You went on a girls' trip to Essence Festival. You knew you were skating on a ten-day notice. Not to mention your utilities were about to be shut off. I didn't have anything to do with that."

"I told you to—"

"You *told* me," Marilyn shot back, waggling a finger in her daughter's face. "You didn't *ask* me a damn thing."

Crystal nodded, then shrugged and took a seat on the leather ottoman. All she needed was popcorn to complete the scenario.

"And between me, you, and the wiretappers, I thought it was high time you learned a lesson about priorities." Marilyn flicked an index finger in the air. "Rent comes before pleasure trips." Another finger went up. "Light bill comes before designer purses." Yet another finger. "Gas comes before nights out at fancy restaurants." All four fingers now. "And gratitude comes right after someone has done everything in their power to cover your ass. You don't seem to know any of that, despite having a degree in business management."

"But you gave Crystal a down payment for her new house," she protested, throwing a scathing glance at her sister who wore a neutral expression.

"Yes, I do help people who are at least trying to help themselves," Marilyn countered. "Why would I keep throwing money your way when it doesn't do you any good? Yet, you're all up in my business about what I need to be doing. Telling me to get my life together when you don't know the first thing about managing yours."

Marilyn cupped her hands about Wanda's face. "You know, my grandmother once told me a humorous story and I didn't understand it until now."

Hiram perched on the arm of the sofa, a few inches from Crystal who perked up. Marilyn sharing something funny was a new one on him. Evidently, for the oldest one, too. As a woman who had worked for a state department for twenty years, Marilyn was as serious as eating Frosted Mini-Wheats without milk.

Listen closely, so you'll learn a little something.

"A buzzard and a vulture were sitting on a fence. The vulture decides to school the buzzard on that bird life. 'You're not living life right. You're always eating things when they're way past dead. You have to eat them when they're still alive; the blood's still pumping, and they're

still slightly breathing. See,'—he points to a mouse running across the field and says, 'watch this. Let me show you how it's done.' So, he flies down, swoops and turns, does a one-eighty. Just as he's about to grab that mouse in his claw-BAM!" Marilyn slapped one hand against the other, causing everyone in the living room to flinch. *"He slams hard into the fence and falls out. He's stretched out there for several moments before his friend on the fence realizes he's dying. The buzzard stretches, yawns and says, "Well, let me go show this smart ass muthafucka how it's done."*

While Marilyn had told the story with a straight face, it took everything inside Hiram not to burst out laughing. Crystal didn't bother to try. She let it rip and Wanda turned red.

"So, let me show your little smart ass a thing or two." Marilyn walked toward the front door and yanked it open. "No weapon formed against me shall prosper. Even if it's my own daughter." Her voice cracked and she gestured to the other side of the threshold. "Get the hell out of my house. Correction—*his* house. Do not ever set foot in this—or my place again."

Wanda finally recovered from the shock and moved toward the door. She snatched up another throw—his favorite—along the way.

"And tell your daddy you failed," Marilyn said, causing Wanda to pause mid-step. "Failed at trying to destroy the best thing that's happened to me since I gave birth to both of you. You failed at trying to take this little slice of happiness from me." Then she wiped away a tear with the back of a trembling hand. "Let's see how your daddy will take that."

CHAPTER 3

"Aren't you under investigation as one of the men who might have impregnated her?"

Equipment beeped, filling the silence while the nurses gasped at the staunch accusation from Dr. Christian that swirled around them.

Jai barely held onto his ability to remain civil with a man who would throw something as ugly as that out there in the open. Eyes narrowed, he fisted one hand.

Nurse Jennifer's caramel skin flushed red. She sprinted around the bed, planted herself between Jai and Dr. Christian to keep him from throwing that well-deserved punch.

"Doctor—"

"My apologies." Dr. Christian held up a weathered hand to ward off any further discussion, then massaged his temples before letting out a long, weary sigh. "That, too, was uncalled for."

Jai took a deep breath and mentally told his anger to stay put.

Nurse Jennifer looked over her shoulder at him and raised a questioning brow.

He nodded, and only then did her shoulders slump as she relaxed. She stayed in place, as if she knew Dr. Christian would make another blunder that could land him on the wrong end of a can of whoop ass.

"You have to be aware that the care her body will need after a C-section is much more involved than a vaginal delivery," Jai said in the calmest tone he could manage.

Dr. Christian threaded his fingers through the whisper-thin hair that barely covered the top of his head. "You're acting as though she's an active participant in this endeavor. You do realize that there's a great possibility she will die from this, don't you?"

"Not if you go into it with the better possibility that she will live." Jai gripped the bed's railing and Nurse Jennifer placed a hand over his. "I repeat. Do *not* cut her unless she or the baby is in danger. Understand?"

All these years, Jaidev had held fast to what he'd learned from a book Khalil Germaine had given him in his last year of high school. *The Miracle Man: An Inspiring Story of Motivation and Courage.* The autobiography told of Morris E. Goodman's recovery from a plane crash which left him paralyzed and unable to move, breathe, talk, or swallow. The man's inner determination led him through a series of surgeries and rehabs that ultimately had him walking out of the hospital a whole man who could tell of his triumph.

The story alone led Jai to research and compare tragic physical experiences along with the mental and spiritual connection in healing. He studied everything from ancient healing practices, Reiki, holistic medicine from all cultures, especially Africa, First Nation, East India, and Asian. His approach to, and success with, medicine in this manner had been a bone of contention between the medical industry and doctors who only wanted to hold ground with outdated methods. Ones like this very doctor who would dismiss the fact that Temple had been surviving quite well under Jai's care. Birthing this child didn't have to change that status.

"Dr. Christian," Nurse Jennifer called as the other nurse's expressions went from calm to shock. "Dr. Christian."

"Yes," he snapped, still focused on Jai who hadn't moved an inch.

"Your argument is no longer valid," Nurse Jennifer said, gesturing to the lower area of Temple's body.

Dr. Christian rounded the nurses and came to the opposite end of the bed.

"The baby is crowning," she said, louder than necessary.

The words filled Jai with more relief than he thought possible.

Temple's body was taking over the process of bringing her little one into the world.

"Well, there's that," Dr. Christian said in a dry tone, frustration etched on his face as he scrambled to get into position to deliver the baby.

"Aaaaaaand we have another complication," Nurse Jennifer offered, and this time her awestruck tone mirrored the expressions of everyone else.

Dr. Christian's shoulders dropped as he lifted the sheet to get a handle on what was happening on the opposite end of things. "What is it now?"

"That patient just opened her eyes. She's trying to speak."

* * *

"Temple," Jai whispered as he took her hand in his.

Her dark-brown eyes focused on him and her breathing that had been coming at a steady pace, now amped into rapid succession. Her peaches and cream skin was smooth, an unblemished complexion with warm coloring touching her cheeks. Her form was curvy and had only diminished by a few pounds under his care. She had the elegant beauty of Lena Horne and Dorothy Dandridge combined.

The words he intended to speak dried up in his throat.

Fear and then anguish held their ground as Temple squirmed, and the nurses tried to hold her steady. The unexpected pain had to be unbearable.

Jai's mind went into overdrive. "You're going to be all right," he crooned, but his heart ached because she was in the middle of a major life-altering experience, and a child was being forced to enter this world under the most questionable of circumstances. "You're in the hospital. In the middle of delivering a baby."

"Actually, she's on the tail end, the baby is almost here," Nurse

Jennifer said as the red-haired female next to her nodded, eyes wide with wonder. The three women worked in tandem, nearly moving Dr. Christian out of the way and it was a sight to behold.

"Never seen anything like this in my entire life," Dr. Christian said as Nurse Jennifer moved past him and practically took over.

"Does she need to push or something?" Jai asked, barely able to pull his gaze from Temple. "And what about the pain?"

The doctor didn't reply, so Jai snapped his fingers in front of the man's flushed face to get his attention.

"We're way past that point," he said, finally springing into action. "She's going to have to ride this one out because that part is over," Dr. Christian said, still focused on the business end of the delivery. "Pushing is for getting the baby to the canal. This little guy is swimming on his— Ooooops, I mean … her own."

"Can we get a team in here to focus strictly on Temple?" Jai asked.

"The team we have now is just fine," Dr. Christian reverted to his dismissive tone.

Jai was ready to throttle the man to shake some common sense into him. He'd better be grateful for Nurse Jennifer who kept him from receiving the ass-whipping he'd been asking for since they wheeled Temple through the doors of Meridian.

"That baby has already been through hell and back," Jai said, fed up with this doctor's nonsense. "The nurses in here need to focus on the baby. I want someone here solely to care for Temple."

Dr. Christian pulled his shoulders back and glowered at Jai.

"I'm not trying to tell you how to do your job," Jai continued in a softer tone. "But the baby's going to need a lot of special care. She hasn't been through what anyone would call a normal process."

"I hear you," Nurse Jennifer said and rushed to the phone hanging on the wall.

Jai dipped his head in acknowledgement. "Thank you."

"I'd swear up and down that you're the father," Dr. Christian said as he wiped both hands on a white towel and tossed it into the nearest bin.

"For all intents and purposes, I am," Jai countered as Temple scanned the strange faces around her. "Do your best for both Temple and her baby."

When Temple's eyes locked with his, Jai moved to the front end of the bed. "I am Jaidev Maharaj," he whispered to her. "And I'm going to take excellent care of you."

A single tear slipped from her eye before Temple said the first words she had spoken in an entire year. "I believe you."

CHAPTER 4

Hiram's brows rose, then lowered as Wanda rushed back into the living room, traded the throws by snatching up her clothes and didn't bother to put on any underwear as she slipped the dress over her head. Then she grabbed her shoes and ran toward the door. She cut an ugly look at Crystal on her way out.

"Aren't you going after her?" Marilyn asked in the softest tone she'd used during the entire exchange.

Crystal lifted the remote from the coffee table, propped her legs up and fully stretched out and claimed more space on the sofa the same way her mother had just reclaimed every second of her time.

"Nope." She looked up at Hiram. "Got any popcorn up in this camp?"

Hiram simply shook his head.

"I just came here to keep her from making an even bigger fool of herself. Daddy was being all vague when I questioned him about that text he sent both of us, which he said was a joke. Daddy said he didn't need me because he had things under control. Then I saw that someone used my ride-share account and knew Wanda was headed here—straight into trouble." Crystal gestured toward the window that faced the front of the building. "I changed the password to my account, so she will definitely need a lift to get home. I'll just give her time to cool off. Then she won't use me as a sounding board all the way to Daddy's house."

Marilyn's chest rose and fell a few times before she asked, "Not your house?"

"Oh, hell no." She waved that thought away with exaggerated hand movements. "Remember, I'm the smart one. I take after you. I am not co-signing this madness." Then she gestured between Hiram and Marilyn. "For real, Mom. You do you. After everything he put you through, you need to find your happy place."

Marilyn left Hiram's side and stood near her daughter. "So, you don't have a problem with us being a couple?"

Crystal schooled her features into a neutral mask. "Truthfully, I didn't realize you had cougar tendencies."

"She doesn't, because I'm nobody's cub," Hiram shot back.

Crystal flinched, then snailed a nod. "I can feel that. All of that."

Hiram looked sideways at Marilyn who moved to be with him. "And I'm not looking for a hit and run either."

"Neither am I," Marilyn added, splaying a hand across his chest.

"Honestly, I kinda do have an issue," Crystal confessed, frowning. "Not because of the age difference or anything like that."

"Then what is it?" Hiram asked, putting his arm around Marilyn's waist and pulling her into him.

"If all you women over forty keep stealing from the only available male pool, there'll be nothing left for us youngins around this camp."

Marilyn stiffened at first, then she roared with laughter and Hiram joined in.

"Oh, there's a few eligible bachelors I know," Hiram offered.

Crystal's smile disappeared as she perked up. "Seriously?"

"One of them is a lot like me, and he's good people."

"Hey." Marilyn elbowed Hiram in the side. "This isn't Match or Christian Mingle."

"Facts. But I can give her a nudge in the right direction," Hiram countered, laughing.

"And speaking of nudging," she teased with a low chuckle as she pressed her body to his.

"And speaking of TMI." Crystal stood and smoothed her leather skirt. "That's my cue." She went to the window and looked down at the parking area. "Damn, she's sitting her entire panty-less behind on the hood of my car." Crystal scrunched up her nose. "I'll need to get it washed tomorrow." Then she craned her neck a little. "Okay, she just got off a call and now she's running back toward the building."

"What are you going to do?" Marilyn asked, moving toward the window.

"She's not wearing any underwear. No way I'm driving that naked tail in my car. Wanda's going to have to walk. It'll clear her head. Maybe she'll call Daddy to pick her up. She'll figure it out. Trust me, she'll be all right, eventually."

A bang on the door snatched their attention.

Hiram looked to Marilyn who nodded. He opened the door and barely moved out of the way before Wanda ran to the sofa and yanked up her purse. Somehow the broken woman who rushed from the apartment several minutes ago, had morphed into a confident one with an evil grin and a glint in her eyes that spoke to nothing but trouble.

"Daddy says to ask you one thing."

Hiram braced himself. So did Marilyn and Crystal.

"How will Jaidev Maharaj take hearing the news that one of his employees is sleeping with the woman who's trying to shut his center down?"

CHAPTER 5

Twenty years ago . . .

Pain had been a constant companion the moment the stranger entered her bedroom and it remained with her when he left.

Her mother and stepfather had closed the door behind him, and Vaunie had stifled a scream. He would come into her room again. She was certain of it. Earlier, after dinner, she had overhead her mother, Carl, and his brother Dane talking . . .

"I won't let him do this to her," Sharon said to her husband. "She's only ten. We don't need the money that bad. Not enough to do something so ..."

"You've never cared for her, so what does it matter," Carl shouted, which made Sharon flinch. "We don't need her," he said. "We need the money that little bastard has tied up in her father's trust."

"Unless you're willing to let me go to prison," he said after a lengthy silence. "And that'll leave you with three children to raise all by yourself. We all know you've never worked a day in your life. That's why you're on husband three."

"She's only ten," Sharon whispered, then pressed one hand to her mouth.

"I have to come up with that money or ... you can wait for her to find her father, and she'll tell him exactly how you've been treating her.

You'll never see a dime. Or, you can move forward with my plans and get that money within a year. Get her pregnant and marry her off to my brother. She's had a cycle so she's a woman now."

"She's too young," Sharon protested.

"She menstruates and can get pregnant," Uncle Dane said, "That will be the way to the money. Or it will be in eight years. I'd say let's get to it now."

"She's only ten," Sharon cried out. "I never believed the rumors about you before now. You're all too willing to hurt my little girl."

Dane smirked. "I'll be as gentle as I can be."

Sharon crumpled to the floor and launched into a fit of sobs.

Fear gripped Vaunie to the point that she couldn't move. Then she tipped back into her bedroom. Her gaze skittered around the small room, which contained only a bed, a few clothes, and window dressings. They had stripped almost everything because she had run away several times before, but everyone knew Carl Webster and brought her back home. They didn't believe that her mother or he had been abusive. But this was something different. Something ... sinister. When she heard the voices start up again, she inched her way back out to the hallway.

"And the law says we can marry her off if she's a minor who's pregnant," Carl said, and his voice grew even harsher. "That's where our focus should be. Make sure Dane keeps at it until she's with child."

Uncle Dane moved to pick Sharon up from the floor as he said, "We have a judge, who has a mistress with two children he doesn't want anyone to know about. He'll sign off on a marriage as long as one of those conditions are met. Pregnant minor is one that fits the law and keeps his nose clean."

"Then we'll find a way to kill her." A few seconds of silence ticked by and Carl continued, "That money will be all ours."

"No, you won't kill her," Dane said. "If she's my wife, then she will remain that way." Then he let out a bone-chilling laugh and added, "At least, until that child comes of age. Then she'll be the perfect replacement. Then I find a way to make my wife ... disappear."

Vaunie had been locked in her room ever since the police found her hiding in the Wilson's garage. The dogs were able to track her scent. She could get away, but she could never stay away. The windows had been nailed shut. Breaking the panes would not give her enough room to slide out. She was stuck. At the mercy of whatever they planned. And she understood enough to know that what they had in mind would be even worse than what they'd already done to her all this time.

An hour later, her worst fears were confirmed when Uncle Dane, the spitting image of her stepfather, had hurt her more than her mother and stepfather ever had. Her stepfather stood at the head of her bed, covering her mouth and holding her down through the entire ordeal.

Hours later, her sister, Ebbie, and brother, Donny, tipped into Vaunie's room. She squeezed her eyes shut, pretending to be asleep just as she had when Uncle Dane had come in to "make her a wife" as he said. Were they going to hurt her, too? Her brother and sister had always tried to protect her. Sometimes even getting between Vaunie and the belt, extension cord, or whatever was in hand, to take the blows themselves. Their action seemed to anger their mother even more.

"I'm glad we came home when we did," Donny whispered. "They're trying to marry her off to that old man."

"They must mean when she gets older," Ebbie said. "I'm not even old enough to get married. But they sure are acting strange."

"That's because Mom has always been angry that she only gets a little of Vaunie's money," Donny whispered to Ebbie and for a moment Vaunie felt a sliver of peace. The truth that no one would mention before was now out in the open. "Let's just take her away right now. I mean, right now."

"And then what?" Ebbie shot back and he gestured for her to lower her voice. "They would find us and she'd be right back here again, just like all the other times. Then we really can't help her because they'll send us away again. We need a grown-up to help us."

None of the grown-ups had. They all feared Carl Webster because his family was one of the biggest employers and property owners in the county. They had old money, but it didn't translate to Carl and Dane because they had somehow fallen out of grace. No one would say why.

But despite their unknown sins, their name still carried some weight anyhow.

"We're the only ones who can do this," Donny protested. "The police didn't help us. Even Mr. Williams tried and they didn't believe him. Everyone is afraid of him. Pastor Kae isn't. She's not going to fall for their crap. She will help us because she doesn't fear nobody but God."

"She doesn't live here," Ebbie said in a lower tone.

"She doesn't have to. Ms. Crenshaw will help us to get Vaunie to Chicago." Donny glanced at the bed and Vaunie locked gazes with him before she closed her eyes again. He moved closer and held her hand. "We can't let her stay here."

Ebbie bit her lip then said, "Okay, they just left the house to go on the other side of town, so we'd better do it fast."

"How do you know where they're going?"

"Said they were going to talk with Parker's father," she replied. "He's got something to do with what they're trying to do."

"Vaunie, come on," Donny said, shaking her awake.

Ebbie stood behind him, peering over his shoulder. "We have to go. Now."

"Now?" she choked out, willing her legs to move, but they wouldn't listen.

"Yes, right now," he insisted, shooting a glance at the door of her bedroom. "We have to get you out of here before they get back."

Vaunie struggled to sit up, but the stabbing pains meant staying in place was the only relief.

Ebbie yanked back the covers, then gasped when she saw the blood pooled around Vaunie's thighs.

"We're too late," she sobbed and hid her face in the palms of her hand, then she nearly slumped to the floor.

Vaunie reached out, trying to get a hold of her sister, but the agonizing pain that came with any movement kept her immobile.

"But still ..." Donny said, and his voice cracked with emotion. "If we don't get her out of here, it will happen again. And again. You heard *what mother said. They can't marry her off to Uncle Dane until she gets pregnant. If it doesn't happen now, they'll keep doing this to her until she is. We can't let them hurt her anymore."*

Donny had already gone to their teacher to let her know that their mother and stepfather were mistreating Vaunie. They had gone to the police, who, upon learning that Carl Webster was involved, declined to do anything to bring him to justice given his status. They did, however, inform their mother of the allegations and she proceeded to beat them, but not as much as she hurt Vaunie. When their mother finished with her, Vaunie's eyes were swollen shut. She wasn't able to go to school for a whole week.

That's when things grew worse. Donny and Ebbie told their father what was happening in their home. Their father went to court to gain full custody of his own children, but refused to do anything to help Vaunie who was the result of an affair that ended the marriage.

Then one of their teachers spoke with a high school friend, a visiting pastor who had a network of people to help people in need. The clients were always women and their children, never children by themselves. Hopefully, she would make an exception.

Donny scooped Vaunie from the bed, ignoring her whimpers as he carried her from the house. They ran across the field, and all the while Donny prayed they would get Vaunie to safety this time. They took the back roads until they reached Ms. Crenshaw's home.

"You can't be here right now," Ms. Crenshaw said, her voice filled with panic. "Everything won't be set until later tonight. If they find out she's missing, this is the first place they will look."

"She won't live that long," Donny said. "This time they did something worse."

"What do you mean worse?" she whispered, gathering them into the house, before scanning the emptiness of the tree-lined street.

"He. Means. Worse." Ebbie let those words stand and Ms. Crenshaw's eyes widened with shock.

"No, no, no, no, no," she chanted.

"She has to get out of here now," Donny insisted, arms aching

under the weight of carrying Vaunie for so long, but he refused to put her down. "We can't wait for later."

"I'll call Pastor Kae."

Once the pastor in Chicago was aware of the urgency of the situation through speaking with Vaunie, who relayed only a small portion of the acts that had been committed that night, she said, "Go on to the Greyhound station. A ticket will be waiting under the name of Willa Jones. You'll have to ride with Vaunie until you make it to the next town on the bus route and hand her off to Willa."

"I can't do that," Ms. Crenshaw cried, folding and unfolding her hands. "I can't get any more involved than I already am."

"I'll ride with her," Ebbie offered, cradling Vaunie in her arms where she sat next to her on the sofa.

"No, you can't," Donny said. "Two children on the bus is going to look strange. It has to be an adult."

"But how will I get back?" Ms. Crenshaw asked. "That's too far to walk, and buying a bus ticket back to this town when I have a perfectly good working vehicle, will raise suspicion."

"I can drive your car and bring you back," Donny offered.

Miss Crenshaw laid both hands on her fleshy hips. "You don't even have a learner's permit."

"I know how to drive," he insisted, pulling his shoulders back. "What other choice do we have? You can't drive her there because the dogs will find her scent in your car."

"They will hurt you too," Vaunie squeaked to her brother and sister as her hold tightened around Ebbie.

"No, they won't," Donny reassured, lowering to his knees so they were at eye level. "Our father isn't rich like yours. They want that money he left for you. You have to go."

"I won't see you again," Vaunie said, reaching for him.

"Someday, it will happen," Donny said, smiling. "Lord willing and the creek don't rise."

Vaunie tried to smile at his usual saying and she came back with her normal answer, "There ain't no creeks around here."

"True," he said. *"But there is the Good Lord and He's everywhere."* *Donny embraced her again and so did Ebbie. "When you're older and they can't do anything else to hurt you, then you find us. Right now, we have to make sure you're okay."*

"We love you, baby sis," Ebbie said, pressing a kiss to her forehead.

"We love you," Donny said.

"I love you too," Vaunie replied and she could barely see them through her tears.

* * *

Temple Devaughn was snatched from that frightful childhood memory, opened her eyes and locked in on a man who stared at her with a concerned expression in place. His eyes carried the same sadness she had witnessed in her brother and sister's eyes that night she left Virginia for good.

"My name is Jaidev Maharaj," he said, giving her a reassuring smile. "And I'm going to take excellent care of you."

Through the unbelievable pain and a heavy weight in her nether regions that kept her pinned to the bed, she inhaled a steadying breath, then said, "I believe you."

CHAPTER 6

Hiram held his peace but reflected on the first day Marilyn made her presence known.

"You came here, to my place, for a reason," Hiram had said to Marilyn Spears a few months ago. "We could've had this conversation at my job, or at a café somewhere, right? What's really going on?"

Marilyn sank into the cushions of his sofa and folded her pink-manicured hands on her lap. The act alone made her seem small, vulnerable, and beautiful. "Not for what I have to tell you."

Hiram leaned against the door jamb for a few moments, then he moved away, closed the door, waiting.

"The latest audits and investigations need to be taken up to a senate oversight committee to put an end to them once and for all. Mr. Maharaj needs to figure out why Donald Amos is gunning for him or he will lose everything. It seems personal."

With both arms folded across his chest, Hiram said, "You're not supposed to tell me that."

"No, I shouldn't do any of this. But my conscience won't let me sleep." She nodded slowly. "I've read up on Mr. Maharaj and I like what he's trying to accomplish."

"Okay, I get that. Thank you. I'll find a way to help him." Hiram grinned, then crossed the distance between them. "But since that's out of the way ... why are you really here?"

Her gaze locked on his. She slid off the sofa and made her way to the door. Defeat shadowed every step.

"So that's how it is, huh?" He shrugged as she looked over her shoulder. "Just come all up in my joint, side-step the real issue, and walk out like I'm not supposed to know something."

She blinked twice, and he witnessed the war going on within as her expression went from fearful and ended up as total confusion.

Hiram moved forward, placing a hand on the door to close it but still kept a three-inch space between them. Her eyes were so beautiful in their hazel-green glory. A flicker of desire lit in them that was so fleeting he wasn't sure it had been there. Then her lips quivered and parted slightly. An invitation? Maybe? Wanting to say something? Maybe that too.

"Tell me what you want," he whispered.

"I don't know."

"Oh, you know all right," he teased, resisting the urge to pull her to him and let her feel exactly what he wanted. "You're just afraid to say it."

She didn't respond.

Hiram moved away to take a seat on his tattoo bench. "Why don't I sit right here until you find the courage to get to the point you need to make." He smiled. "I'm not going to make it easy. Your being here says a whole lot, but to be sure I'm not overstepping any unspoken boundaries, you're going to need to say something else."

"I ... I ... shouldn't." She shook her head. "You know, this was a mistake."

Frowning, he said, "This what?"

"Coming here."

"Okay. So, you came to tell me that Jai's business is in danger from the people you work for. I already knew that. What else do you need me to know?"

She swallowed hard, her body trembled a little and the heavy warmth of arousal fueled his next action. He was with her, pressing a kiss to the softest lips he'd ever touched. "Talk to me," he whispered into her hair.

"Speak what you want me to know." He trailed his tongue along the fullest part of her lips, and she whispered his name.

The sound, both a plea and a prayer, was his undoing. He held on to his sanity long enough to say, *"You have to tell me what you want."*

A tear slipped from the far corner of her eye as she tilted her head back and looked directly into his eyes. *"I want to know what love feels like."*

That sobered him. All thoughts of making this woman lose her absolute mind went out of the window.

"I want to know that I am worthy, and needed, and ... loved."

Marilyn was asking for much more than sex and physical gratification. She wanted more from him than any woman had ever asked. For her to be this open, this vulnerable meant everything to him. Hiram pulled her into the wall of his chest, trying to calm the storm he felt was rising within her. *"Let me see how we can make that happen. Are you down for that?"*

Her breathy answer was all the confirmation he needed. *"Yes."*

That night he devoted himself to adoring and pleasing Marilyn, leaving her in no doubt that he desired her. Since then, he'd done everything to make her dreams resemble what she wanted to be her reality.

"So how does this work?" Hiram said after they made love. *"I work for the man your department is investigating. Wrong move, I might add, but still. Does make for interesting dinner conversations, though."*

"We keep work out of this," Marilyn answered. *"The investigation is going to be over as soon as the patient has the child and the police gather what they need. And if Mr. Maharaj can uncover Donald's hand in this or he waits for the evidence that will prove you all are innocent, everything will be fine."*

Everything will be fine was the biggest lie Marilyn could have told. Because right now, with her ex-husband's blackmail hanging over their heads, everything was far from fine.

Wanda relished their angry vibes, swept toward the door, haughty posture back in place.

Crystal was on her heels, saying, "You don't learn, do you?"

When the door closed behind them, Hiram's heart was heavy with concern, "I'll take care of it," he said, lowering himself next to Marilyn who slumped down onto the sofa.

He had never wanted this new relationship to be affected by their jobs. When he laid eyes on the beautiful, curvy woman the day he'd walked into Jai Maharaj's office to drop off the latest reports, it was as though a bolt of lightning had shot through him. Nothing else mattered to him in that moment; not the fact that they were on opposite sides of a major issue that could threaten his livelihood; not the fact that she had a few years on him and people might certainly give them a side-eye about the age difference; and certainly not the fact that he wasn't looking for love in any shape, form, or fashion.

Marilyn changed all that, and he was a better man for it. Even going along with keeping their relationship a secret, so that her job with the Bureau wouldn't be threatened. His too. He wanted to shout their love to anyone who would listen, but he understood her need for privacy.

Somehow, her bitter ex-husband had gotten hold of that information and planned to hurt her more than he already had. The depths that man had already gone to inflict pain and distress on her was unreal. All because the minute Wanda turned eighteen, and Marilyn had the presence of mind to say "deuces" and left him inhaling her dust.

"No, it's fine." Marilyn waved in a half-hearted gesture.

Hiram shook his head. "I'm not going to let him blow up your twenty-year spot over this."

"I can always find another job." She cupped his face in her hands and planted a gentle kiss on his lips. "But I can't find another you."

"Damn, what a comeback," Hiram teased, tightening his grip on her waist.

"I've lived my life for everyone else," she confessed laying her head against his chest. "A husband who cheated on me, then tried to make me believe it was my fault. One child so into her own life, she barely has time to call unless she wants something." She changed positions and straddled his thighs. "This right here … is just for me. As much as

I wanted to deny it, I felt something so strong it wouldn't go away. No matter how much I tried." With one hand, she stroked his cheek. "And I did try. I was embarrassed because I haven't felt anything for anyone in a long time. And there was so much fear, so much doubt. Did I deserve to have you? Someone who loved me for me, and not because I was simply there to boost your ego, or replace your mother or some other woman you'd been with? Men have a strange set of needs these days."

He let the silence settle around them for a while as his gaze roamed her face for a few moments, taking in her solemn expression and vibe.

"I get it." Hiram shifted her until she was cradled in his arms. "I do. But none of that is me. I don't need taking care of, I need the same things you want out of a relationship."

Hiram let silence fill the space so she could absorb those words.

"He's going to make me pay for being with you," she whispered into his chest. "So, what are we going to do about that?"

"What do you mean 'We' White woman?"

Marilyn gasped and pulled away with her eyes widened and her creamy skin flushed with reddish color. "I'm not white—"

"I know, I know." He held up his hands in mock surrender. "It's how we tease Jai all the time."

She released a long, slow breath as she always did with issues surrounding the color of her skin. "And I admire what he's doing, but …"

"No work, remember."

"To hell with that," she snapped and placed a hand on his chest. "What Mr. Amos is doing to him is so wrong. First, it was that substantial audit months ago that didn't turn up anything, but cost Mr. Maharaj a great deal of time and money. Then the way this case was handled in the media—all to embarrass Mr. Maharaj—was wrong. How he's coming after him is unethical and borderline illegal. We have places higher up on the list that need shutting down."

She raised both hands in exasperation. "He's not only coloring outside the line, he's moving the line to match the coloring so no one can tell what he's doing. Then this case dropped at the wrong time. People up top are not going to bat an eye at any of his wrongdoing with so many of them owing him favors. He's slick, and I have it on good authority that he's also deadly. I should get out while the getting is good."

"How will your resignation affect anything?" Hiram asked. "Your ex is still going to try and destroy your credibility. You need to take your time and figure things out so you're still in a position to do damage control. You can't do that if you're not in-house, although I can take care of you."

She mulled that over and he could practically see the wheels turning in her mind. "I have some savings, so I'm good, but I thank you so much for being *that* dude."

Hiram grinned at her use of slang.

"My house is paid for, bought it in a short sale. Took a minute for everything to pull through with the bank, but when it did, I paid pennies on the dollar. So, I can walk from that place and still be all right for a little while."

Hiram extracted his body from hers and went to a miniature dollhouse she'd fashioned for a friend's daughter. "This right here, can bring in how much?"

"I don't think about that," she answered, shrugging. "I just love doing it."

With both brows raised, he said, "Love it even more if you got paid, yeah?"

Her gaze narrowed on him and she perked up as if she felt his excitement. "So, what are you thinking?"

"Your job can't hold you hostage if you have an escape plan. Not just to survive, but to thrive." He went back to her side and stroked her cheek. "It's time to stop playing at this part of your life and go ahead and do the damn thing. You're the only one holding you back."

Marilyn was silent for a few moments, then left the sofa and stood in front of her artwork. "You really think I can?"

"I know you can." Hiram was by her side in the time it took to blink. "Just like I know between the two of us, we can find a way to save Jai's center before Donald Amos and Big Red tear it so far down we can't get it back up again."

"Big Red?"

"That's the name we gave your boss," he replied. "Amazon size, big bod, big hair, red freckles, big everything."

Marilyn placed her hands in her lap. "Tell me about him. Jaidev Maharaj. I need to see what we're working with. Then we'll know how to work against them to at least allow Chetan to become operational again."

Hiram guided her to the sofa, curled his arms around her and started with, "We work on the premise that they can still hear, feel, and sense; that every one of them will wake up one day. And we want their bodies well enough to accommodate them. That is the major mistake that rehab facilities make, thinking they're supposed to bide their time until the patients die."

Over the next hour, Marilyn learned that Jaidev Maharaj came from an East Indian family who settled in the heart of Devon—a fifteen block stretch on the North Side housing a South Asian community and commercial district with an array of jewelry stores, restaurants featuring East Indian and Middle Eastern cuisines, Taj Sari Palace, Patel Brothers—the largest Indian grocery store in North America, and worship centers. The area, now known as Chicago's Little India, began growing in the early 1970s under the watchful eye of Ranjana Bhargava, a community activist who was among the earliest Indian immigrants.

Jaidev had his life planned out—education at Loyola, family merchant and trading business, marriage to an East Indian girl from a high caste family, and two children to round out their dreams for him. Unfortunately, that wasn't what he wanted for his life.

His first break from their plans started when he insisted on attending the Macro International Magnet School, which put him in the hands of a mentor and further in line with six other scholars from backgrounds that differed vastly from his own. The argument was epic, but it wasn't the first time his parents ever fought. That was the first time his mother had ever won.

Jai incorporated a spiritual, not religious, approach to the patients in his care. His methods had not been widely accepted in the medical and scientific community, but the number of patients who successfully recovered made his institution sought after, even from his detractors. Along with health professionals—doctors, nurses, medical assistants, he employed doulas, who were mainly known as spiritual midwives for women giving birth or people leaving the earth scene, and were used at Chetan to provide care for patients in suspended life experiences and provided comfort to those closer to transitioning.

His therapies for patients included music, assisted aqua aerobics with essential oils to keep their bodies flexible, limber, and hydrated so their return to life would mean their bodies hadn't failed them. Some therapy also included playing comedic movies and shows from standup comedians that would appeal to the patient, based on what their families had to say. Overall, a combination of things that would stimulate the patient's mind, body, and soul were created and then revisited from time to time. This approach had resulted in a high percentage of patients recovering from injuries and comas despite medical professionals saying that death was the better alternative.

"No wonder Donald has such an issue with him," Marilyn said. "First, he's one of the biggest racists there is, but there's something else driving him on this. It has to be more than just the fact that the lobbyist and politicians have him in their pockets."

Hiram thought that over for a moment, then the most plausible explanation he could think of came to him. "I think it has something to do with The Castle."

CHAPTER 7

Jai grimaced as he settled into the executive chair behind his smoke-glass desk. A few minutes to clear his mind would have been appreciated, but so much for that.

Kelly had sent a text saying he needed to high tail it back to Chetan because Donald Amos had arrived at his facility. He'd also brought two women with him.

The effort to keep the distaste off his face took everything in him, but one of Khalil's gems centered him. *Never give your opponent an advantage. Keep him guessing and that will throw him off-balance.*

"You know, if you sign over your controlling interest in The Castle," Donald began. "I can make all of this go away. Then you can get back to doing what you love. Playing around with dead people." He held up a hand to ward off Jai's protest. "My bad—*nearly* dead people."

Jai's gaze narrowed on the man's pale skin, beady blue eyes and a combover that was on its last stint at being an actual covering for his shiny pink scalp. Someone who seemed above-board at first glance, but was as dark and dirty as bureaucrats could go. "I hope there's never a time when—"

"I certainly wouldn't need your little 'magic' facility, if I did," he snarled, his face a mask of disdain as he scanned the office taking in the modern furnishings and abstract paintings as though they were beneath his personal taste. "My luck never runs that way."

"From your lips to God's ear," Jai quipped, giving the man a smile he was sure didn't reach his eyes. "In a blink, *anyone* can become disabled or somewhere in between living and dead. Never forget that."

Donald scowled his displeasure. That statement alone always seemed to get through to the hardest of people who wanted to believe they were invincible. That's why Jai always opened every fundraiser speech with that line or something similar. People tended to fall under the belief that all disabilities started at an equal point. They never thought that a car accident, workplace injury, or genetics could wreak havoc on their bodies and life at any moment.

"You could serve up one of those felons and buy yourself some time," Donald suggested, sliding a heart paperweight off Jai's desk, curling his pudgy fingers around it.

"We can wait for the DNA results to come back," Jai said, as someone knocked on the office door. "I can bide my time. The truth will come out. Eventually."

"But by then the damage will be done," Donald pointed out, grinning. "Then, you won't have patients, a facility, or anything else to speak of. You're losing ground every day that you don't accept my offer." He laid the paperweight back on the desk, then gestured behind him. "I thought you'd need a little incentive, so I brought along a couple of friends to help me out. Make you understand exactly how ugly things can get."

He opened the office door to find Kelly standing outside. "His minions are getting impatient."

She stepped back and his gaze fell on two women clad in power suits and wearing austere facial expressions that held an ominous vibe. He immediately recognized the red hair and freckled face of Tina Drew-Miller—Big Red—as the woman who had been all over the news the minute Temple's pregnancy was leaked by a police source. Quite possibly at the urging of the man who'd been smirking at him seconds ago. The other woman he also recognized as Marilyn Spears, the one who'd been in charge of fielding documentation that had been required as part of an ongoing witch hunt. For some reason, he had the feeling that she was not enjoying this process as much as Donald and Big Red. At times, she would hint at ways to close the gap on the process, but then Big Red would throw something else into the mix and start things all over again.

Pointing over his shoulder with one thumb, Jai said, "So he somehow talked you into expediting this whole process, right?"

"We didn't have a choice," Big Red said, and actually managed to keep a straight face behind that lie. "The press coverage alone demanded that we take immediate action."

No, that "immediate action" came after Donald found out that Jai was in line for managing member of The Castle, which would set the stage for ousting Donald and the other men who had control, he moved some key players into place and rained down all kinds of unnecessary audits and investigations on Chetan. He also worked the most vicious angles pertaining to this current unfortunate situation with Temple, trying to get Jai not to sign the paperwork. With eight other men who had his back, Jai was not going to be strong-armed into giving up something so important. Not when he understood the depths that rich men would go to keep their dirty deeds hidden. The Castle was mired in so much filth his fellow kings—eight men who had been commissioned to unravel all the wrongdoing within the organization—it was taking much longer to weed out the source of so many crimes.

Right now, it was taking full resources to unravel the mess the former board had made. An unknown individual attempted to assassinate Khalil and his son, Vikkas. That action netted Khalil a two-week hospital stay and Vikkas, a graze wound on his upper arm. All nine of the kings were filtering through leads, trying to figure out who would be so bold to harm such a peaceful man. Thanks to Daron's handle on the security and surveillance systems, and Dro doing some major digging into the backgrounds of all The Castle's members, the answer would present itself soon. But, before that, he had to deal with this immediate challenge.

The two women followed him into the office and sat after he waved them toward a couple of chairs.

"All of the male employees are on leave," Jai countered, reclaiming his seat across from his unwanted guests. "So, the more pressing issue has been eliminated. I don't see why the patients have to be moved."

The quieter woman's body language hinted that she didn't agree with the actions of her superior. She leaned away from Donald and barely kept the disdain off her face when she looked at him. Donald must've had something on Big Red to force them to pull a rope around this process so fast, without proper planning or a good contingency effort in place.

Big Red crossed one leg over the other, her chin lifted in a haughty manner that signaled her authority as the director was absolute, but so it was with the men who had banded together to take on people like her boss. "They're going to be placed in state care for the time being. Even when this is all resolved, you won't be able to operate the way you have been all this time." She inhaled and let it out slowly. "The fact that Dr. Taylor was the only one in the medical community who spoke up on your behalf is telling."

Marilyn straightened her skirt, but didn't say a word.

Jai absorbed that whole spiel and felt the need to educate Big Red on the truth of things, but also as a way to reach the silent one who might have a conscience under that conservative exterior. "Let's call it like it is, more people didn't come forward because my methods don't feed into the pharmaceutical pipeline—an industry that makes billions off people, since they have a focus toward treatment and not full cures. These new meds that get FDA approval without the years of testing, or after the right money changes hands ..." He flickered a gaze to Big Red, who seemed bored by all the logistical information. "... sometimes create more illnesses that require patients to take even more medicine." Jai steepled his fingers under his chin. "Who benefits from that? The people who are putting money directly in his pockets, not yours. Yes, I can see where that question could pose a problem for your friends."

"As a former pharmacist and someone who works with those companies," the silent one finally spoke up, "I say not to vilify everyone in the industry. There are many aspects of Big Pharma that aren't bad. And everyone wants a cure, a pill, a quick fix to get better. No one wants to be told there is no cure, suffer through the pain, or just too bad so sad. Sometimes drugs are risk versus benefit."

Jai slid to the edge of his seat, all too ready to debate the issue, realizing she had valid points. Donald and Big Red shared a bored glance.

Marilyn's hand went up to ward off the attack. "I'm not absolving Big Pharma for all its sins. But, there is a middle ground here and we need to find it. Without some of those companies sinking their funds into medical research, cures would not be created, and they do cost money. And there are often gross misuses of the system. I just ask that we all use a little perspective on both sides of this argument."

Big Red and Donald glared at Marilyn and she quickly added, "I will comment no further on that point."

"And regardless of *your* point," Big Red said, as her hard glare was on Marilyn before her eyes flashed in Jai's direction. "You're going to lose your patients and right after, your business as well.

"Fortunately, the law is on our side," Jai countered, but he was well aware that they were right in some regards.

"Will that be enough?" Big Red shot back, a malicious grin punctuated her point. "Donald, here, has enough power to keep you on ice until he gets what he wants."

A chill crept over Jai's skin as Donald's thin lips curled into a sinister smile. Despite his discomfort, Jai refused to show any outward sign of his unease. He'd worked hard to establish his clinic, which had a stellar reputation and he'd be damned before he let this evil trio ruin what he'd sacrificed everything to build.

CHAPTER 8

"You would think that someone who has been asleep for an entire year, would stay awake as much as possible."

The harsh words, unexpected voice, and ugly tone snatched Temple Devaughn from a not-quite-peaceful sleep. She didn't appreciate being disturbed, especially since her dream world was much better than the reality that faced her.

The brilliant lights in the ceiling and the bright-white hospital walls hurt her eyes as she locked gazes with her scowling mother and shot back, "You would think that someone who had three children would realize how exhausting childbirth could be." Then she lifted the corners of her mouth in something that couldn't be construed as a smile. "But then we'd be talking about someone with empathy and compassion for others, of which you have none."

Sharon Liscell flinched and so did Curtis Burnside, Temple's ex, standing next to her mother and whose sour expression marred his Nordic features.

"What are you doing here?" she said to Curtis, unable to hide the disgust in her tone. "Besides seeing for yourself that I'm actually functioning well on my own."

Temple realized too late that she had made a major mistake in falling for the charms of a man like Curtis. She had met him at an interfaith worship service and that suave exterior, coupled with the high-level position he held in his church, led her believe he was a true Christian which had made her fall for him so hard she couldn't get back up again.

Their relationship was a whirlwind of dates where he wined and dined her at some of the best places in Chicago. She didn't realize, until later, that a great deal of his conversation was long on promises and short on substance. Then he began pressing her to take a test drive before making that ultimate last step—marriage. Something always made her hold back.

Unable to tie down what made her unsettled, she finally had a conversation with the minister at her church several months into their relationship. Pastor Kae warned, "Make him wait for marriage. You deserve a man who respects your faith, yourself, and your body enough to slide you down the aisle before he slides you into his bed."

"He's a good man, has a good job, isn't dependent on anyone, and has his own place." Temple's list of Curtis's attributes rang hollow even to her own ears.

"As he should," Pastor Kae agreed, leaving the glass wall that separated her office from the sanctuary. "He doesn't get a bonus round for doing what a grown man should. And all those points you made might be true, but he's still a man. Sometimes righteousness takes a back seat when that peen starts doing all the talking and thinking."

Enough said. Temple stalled any attempt to take her for a "test drive" to make sure they were a good fit. For some reason, that didn't sit too well with Curtis.

And if her memory served at all, that was the argument they were having the night of her accident, then … Temple closed her eyes, as another scene came to the forefront. She had rushed from her condo that night because he tried to … he had …

Her eyes flew open as the scene swirled out of view and a throbbing headache commanded every ounce of effort. Her mother's face hovered to the point that she blocked out everything else.

Nurse Jennifer walked into the room and quickly maneuvered by her bedside. With a smile, Temple let her know she was okay. The nurse faded into the background, but stayed in the room to keep watchful eyes on Sharon and Curtis. They did give off the strangest vibe.

"We're bringing in a priest so you can go through with the marriage," Sharon said in a matter-of-fact tone that matched her stance. "At least he'll be able to make sure your extensive hospital bills are covered. Since you have no assets to speak of."

Money. That's what it always came down to with her mother. Something about their unwanted presence, and the fact that she could vaguely remember turning Curtis down more than once bolstered Temple's courage. "Jaidev Maharaj is footing the bill for my stay here, along with everything else. I am well taken care of. No need to rush into any long-lasting thing. Especially since I need to recover first and foremost, then I'll get back to my regularly-scheduled program."

Sharon shared a glance with Curtis that spoke volumes to their anger. Why wouldn't they be pleased that someone else was paying the costs? What was their game? She glanced at her finger and didn't find an engagement ring there. Somehow, she believed one was never there in the first place.

"You agreed to the marriage before your ... unfortunate mishap."

Mishap? Car crash in the middle of the Dan Ryan Expressway. From what the nurses told her, and the information she was able to locate online, she'd barely made it out alive. They were calling her the Miracle Woman, and the newborn babe, The Miracle Child. The baby. That ... stranger.

Temple gripped the railing and closed her eyes as a flash of light and the crunch of metal on metal echoed in her head. A dark blue car of some type. Her heart raced and her body went hot, then cold. In her mind's eye, she was running from something, but what? She opened her eyes and found Curtis peering at her in a curious manner. Something about him left a sour taste in her mouth. His scent was pungent and heady, not in a good way either.

Engagement? Not bloody likely.

"Be that as it may, I'm of a different mindset now," Temple said, drawing the covers around her body. "There won't be a marriage to him—or anyone, any time soon."

Curtis leaned toward Sharon and tugged at her sleeve as though to lead her from the room.

"No," Sharon said, pulling out of his grip. "Not until we secure her future and yours. She has submit the DNA results needed to establish that she's actually Siobhan Liscell." She glared openly at Temple. "You've always been difficult," she snarled. "No wonder your father left us. He—"

"Get it straight, Mama," Temple countered, meeting her mother's glower with one of her own. Over the years, she had given much thought to the "why's" of it all and pieced together snippets of what she'd overheard to figure out her parents and that whole sordid ordeal. "He left you. I had nothing to do with the fact that you became pregnant with the sole intent to snare him in a marriage he clearly didn't want. How'd that work out for you?"

"You little b—"

"I'd like to see the documents for the Trust set up by my father."

"Not necessary," Sharon growled., but she flinched and stood ramrod straight as though a lightning bolt had zapped through her. "Those papers are locked away for safe-keeping."

Which meant Temple couldn't get her hands on them without some type of court intervention. That also meant her father was still alive. If her father had died, the Will would be recorded and made public, but not so with the Trust.

"Nurse Jen, could you escort my guests out of my room?" Temple said in a firm tone. "And see to it that they're not allowed to return."

"How dare you," Sharon growled and waved Nurse Jennifer away. "I'm your mother."

"I can't tell," Temple said, gesturing for the nurse to hold off for a minute. "Truthfully, I never could. Thank God I got away from you and that I've done well on my own." Temple relished their thunderous expressions. "Trust me when I say that I'll continue to do so—without you or him." She dismissed them with a flick of the wrist. "I'll be leaving here the moment they get through with all of the tests. I'd prefer it if we never laid eyes on each other again." Temple met her mother's angry glare head on. "Someone who hurt me the way you did, has no place in my life. Someone who tried to sabotage my career has no place in my life. Someone who never loved me has no place in my heart." She shifted her gaze to Curtis. "And someone who disrespected and belittled me at every turn, trying to make me insecure so he could get what he wanted, has no place even thinking I'd walk down any aisle with them. It's more likely that I'd run in the opposite direction."

"Sabotage your career?"

Temple laughed, sat up and threw her legs over the side of the bed, and signaled to Nurse Jennifer that she was fine. Out of all her accusations, those words were the ones Sharon decided to hang her hat on? "You think I don't know how you ruined my life? I mean, in addition to everything else you did to please that husband of yours and his brother all while trying to line your pockets at the expense of my body and my well-being?"

The memories of *that* night were back in all its nightmarish forms. But the details of what happened the evening she landed in a coma were also coming back, little by little. She had been running from something or … someone. Then someone had rammed into the back of her car. A blue car, bright headlights that still flashed in her mind at the time. The police hadn't figured out who or why.

The sabotage to her talent, though, didn't come to light until she'd finished high school, and was sitting in front of Petal Gowie in the office of admissions for the Art Institute. She had been shocked to find one of her own paintings hanging on the wall. When she completed that particular piece, she'd been ten years old. Painting was her only escape from the abuse she suffered at her mother's hand. And it seemed her only connection to her father.

"How did you get that?" she asked the robust woman who turned to identify what Temple had referenced.

"I acquired it on a trip to Virginia. So many of this child's work, and her father's ended up in thrift stores in that area." She glanced at

Temple's application, then focused on the painting for several moments and her eyes widened with recognition. "Temple Devaughn? You're actually Siobhan Liscell. It's been years, but I should have recognized you right away."

"Yes, ma'am. That's me." She wasn't sure if she should have been startled that the woman knew who she was simply by connecting her to the painting. She gestured to the abstract and a father-daughter portrait blend that was reminiscent of the hope that she would connect with her father one day. "And that's definitely my artwork."

Petal nodded, clasped her hands and placed them on the wooden desk. "I was so disappointed when we received the letter declining the scholarship package that I put together specifically for you."

Temple's head whipped away from the painting and her gaze latched on to Petal. "What letter?"

Petal blinked several times, pursed her lips, then left the desk and went to the bottom drawer of a metal filing cabinet. She took several moments, then retrieved a slim manila folder that was a little worse for wear, and slid the contents across the desk. Temple scanned an unfamiliar document with a very familiar signature. Though the art school had given her a full ride in combination with a private school and a host parent, her mother had sent in a letter stating that Temple had decided not to accept and would continue with a normal course of study.

Further notes on the file showed that Petal had attempted to reach out several more times over the years and ... all calls were not returned. Sharon had told Temple that they had retracted the offer because they wanted to give the scholarship to someone who had more promising talent as they were mistaken about Temple and her prospects. Donny and Ebbie, with the help of Ms. Crenshaw, had managed to send several of Temple's paintings to the school, believing that her talent would be the way to get her out from under Sharon Liscell and her latest husband. Every time they tried, someone had blocked their efforts.

Once again, her mother had lied. And that, too, had changed the trajectory of Temple's life and served a vicious blow to her thoughts of following in her father's footsteps. That lie had kept Temple tethered to that house, instead of being moved to a safer space as her siblings intended.

Tendrils of fear overcame her the moment Curtis stepped closer to her bed. His scent made her lightheaded and ready to lose that scrumptious breakfast she'd consumed.

"Do not come near me again," she warned them once more.

Sharon's face darkened with anger. "You're going to need me long before I'll ever need you," she threatened.

"I certainly hope life doesn't work that way," Temple replied, tipping over to the chair. "With everything else you did to me, correction—let them do to me, if you were on fire, I'd pour some gasoline to keep the party going."

Curtis gave her a lingering look and swept out behind Sharon, who had stormed from the room.

Temple addressed the nurse, who stood against one wall. "Jennifer, I know with all this drama, you all are ready for me to go."

"Honey, we are not trying to see you get up out of here," Nurse Jennifer said, glaring at Curtis's retreating form.

"Why?" Temple asked, mystified.

"We're getting spoiled," Jennifer said with a grin. "Mr. Maharaj sends each one of us thank you notes, flowers, and the entire wing and staff gets breakfast from Batter & Berries, lunch from Dixie Kitchen, and dinner from Miss Mabel's Jamaican Joint every day. We had to bring in a nutritionist to approve your meals. Kind of helps that she slides through every day for a plate along with everyone else. We have to fight off co-workers from the other floors." Jennifer assisted Temple to the chair closest to the window overlooking the gardens. "Not that we're looking at it as a bribe or anything, but we've never experienced this level of appreciation from anyone. Ever. Found out that he has a standing order for the food and gifts to continue for months after you check out. We don't take that lightly. Some of us are even considering coming to work for him when all of his affairs get sorted out."

"Affairs?" Temple said, trying to remember if she'd seen a ring on his finger. "What affairs?"

"Oh, not those kind of affairs," Jennifer said with a laugh. "I'm talking about the situation that landed you in this hospital in the first place. He's been hard at work about finding out who did this to you."

Temple mulled that over, along with some of the information she'd been able to glean on the iPad that Jaidev had bought for her to use. "It has to be one of the male employees, right?"

"So that's why he paraded those guys in here a few days ago?"

"Yes, I asked him to do that," Temple replied. And all but two of them had complied, against her doctor's wishes and their lawyer's advice. Temple had asked to be blindfolded. None of them smelled remotely like the man whose scent she would never forget as long as she lived.

"You are his top priority right now. And the baby," Nurse Jennifer said, snapping Temple back to the present. "You know, he's here every second he can, in the nursery. Holding her, singing to her, and talking to her." Her smile widened. "He's going to make some woman an excellent husband and be an awesome father to any child."

Yes, a lot better father than Temple would ever be a mother. No way in hell did she want a reminder of what had been done to her.

No way. No how.

CHAPTER 9

Jai leaned back in his chair, fixing his attention on Big Red. "At least she has a point of view that's based in reality and not revenge."

Big Red's ivory face turned a shade that lived up to her nickname. "You know what?" she spat, getting to her feet. "I'm going to let you two hash things out." She gave a dismissive wave of her hand before she gathered her things. "We can at least put in the report that he voiced his dissent. It won't change anything. Make sure he understands that."

Jai waited until Big Red and Amos cleared the room before focusing on Marilyn Spears. Honestly, he liked the woman's perspective, but he couldn't work with her agenda, especially since she was on the other side of the fence from him.

He checked the phone and saw a note from Nurse Jennifer giving an update on Baby M. Every moment he wasn't at Chetan, the new center site or at the Castle, he'd been at the hospital with Temple, and in the nursery holding the baby as Temple had not laid eyes on her since delivery.

He, along with everyone else, kept thinking she would come around. Unfortunately, she was adamant about having nothing to do with the child. Seeing how she was struggling to put her life together was inspirational. The only fly in the ointment was her aversion to the baby. Understandable, but still painful.

"I get it," he said to Marilyn. "You're not trying to provoke, simply providing food for thought. And what was your background again?"

"I was a pharmacist many years and a researcher-liaison before I put in for a position with the Bureau." She tilted her head, peering at him. "But I truly appreciate what you've accomplished here. It's admirable on so many levels."

"Then you'll understand when I tell you that the only pills our patients receive are ones that are absolutely necessary," Jai said. "We monitor their vitals and blood work—everything. Test them for allergies so we know what works for them and against them. Our focus is on healing, preventative care—not on how much we can rake in before we put patients in the poor house or the grave."

Eyes narrowed, she said, "That was a low blow."

"Well, since you feel that I'm going so low, I might as well hit a little higher up on the below the belt scale." He gestured to the bracelet. "Riddle me this, Bat Woman."

"There was never a Bat Woman," she said, with a wide smile as she lovingly fingered the charm she didn't realize had identified something she probably would have preferred to keep secret.

"Yes. I always wondered about that, too." Jai leaned against the wall near the window. "And my earlier assertion wasn't a low blow, it's the truth," he shot back. "People are dying because they can't afford insulin, or even allergy medicine."

"On that, we can agree," she said.

"So, yes, we've been a problem for the industry for a hot minute. But that isn't what any of this is about. He's pulling your strings, and you're letting him, too. I can tell you have a problem with it. You need to work on your poker face."

Marilyn flinched, but a small smile played about her lips. "I've been with the Bureau for nearly twenty years, I can retire in a few more. This is the job, whether I like it or not."

Jai assessed her for a moment. "Politics aside, let me ask you this." He left the window to perch on the edge of the desk, so he was a few inches from her. "Of all the places you've investigated over the years, if anything happened to you or one of your loved ones … where would you—or them—want to be?"

Marilyn snatched up her belongings, and made her way toward the door. Then she paused as though giving his words some thought. She looked at him over her shoulder. "On a personal level, I mean it when I say that I admire what you're doing, Mr. Maharaj," she said. "I'll give you that. But we have laws in place—and regulations for a reason. Everyone can't just go off and do their own thing. We'd have chaos."

Jai moved from the edge of the desk. "I do follow each and every protocol that is in place. I'm not trying to get around any of that. I simply want something better for my patients. This society disregards the elderly and children, the disabled rates up there, too. No one considers that they, themselves, could be disabled." He snapped his fingers. "In a split second."

Jai pulled up the remote and flicked it so that the screen on the back wall projected his latest numbers related to the success rate at Chetan. "Somebody has to do things a little different, otherwise the health and well-being of America as a whole will decrease to the point that only pills and potions will be considered the norm for everything."

Marilyn scanned the screen taking in the text and images, before releasing a resigned sigh. "I will help you as much as I can, but you have to know this goes above my pay grade. When those results come back and one of your men has been found liable—you can forget all of those plans. Doing something different is admirable but not when you're under fire from the very establishment who licensed and still regulates you."

"I don't say anything or speak out on their methods," Jai protested, miffed that she would take that stance.

"You don't have to." She gestured toward the screen. "Your actions say it for you. And you don't even publish papers or hold any kind of symposium to share your findings so that others could be included."

Jai closed the distance between them, taking in the emblem on her bracelet, trying to recall where he had seen a similar one recently. "Does that mean I shouldn't do it at all? Or that no one should try? I'm trying to perfect a method and make sure it actually works before I put it in the public domain. And it's hard for me to do anything where every success is seen as suspect."

Jai took a calming breath and lowered his tone. "The bigger question is why would the industry want to ply us with one drug after another, rather than finding ways for people to live healthy, wonderful lives without costing them an arm, a leg and a couple of toes." Jai stroked the bracelet she wore, as a memory clicked into place. "And maybe you can answer one other question."

She stepped back, suspicion clouding her eyes. "And that is?"

"How long have you been sleeping with Hiram Fosten?"

CHAPTER 10

The room in which Temple lay was overcrowded with bodies, and Jai hoped the place would empty out sooner, rather than later.

Terri Ann Rayford the social worker who reached out to him the moment Temple decided she wasn't leaving the hospital with Baby M, turned an expectant gaze on him. The nurses had christened the sweet infant Baby M for the first letter in his last name.

Jai threaded one hand through his hair as his chest expanded with a deep breath. He had weighed all the options and the best scenario he could come up with was . . .

"I will take her," he said to the nurse whose forlorn expression also signaled long-held frustration with Temple Devaughn.

He repeated his words and a lengthy silence followed, along with shared looks of surprise from Ms. Rayford, Nurse Jennifer, and Nurse Donisha.

They had called him to talk some sense into Temple, but he already knew and understood her stance. He didn't have to agree. Her position on this mattered a great deal. To force her to take the child was equally as damning as the action taken to impregnate her in the first place.

"This happened because …" He shrugged. "It doesn't matter. I will care for the little one."

Since he had been the one in the nursery several times a day, crooning to her, promising her that everything would be all right, he had to follow through on that part of his promise. He couldn't do any of the above if she went into an already overwhelmed foster care system. Jai didn't have the best relationship with his father, and he definitely wanted to be certain this little one did. Given the violent way she'd been brought into this world, he could at least ensure that the rest of her existence wouldn't impact her in a negative way. Healing for both mother and child was paramount, and that meant they might live apart.

"There are channels that we have to go through," Ms. Rayford said, adjusting her documents so they were stacked in a neat, orderly pile on a table in one corner of the room. "And personally, I think you're too close to this situation to be a good placement."

"Is the place you're aiming to take her planning on caring for her for the rest of her life?"

She grimaced as though trying not to see the logic and simplicity of what he offered. "Mr. Maharaj, I can't make any guarantees about that."

"Go through whatever paperwork you have to in order to make this happen," he said, rocking the baby gently in his arms. "My background check and fingerprints are already on file with the Illinois Department of Health and Human Services." He stroked the baby's back, then patted her back gently three times. She answered with a hearty burp.

"Oooooh. All right judges, what's your call?"

Nurse Jennifer held up eight fingers. Nurse Donisha held up six. Temple's hands slowly snaked upward for five, and Ms. Raye shook her head and put up six fingers and smiled.

"Well, that's a solid seven," he teased and nearly everyone in the room laughed. Even Temple who graced him with a smile as she looked on. He smiled back and he could swear she blushed.

"I don't want her to end up in the system—even for a short period of time," he said to Ms. Rayford and two of the nurses sighed with relief. "When things are clear, we'll arrange a private adoption."

"This is highly irregular." Ms. Rayford glanced at Temple, who was struggling to keep a neutral expression.

"He has my consent," Temple said folding her hands and dropping them on her stomach. "I'll sign whatever you need so he can have the baby."

Ms. Rayford snatched up a yellow legal pad and scribbled a few notes. "The father needs to consent as well."

Jai's head whipped up. "The father is a rapist," he countered, barely able to keep a civil tone. "He doesn't get a say."

Temple adjusted to a sitting position and nodded as Jai held out his free hand and she quickly grasped it. "The moment they find out who that monster is, he'll be going to prison. He'll never get his hands on her. I trust Mr. Maharaj with her."

"But isn't he also under …?" The social worker peered at their conjoined hands, then flickered a gaze between Temple and Jai as though working out details in her mind. "I'll look into it. For now, I need to tear up this paperwork," she said, holding up a set of documents that would have committed Baby M to an uncertain future.

Jai had heard enough stories over the course of his short career to know Baby M already had a rough start and placing her with family after family would not be a good thing. One of the reasons he started Chetan straight out of the medical rotation was to give a better placement for patients that fit a narrow criteria.

"Sounds good to me." Temple glanced at Jai, who reluctantly allowed the nurse to lift the sleeping baby from his arms. "We'll do something private."

"I'm still going to run another background check just in case," Ms. Rayford said and her tone was far from happy, more like resigned to a situation that was out of her control.

"That's fine," Jai said.

"Whatever," Temple offered in a dismissive tone that had become her norm.

Nurse Ashley tipped in, slid the baby from her fellow nurse's arms, frowned and moved toward the bed. "Don't you at least want to … at least once?"

"No, I don't want to see her," Temple replied, turning her head, but there was a break in her voice. "Just … just please take her and go."

Jai gave the nurse a warning look—and not for the first time. This one, more than the others, was having a hard time with Temple's stance when it came to Baby M. Nurse Jennifer had schooled the others on the situation, but he'd have to insist that Nurse Ashley be kept away from Temple because the warnings had gone in one ear and slid out the other.

They'd all fallen in love with the child, as had he. Baby M seemed to know when he was around, and was especially impressed with his singing. The infant cooed at the sound of his melodious notes. He gestured for her return and Nurse Jennifer smiled as he accepted the baby again and cradled her in his arms.

Temple turned her head to watch him, but was just in time to see the nurse and the social worker gave her a lingering look as they filed out of the room.

"If you will do one favor for me," Jai said.

Temple focused a steely gaze on him.

"Would you at least provide milk for the first few weeks?"

Temple blanched and was almost as pale as the pillow behind her.

Jai instantly regretted the question, but pressed on. "She already has so much going against her and she'll need the best start in life."

Temple averted her gaze but a micro-expression conveying her confusion crossed her face. A second later, she schooled her features into something bland and unreadable. "It's supposed to do a body good, right?"

"Well, I'm about to be a single dad," Jai answered, trying not to smile at her joke. "And we'll both need all the help we can get. Thankfully, a pump would work and I'll be sure to pick up the milk every day."

The low hum of the nightly news echoed in the background. Reports of yet another teen missing from the South side of Chicago.

"This should never have happened," she whispered.

"You're right," Jai conceded. "And we're going to find out who did this to you. They *will* be brought to justice."

"You're so sure of that?" she asked, her gaze firmly on the baby. "The justice part?"

"DNA will pinpoint that monster and the police will have no choice."

She watched a moment as he murmured comforting words to the baby. Then a frown crumpled her face. "How could you take on a child that …"

"Because she's beautiful and vulnerable," he replied, caressing the baby's cheek with one finger. "Putting her in the system would be cruel. Especially when I have the time and means to care for her."

Temple's expression went dark as she narrowed a glare at him. "So, you're one of those pro-life nuts?"

"Not at all. Very much pro-choice," he replied, lowering himself to the leather chair next to the bed. "Means I care about the woman's choice and about the woman who decides to bring a child to birth and beyond. I provide careers for men who are looking to have a second chance at life. One of the first things each one of them did was start shelling out money for child support."

"You're proud of that?"

Looking sideways at her, Jai said, "Speaks to their character."

Eyes narrowed, Temple asked, "You don't think one of them did this to me?"

He glanced at the baby before answering. "Would it be painful for you to hear me say 'no'?"

"No, you seem like the loyal type and you might be right." Temple stared across the small room, then continued. "Since I've been here, I get flashes of things. The scent of whoever it was. I would know that smell. Maybe even the clammy feel of his skin. The sound of his voice." She sat up straight in the bed. "Can you bring them here?"

"I don't think that's a good idea, since they're the center of the investigation." After giving Baby M another smile and thinking a little bit, Temple added, "You're right. But since I can identify his smell, maybe you can bring a piece of clothing or something."

Nodding slowly, Jai admitted, "That might work."

"I think I might … I don't know. I just want to do something besides lying here being taken care of by everyone." Temple's expression and voice turned sour. "Except my mother. She only comes to demand that I stall on giving the police permission to do any DNA testing and to insist that I marry quickly, so that a man I have no affection for can take care of me."

"You don't have to do that," Jai said, uncomfortable with the sense of alarm spreading inside him. "This situation happened on my turf. Everything related to you and her is my responsibility."

Temple craned her neck to steal another peek at the baby. Then as though remembering she shouldn't do even that, she abruptly turned away.

Getting to his feet, Jai announced, "I'll take her to the nursery since her presence disturbs you so much."

Jai made it to the threshold when she said, "The nurses are looking at me like I'm some kind of monster."

Yes, he had seen the reaction from one in particular. "I'll speak with them." *Again.*

"No, don't bother," she said in a resigned tone. "They're right I should feel . . . something."

Jai turned back into the room, claimed a seat on the chair next to her bed. "Temple, most women have months to come to terms with changes that happen to their bodies and to bond with their child. Months. You had thirty minutes—and that's a stretch. Then had to come to terms with the fact that you were in the middle of a full-on delivery of a child you knew nothing about, and a violation that was of the most horrific kind." He searched her eyes for a moment, hoping his words were getting through. "Trying to distance yourself from a child who feels foreign to you is understandable. So, give yourself some credit. Right now, I'll just have to provide enough love for both of us." He looked down at the baby. "Isn't that right, India?"

Temple perked up, tried to get a look at the baby yet again. "You're naming her India?"

"Did you have something else in mind?" Jai raised both eyebrows. "I'm a little weary of everyone calling her Baby M."

"But ... but why India?"

"I named her for the country in which my parents were born," he said, locking hiseyes on hers. "The place has a history of overcoming the British invasion and rule but still has shadows of pain from their presence on our land. So many died for their greed and the need for them to conquer for financial gain. We survived when Gandhi made the mistake of partnering to give away our land to Muslims in an area now called Pakistan. He was beloved by a lot of people around the world for his efforts to bring peace, but he has been hated by many Indians for that action alone." He stroked a hand across the downy silk of India's hair. "Though parts of the country are still ravaged by poverty and there is still an issue with an underlying caste system, India is still one of the most beautiful places I know."

"But all countries have a flawed foundation," Temple said, folding her arms across her ample bosom. "America, Africa, China, England."

"And Canada," he added. "But they don't have quite the same ring."

Temple's lips twitched before settling into a smile. "I like India. India … Maharaj?"

"Good to hear." He stood, rocking the baby a little as he sang to her.

Temple closed her eyes, and settled into the bed, listening to the words of *Just Ordinary People*, a gospel song that Khalil had given Jai in high school. He still had the Walkman and the cassette.

When the last words, *little becomes much when you place it in the Master's hand* echoed in the room, Temple's eyes flew open and locked on his. India definitely enjoyed his singing. Evidently, so did her mother.

Jai thought it was high time to have Temple out from under the doctors, who were bringing in specialist after specialist trying to figure out what factors contributed to Temple being in such a healthy state. They couldn't believe nothing was seriously wrong with her after being in a coma for a year. Seemed they were inventing reasons for her to remain in the hospital's care.

He was certain she had tired of all the poking and prodding—their attempt to find something contrary that they could lay at his feet.

"Let me go see a doctor about getting you up out of this camp."

CHAPTER 11

Hiram, along with his fellow co-workers from Chetan—Ryan, Chuck, Andre, Michael, Falcon, Jared, Chris, and even DeMarco stood in a cluster inside an impressive meeting space. They had been awed by the opulence of The Castle even before they entered. Now, they faced a circular boardroom table seating another group of equally impressive men who might be strangers to his co-workers, but Hiram remembered when Jai had asked him to look up the names on his first journey to the Castle when Khalil had been shot.

If he remembered correctly the men at the table were named Dro Reyes, the "Fixer" who was of Mexican descent as evidence by the olive skin and dark hair; Vikkas Germaine, Khalil's son, and international lawyer; Shaz Bostwick, with signature locs that nearly touched his waist, was a family and immigration lawyer whose family was from Jamaica; Grant Khambrel, a commercial architect for Houston who also had dark hair and brooding eyes; Reno Deluca, founder and director of a women's shelter and came from an Italian family in Chatham; Dwayne Harper, owner of a private college prep school with a haircut that was as chiseled as his medium brown features; Daron Kincaid, an inventor and security specialist whose family came from the Philippines; and Kaleb Valentine with light brown skin, slightly wavy hair, a commercial and residential real estate developer. None of them had anything in common with Hiram or the men standing next to him. Why were they here?

Several weeks ago, Jai had called Hiram into the office and asked him to create the special tattoos for all the Kings at the table. This took place under the direction of Daron Kincaid, who seemed most familiar today, even without his trademark hat. Hiram wasn't sure what the silver markings the man added toward the end signified, but now he was beginning to wonder exactly how far this whole Castle thing went, and what more would be required of him and the men who were walking into this situation blind.

Jai stood, beckoning them to come forward. The woman who guided them through the maze leading to an inner chamber of The Castle, disappeared as quickly as she had shown up when they first arrived at the golden doors of the front entrance.

"Man, this is some medieval kind of bull—"

Hiram nudged Ryan into silence. The two sets of men assessed each other—professionals in designer suits versus uniform scrubs and tees—but it was Hiram, the designated spokesperson for his co-workers, who stepped forward and said, "You wanted us here. So, what's the deal with all this cloak and dagger stuff?"

"Yes, we'd like to know that as well," Shaz said, moving his locs off his shoulder so they streamed down his back while tamed with a leather band.

Jaidev scanned the men at the table and said, "Khalil made a grave error in not having men already lined up, or a succession plan. I am asking for two things here. One, for each of you to mentor my employees in your specialties. Two, for you to consider that while we are Kings of the Castle, we should have a few Knights as well. Ones that learn from us, grow with us and become Kings in their own right."

"The difference is," Reno said, sliding his glass toward the center of the table. "We have a common denominator. Khalil Germaine. They have none."

"Incorrect," Jai shot back, his tone causing the rest of the men at the table to snap their focus toward him. "They have me, and they will have us. That's a lot more than most. And in my estimation, it will be more than enough."

Grant tapped the file in front of him. Hiram recognized the document on top—the résumé he had submitted to apply for the position at Chetan. Why would they have them?

"Come a little closer," Grant said. "We don't bite on Mondays."

"Unless you're into that sort of thing," Dwayne joked, causing the rest of the men at table to glance at him.

The Kings chuckled. The others did not.

"Well, just so you know, we'll bite back," Hiram warned, squaring his shoulders so he stood at his full, towering height. His co-workers did the same. "We might not have your degrees, or status, or anything like that, but we ain't no punks either."

"What are you riding?" Kaleb threw out, narrowing a piercing gaze at Falcon who stiffened at hearing such a loaded question.

"What are we riding? Jaidev Maharaj's program all the way to success," Michael shot back, his dark brown gaze narrowed on Kaleb. "But if you mean if we have—"

"Had," Hiram corrected, keeping his eyes on Kaleb.

"*Had* any affiliations," Michael continued. "Then we're sorry to disappoint. Maybe a few of us did at one time, but we put that life—and a whole lot of things—behind us when we stepped into Chetan. That's the life we're about now."

Hiram moved forward so he was closer to Kaleb and tilted one eyebrow. "Maybe the better question should be, what are *you* riding? The person throwing it out there, had to bring that from someplace."

Shaz gave a low whistle and a few others at the table shared a speaking glance, along with smirks that said plenty. Hiram had hit the mark—spot on.

"Former Sovereign King, heavy emphasis on former," Kaleb offered, seeming a little taken aback at having to admit it.

Hiram's low throaty chuckled echoed in the boardroom. "Yes, you did seem to have that … edge. Success can't always hide our pasts, but we can refuse to let it—or anyone—define us by it."

Vikkas applauded, soon followed by other men at the table, even Kaleb. "And therein lies the truth," he said. "But I'm not too cool with having them given that name in relation to the Castle. They have to earn it out, first."

"Why," Jai shot back. "Khalil didn't call us students, he called us scholars until we became exactly that."

"That's truth," Grant said. "Everything is in the name that you embrace. We did when we became Kings."

Reno chimed in, "We're here to make sure they live up to that name. And that means they'll be given the same, or better opportunities than we had."

"I'm still going to need to check out their background a little further," Daron said. "You're asking us to trust them with a lot for all we don't know about them."

Hiram's shoulder pulled back. "And I don't have a problem with that. Do whatever it is you have to do. Jai called us Knights, and that's exactly what we'll be, whether you sign on for it or not. We know him. We don't know you."

Silence met that declaration, but Hiram and not a single one of his fellow Knights had any signs of backing down. They would own their process and no one would take it from them.

"So how is this going to work?" Dwayne asked Jai.

"I'll let each Knight speak to what their interests are, then we can pair off that way," Jai said, placing a hand on Hiram's shoulder. "But I'd like all of them to be assessed by Dwayne, so he can help craft a higher education plan, and recommend any seminars, workshops, or studies that will put them on the fast-track to their ultimate goals. Same way that Khalil did for us."

"But we had three years of intense study," Dwayne protested, his focus on Jai. "It was nothing like the traditional structured education."

"And they've had years of an intense life that meant doing whatever was necessary to survive. That's an education within itself. They've been through some things neither of us could fathom," Jai said, then leaned toward Dwayne. "And from what you already know, you'll make sure that their education isn't on a boring path," Jai teased with a comedic lift of his eyebrows. "Unless your reputation as one of the top educators in Chicago isn't well-earned."

"You're full of it, you know that?" Dwayne said and both the Kings and Knights laughed along with him.

"This is an ambitious undertaking for all of us," Jai continued, pacing the small area in front of the projection screen. "But we have to understand Khalil's aim. That we work together to do our part to counteract the inhumane issues going on in this world. It takes money, power, but most of all, it takes purpose and passion." Jai scanned the faces of everyone in the room. "Every single man here today has most of this in some form or fashion. Any one of you who needs to be bolstered in any area, only has to tap into your fellow Kings or Knights to get what you need."

"You said, that in a year's time we would all be on the same page." Hiram scanned the anxious and concerned expressions of his co-workers that mirrored what he felt at the moment. "This whole thing seems like an entirely different book. I can get that dude is going to bring us up to speed on an educational level. Much appreciated, by the way." Dwayne gave him a head nod in reply. "But these dudes are rolling with the kind of bank accounts we've never seen."

Jai's shoulders drooped as though he realized his plan might be admirable, but maybe the Knights weren't up to such a monumental task.

"Each one of us started like you," Shaz said.

Grant offered, "With the exception of Vikkas and Jaidev—"

"Wrong," Jai shot back, his face tightening with anger. "My father disowned me the minute I accepted that invitation to attend Macro. He wanted me to have nothing to do with Khalil Germaine. He had like … this insane jealousy when it came to him." Jai allowed a few moments for that tidbit of info to settle in. "My mother encouraged me to follow my heart, then to move on to my dreams of being a healer. None of which my father approved. He wanted a lawyer, international merchant, or politician. Someone with real influence that he could brag about. He even said, I could at least become a 'real doctor' as if what I do is not important. So, if you've thought I've been …" He flicked a gaze at Hiram, then back to the Kings. "Big balling all this time, you're sadly mistaken. I had to start with only that stipend Khalil gave us upon graduation."

The silence beyond that statement was telling.

"What stipend?" Vikkas asked, narrowing his gaze on Jai which caused a chill to fall over the room.

CHAPTER 12

Temple walked into her condo and froze after a few steps over the threshold. That overpowering scent hit her first and she had to brace herself so she didn't lose her last meal.

She scanned her condo and only recognized one thing—an expensive portrait abstract blend by her father. Everything else—the furniture, the walls, the décor was something more suited to a bachelor who was pretending at that "rich and famous" lifestyle, but only had a Ramen noodles budget.

None of these selections would have been his choice. Everything had Sharon Liscell's name written all over it.

"What happened to my place?"

"Your place?" Sharon repeated, and the sarcasm in her tone was enough to send a chill up Temple's spine. "Remember when I said you would need us before we would need you?" She leaned in so she was a whisper away from Temple. "This is one of those times."

"I control all aspects of your life," Curtis said over the rim of a jewel-studded goblet from where he sat across the room. "And it made sense to put my name on the paperwork in order to maintain everything properly."

"You mean, in order to live here at no cost to you." Temple let that hang for a moment but his expression remained blank.

"Well, I was seeing to your personal business and all." His smirk that accompanied that statement infuriated Temple as he crossed his ankles on the edge of the dining table. "Living here was ample compensation."

Sharon sauntered into the dining room and parked on the chair. "And he will continue to take care of you when you marry him and you're done with all of the nonsense."

"Take care of me," Temple scoffed. "The only person Curtis cares about is himself. No wonder you all get along so well." She peered at them, taking in the rigid set of her mother's shoulders. "Why are you all rushing to get me to the altar? Hell, I just came out of a coma and found that not only was I violated, but I have lifetime evidence of what happened. Can I at least catch a break around this camp before folks try to put me in that emotional coma called holy matrimony?"

Sharon crossed into the dining area and closed the distance between them. "Well, I'm sure Curtis will give you a couple of days while you sort yourself out." She gave a dramatic flourish of her hand as she placed a Virginia Slim between her lips and Curtis rushed to light it for her. "Then, you'll need to make a choice. Either marry him to stay here, or …"

Temple scanned the hodge-podge décor surrounding them. "I'd leave first."

"And where will you go?" Sharon taunted, taking a pull from the cigarette. "He has control over your accounts, this place, and everything related to you. Right now, you can't access anything without his permission." The smoke curled around her like a halo of evil. "We went in yesterday and had the court reaffirm his control over your personal endeavors until it is determined that your mental acuity is intact. You know, seeing that you can't be in the right state of mind after being in a coma for so long."

"So, you bribed a judge to do as you wanted," Temple said. All the years of her mother tipping on the edge of polite society, the Black Nouveau Riche, had paid off. She had found a way to make herself invaluable to lawyers, judges, businessmen, and philanthropists alike. So many people had been into Sharon Liscell for "favors" that she never went without anything she needed. Until she married Carl Webster, thinking that she'd hit pay dirt, without realizing he would never see the "pay" part of the equation, and all she had was someone who was lower than dirt.

Unfortunately, their many benefactors' generosity did not filter down to Temple. Beside Donny and Ebbie, various teachers and parents of her friends had been Temple's guardian angels growing up. If anyone had been the wiser, they would have thought Temple Devaughn was adopted. They would be wrong. Temple was simply unwanted and unloved, but she held some value that her mother never quite made clear. Now Temple was of the mind to find out what her mother had been hiding all these years.

"It's all right," Temple said, resigned to the fact that she would face a few unnecessary challenges with her mother and Curtis—now at the helm—and working in tandem. "The first chance I get I'm going to reach out to my father and figure out exactly what happened. I'm still wondering how a man who painted the most beautiful artwork in the world, could have left me with someone with such an ugly soul?"

Sharon almost dropped her cigarette. "He didn't want us—"

"He didn't want *you*," Temple shot back as her mother swiped at the ashes that had fallen on her suede skirt. "And I think I became a casualty of whatever mess you made." She scanned all the rooms within her view, saw that some of the designer items were well out of his financial reach, even in his prime as a top stock broker. And her own accounts couldn't have afforded this kind of living. "Better yet, I'm going to get a judge involved so I can lay eyes on those Trust documents you never wanted me to see."

Curtis bristled with anger at the same point that her mother's expression went blank and he put his feet on the floor.

"Problem?"

"No, not at all," Sharon purred. "We'll send them wherever it is you're staying."

"Well, I'm staying here," Temple said, claiming a seat on a chaise with the most hideous design. "I don't care what fancy paperwork he put in. This is still my place and evidently my money helps to pay for it and this new lifestyle."

"That's not exactly how it works," Curtis said, and there was a bit of censure in his tone. "You don't want to have anything to do with me? Fine by me, sister," he taunted, using the words spoken by Sophia's character from The Color Purple. "But you can't stay here until you have a lawyer to file for it. This is my place now."

"And you expected me to do what? Agree to be with you after pulling a stunt like this," she asked, shifting her gaze to Sharon whose scowl marred her pretty features. "I didn't see it at first, but he has a cold streak that matches yours to a 'T'. I'm happy that your actions have provided more clarity than I ever needed."

Temple turned her attention to her father's artwork. Closer scrutiny showed a portrait of baby Temple inside the image of a sun emerging from the moon's shadow. She went to the kitchen before Curtis could block her path, snatched up a knife then ran directly to the painting and liberated it from the wall.

"You can't take that," Curtis said, getting to his feet.

"Watch me," she shot back. "This is the only thing I have from my father. It took me forever to find it. There isn't a snowball's chance in hell I'll leave it behind for you two to profit from it."

"Don't worry," Sharon said around a ring of smoke. "It's not worth anything."

She wouldn't bother to disabuse them of that notion. Anything from the great Elvin Drescher could fetch thousands on the open market. But that meant nothing to Temple at the moment. Somehow that painting represented more now that she had given birth to her own child. This painting was a message. The fact that it was the sole item of hers left in this place she once called home was telling. The only thing of value she left behind in Virginia was her brother and sister and the only thing here worth anything was the painting her father had done. Many lithographs existed, but this original, she had scoured every imaginable place until she found it and used every penny she had at the time, to purchase it.

"The fact that my father wanted me to know that his sun revolved around me, means everything and more." She looked at Sharon whose lips were pursed in mild disapproval. "Evidently, I've been sleeping on a lot of things. If you were so willing to lie about my father, if you were so willing to sacrifice me to Uncle Dane to get your hands on the money my father left me, no telling what else you've been lying about all these years."

Temple didn't wait for a response as she grabbed up the small suitcase Jaidev had brought for her, struggled to anchor the huge painting under her arm, and left them without a backward glance.

CHAPTER 13

Jai grimaced, seemingly taken aback by his tone. "Well, I thought …"

Daron and Kaleb simply stared at him. Dwayne, Dro, Grant, Reno, and Shaz slowly raised their hands, admitting they had received one as well.

"And I don't get why you of all people would need it," Vikkas said to Reno. "You came from money."

"Came from it, doesn't mean it landed in my hands," Reno countered, and Hiram noticed him fingering the tattoo on his wrists. "Especially when I went into architecture and then opened the shelter. My father and I didn't quite see eye to eye on where my life was going. Khalil filled that void for me as well."

"Dro?" Vikkas snapped.

"I still have it," he confessed, waving it off as a non-issue. "Gaining interest in an account that I haven't touched since high school. Should be a nice little chunk of change."

Dwayne pulled his shoulders back. "I used mine to pay for my education, and for my sister's," he admitted. "Sometimes, I dip into it when my students' families need help. But there's still a great deal of it left. Khalil didn't give us chump change." He shrugged. "I'm just saying."

"Why do you seem so upset about this?" Grant asked Vikkas who bore a strong resemblance to Jai—olive skin, tall stature, dark hair, except Jai's had a silver streak at the widow's peak. "It was his money to do with as he pleased."

"My father tells me everything,"

"Well, not everything," Daron said over the rim of his glass, his short-cropped hair bore a reddish-brown tint. "And I think I didn't get one, and Kaleb either. We didn't graduate from Macro."

"Jai, how about this," Dro said, running a hand through his dark hair. "That money I have sitting around, why don't we divide it nine ways, and have it become the starting funds for the Knights. If you're vouching for them, that's good enough for me."

"You mean, once they complete their education points," Dwayne chimed in.

"They'll need some of it now," Jai insisted, shooting a glance at his brother. "With the investigation going on right now, I'm still paying their salaries. That extra could be a cushion to move out of the places where they now reside and into more suitable arrangements. Once they hit a certain level of success, they'll become targets." He glanced at Hiram. "Church?"

"Most definitely," Hiram said, grinning at Jai's use of his favorite word which meant that whatever had been said was considered "facts" or "truth". "Good looking out."

"So, why bring them here?" Kaleb asked, and Grant gave him a warning look. "We could've met them in Starbucks somewhere."

Jai tilted his head, glaring at Kaleb in a silent move that said, *are you for real right now?* Instead, he answered, "Because I need them to see the finish line."

"The Castle?" Reno asked, his focus on Jai who shook his head.

"No, you." Jai walked around the table, placing a hand on each man's shoulder. "Every one of the Kings. We all come from diverse backgrounds, and some of you from very humble beginnings. They need to see this …" he gestured, meaning them, the place and everything involved. "That they, too, can be on this side of life. Not just living paycheck to paycheck." He looked at Hiram and smiled. "That they deserve to do what it takes to be sitting around this kind of table, discussing solutions to issues that affect their communities and ours." Jai moved forward until he was standing behind the chair meant for him. "It can't be only the nine of us. It started with Khalil, and he put all of these ideas into us for going beyond what we dreamed possible. Now it's us, and then …"

"Makes sense," Dwayne said.

"Spoken by a man who had to be brought into this kicking and screaming," Vikkas pointed out.

"Because I'm not like any of you," Dwayne shot back. "I don't have your wealth, or status, or anything like that. I didn't feel that I belonged among you. Khalil and my Uncle Bubba made me see things differently. That it isn't acquiring lots of money that makes you rich, it's being able to fulfill your dreams, desires, and those of the ones around you who don't necessarily have the resources or tools to do so."

Dwayne stood and faced the soon-to-be Knights. "I rebelled against The Castle because I believed it was a guise to get us into Khalil's religion—the Bahai's Faith. Nothing could have been further from the truth. Not once did he make being part of his faith anywhere in the deal. He took the best elements of his religion and put them in a secular form—elevating all of us on a spiritual level, but through humane treatment of others, protecting those who cannot protect themselves, seeing how each of us are connected spiritually, no matter what religion or faith we embrace. We can't be better as a whole, until we work on becoming better, more enlightened individuals."

Vikkas' face split into a wide grin, and he held out his fist to Dwayne for a pound. Dwayne obliged and said, "I get it now. I understand our purpose is far beyond money and power, it goes to using what we have to balance out the evil that's in the world.

"His own little band of superheroes," Hiram asked, trying not to feel overwhelmed by this overload of information.

"Something like that," Shaz said, leaving the table at the same time as Daron, Grant, Dro, Kaleb, Dwayne, and Reno who now stood next to

Vikkas and Jai. They all faced the younger men in the room.

"And another thing," Jai said.

"Here we go," Shaz mumbled and slid back into the nearest chair.

"We're going to need your help with the investigation we're conducting under the police radar."

"You don't ask favors in small measures, do you?" Shaz shot back.

"They can't trust the police on this," Kaleb said with a pointed look at Falcon who nodded.

"Finally, someone besides Jai who gets where we're coming from," Michael said as Ryan nodded and added, "Now *that's* church."

"There is another set of chairs in the anteroom attached to this one." Vikkas gestured behind him. "Pull one in and slide to the table. We're going to tell you how The Castle came into existence, and then we have major business to handle."

The Kings moved forward one by one and welcomed each of the Knights into The Castle. Well, all except one.

"Speaking of business," Hiram said before Grant could extend a hand to him. "Before we go all brotherly love, sunshine and rainbows, and everything … Jai, we need to talk."

CHAPTER 14

Hiram stood to one side of the boardroom, gesturing for Jai to join him.

"What's going on?" Jai said, ignoring the directive to move away from the rest of the group. "Is it something we need to speak about in private?"

Hiram's shoulders pulled back as he answered, "Actually—"

"No." Reno moved to stand next to Kaleb. "Especially if it's something that's going to keep him from becoming one of the … Knights?"

All the Kings nodded at the term.

"Knights," Reno said. "Everyone here should be about transparency."

"As I was saying before I was interrupted," Hiram replied with a pointed look at Reno who shrugged. "There's something I must tell you."

"Can it wait until after this meeting?" Jai implored, his face a mask of concern at having his plans derailed—even a little.

"Maybe, but what I'm about to tell you means I might not be able to a part of Chetan or anything else," Hiram replied, handing Jai an envelope. "You might want to take a look at this before we get into all this brotherly love."

Jai opened the envelope, scanned the document and his head snapped up at Hiram, his expression pained. "Letter of resignation? Why?"

"Do you know that *why* is the question asked most frequently around this joint?" Hiram teased, placing his back against the wall.

With his eyes fixed on Hiram, Jai said, "You're stalling."

"Because I need a favor. A *huge* favor."

Jai sighed and the other men shared a few questioning comments. "Brothers, can you give me a few moments."

"Make it fast," Shaz said. "My stomach's about to walk out of here before the rest of you."

"Camilla's aunt is delivering some more vittles. Should be here shortly," Vikkas said with a chuckle.

"In that case," Shaz waved them forward. "Take all the time you need."

"Nah, man." Falcon made his way through the men gathered closer to the door. "If it means he's riding solo, and leaving us all to this, then we need to know."

Jai scanned the document again. "So, you're leaving this goodness on the table just when things are getting started for the Knights. All because you need me to do something for you? That makes absolutely no sense."

Hiram scratched his forehead, grimacing as he gathered his thoughts. "I'd like you to hire someone."

Jai opened his mouth and promptly shut it when Shaz gave him the signal to just listen. Then he opened it again because curiosity got the better of him.

"Wait, hear me out," Hiram said, holding up his hand to stall Jai's protest, which caused Shaz to toss out an 'I told you so' look. "This person will be able to help you more than I ever could. They can get you through all the red tape and ensure that Chetan, and the new places are tight."

"All right, I'm listening." Jai moved back to the table, settled his weight onto the closest chair—one normally occupied by Grant, who gave him a stern look. The rest of the Kings claimed a spot close to them as the Knights wheeled in chairs of their own.

Jai squared his shoulders and braced himself. He already had a pretty good idea where this was going. The conversation he'd had with Marilyn put a lot of scenarios in play. At least he now had a better handle on where to put Dro, Daron, and Vikkas' talent to use in protecting him and Chetan against Donald's machinations.

"*Who* do you have in mind?"

In a neutral tone, Hiram said, "You already know her."

"Her?" Jai nodded and laughed, causing Hiram to pause midway into a seat that Ryan wheeled up for him. Now things were making a little more sense. Actually, a *lot* more sense.

"It's not like that at all." Hiram rubbed a hand across his low-cut fade. "Well, it's sort of like that, but—"

"Then what am I missing?" Jai shot back. "You're about to give up a hard-won career in the medical field, and a place among a group of men who will provide valuable mentoring, and you're set for a seat at a newly-formed table for you all to mirror our efforts and come up with some agendas of your own."

Hiram's tone was patient when he answered, "Because we both can't work for you at the same time."

The men around them didn't move, but waited in silence.

Jai thought about that for a moment and flicked his wrist in a dismissive wave. "That's an unspoken rule, but certainly isn't policy. It can be worked out."

Hiram shook his head. "No, not for us."

"Us?" Jai gave a low, throaty chuckle.

Hiram grimaced and rose to pace the open area in front of the boardroom table. As he did, he massaged the nape of his neck.

Jai had never seen the man so nervous.

"There should already be some level of trust between us," Jai said before Hiram reached into a white envelope he'd placed on the table, slid a résumé toward Jai, and pointed to the first line.

Jai scanned the name, and then looked up. "Whoa." He locked a gaze with his right-hand man. "So, you're a couple now?"

Hiram nodded.

Though he already knew the answer, Jai was still grateful Hiram chose to tell the truth. He didn't realize Marilyn and Hiram were so far along in their relationship, they were finishing each other's lives. "And she couldn't apply herself?"

The younger man schooled his features until he put on a stoic poker face. Evidently, Marilyn hadn't told Hiram that she had practically pleaded with Jai to allow Hiram to remain at Chetan and she would resign immediately to let him keep his position. Jai didn't see anything good that could come of losing Hiram, or by not having someone in the Bureau who was at least trying to look out for them.

"She doesn't know you're asking me for this?"

"No."

Jai's eyebrows winged upward. "That's not a good sign for your relationship if you're keeping—"

"This is more serious than anything I've ever been in," Hiram countered. "I see the bigger picture because you gave us the best start. Chetan is only the beginning. The Castle is the next step." Hiram took a few steps to where an architectural scale model was displayed. He tapped the corner of the miniature replica of the building that would be erected on the South side of Chicago within the year. "Six more centers, right? Total of nine. Do you think we—your crew—can't peep what's going on? And Marilyn would be good for the project. She can lay the groundwork in every place, run point on processes that you would never be able to. She knows the questions to ask, and will be invaluable when they're making you jump through hoops just for shits and giggles."

"But that's what Kelly does," Jai pointed out, though he did see value in Hiram's logic.

"Don't get me wrong, Kelly is good at what she does, but you'll need someone like Marilyn, too." Hiram inhaled and let his breath out slowly. "Do you know how good it feels to defy the odds? Like the men working for you who didn't let their records hold them back? Like how you're successful with Chetan even though the suits aren't feeling the way you do things? Temple Devaughn being alive and the baby, too." Hiram nodded. "We don't do things the traditional way around here. And Marilyn can help you because she knows how to navigate both sides and make sure you come out on the winning end."

Jai placed an index finger on the resignation letter as the pit of his belly sank. "Then what are you going to do if you're not here?"

"I'm going to do tattoos and my art," Hiram answered. "I've taken everything you taught us and I don't have any debt, so I can open a shop in the South Loop and—"

"Why not do both?"

Hiram took a step back and tipped his head as if he hadn't heard correctly. "What?"

"Complete the necessary work with your mentors, handle this part of the business while you build that business as well," Jai offered.

A rumble of agreement from the other men passed around the room.

Hiram's eyes took on a hopeful glint. "So, you're going to hire Marilyn?"

"After the conversation I've already had with her, I'm going to listen to what she has to say, then we'll see what's what." Jai waited and was pleased when Hiram smiled. "The bigger question is … why should I trust her with something as sensitive as this? You know I could easily put in a call and part of my battle with the Bureau would be over. Then she'd be the one trying to explain away things that I shouldn't be aware of. She's not being loyal to her job, why would I believe she'd be loyal to me?"

"She's being loyal to what's moral and what's right." Hiram gestured to the other men. "I thought that's what this was all about. Her ethics involves not allowing them to keep doing these things to you." Hiram put his back to Jai as he scanned the rest of the group, then claimed an empty chair between Reno and Dro. Jai followed suit.

"When I was in Menard, I had to be on guard, all the time. Even in my sleep. No real rest, because at any moment violence could break out, for no reason at all. Even ones who claimed to be a friend, could turn"— he snapped his fingers"—just like that." Hiram faced Jai, who folded his hands and placed them on the boardroom table. "For the first time since I got out, I closed my eyes when someone else was in the room with me, and I felt at peace. That's a kind of trust I don't take for granted."

Jai absorbed the words and nodded. "How do you know that she's not playing you? Amos is not above getting down and dirty by using her on the sly."

"Because that's not how she's made," Hiram countered, getting to his feet. "Trust. That right there is just as important as love. I never knew what peace was until I met her. Never realized that I was still doing time—out here on the other side of the bars, because there's so few people I can trust." Hiram tapped a fingertip on the table. "You, the crew. But a woman? I haven't had this kind of love—ever. She sees me. The *real* me. Not an ex-felon. She sees the man. The man I was becoming before the fight that landed me in a place I never wanted to be. That night was a diversion from my path, but it's also part of my path right now. I see that now. Being with her, and simply sleeping with her—and I'm not talking about sex—is an act of trust." Hiram stalked to the projection screen which bore an image of the new center, then returned to the conference table. "And Jaidev Maharaj, I trust you, too."

"Yes, but just so you'll know," he shot back, "I won't be sleeping with you."

"Um, no. I'm good on that man," Hiram quipped, shaking his head.

Everyone in the room laughed.

"You've got a good place in your heart, man," Hiram said. "I've seen the worst that people have to offer—inmates, where guards can be just as ugly—the whole legal system. It feels good to be part of something great. And it's a beautiful thing to have a woman who wants to be part of the solution."

Jai mulled that over a moment.

"So, I'm willing to give that up to get her to a place where she's not having her twenty-plus years at the Bureau being held over her head if she doesn't continue in his efforts to put the screws to you and your business."

Jai thought that over for a moment. "No, we'll come up with something else," he said, as the idea appealed more to him by the minute. "Because I'm not willing to cut my wingman loose. All of you are set to play a vital part in several projects."

"Including that Kings of the Castle business?"

"Most definitely."

CHAPTER 15

"You knew I would come," Temple said, as she entered Jai's home. Her gaze swept across the artwork strategically positioned on the walls to capture the sunlight, then to the Persian rug, the eclectic but warm furniture, and the piano at the far end of the parlor before focusing on him once again.

"I hoped you would," he replied, taking her coat and what looked like a small overnight case and a canvas painting that was nearly twice her size before placing the case in the foyer closet, removing the contents on the hallway table and setting the painting there. "Thank you for this. Although I'm curious about what changed your mind."

Temple perched on the suede sectional in the parlor, closed her eyes and sighed as if the entire morning had taken most of her strength. She seemed sad, almost sullen, more so than he had ever witnessed in the hospital.

What had happened between her exit from Meridian and moving back to her condo to give her this weary demeanor and a heavy spirit? All he wanted to do was wrap her in his arms and tell her everything would be all right.

Unfortunately, he couldn't cross that boundary at this time. She had to invite him into her personal space. The last conversation they'd had was that he would do "milk runs" to her condo every morning to retrieve any bottles she had for the baby. Then she called to say she'd come and breastfeed the baby directly for a time and she said nothing to indicate anything had changed.

When she opened her eyes, they seemingly focused on him, but the faraway look in her dark-brown orbs unsettled his soul. He waited, standing near the parlor's entrance, knowing she would speak only when she was ready.

Several moments ticked by before she said, "He violated me."

Jai released a calming breath and whispered, "Yes, he did."

"In the worst way," she continued and wrapped her arms around her body.

"Yes." He resisted the urge to comfort her, but thought it wiser to hold his ground where he stood, a few feet away on the carpet.

She locked gazes with him. "This is the second time a man has violated me this way. The first time, I was ten."

Jai blinked, trying to keep his expression neutral, but didn't respond. The horror that filled him, knowing that unfortunate piece of her past, could not be displayed on his face. He did not want her to think it was directed at her instead of the ugliness of the situation.

"You're shocked by that," she said, inhaling and fixing her gaze on the portrait of his grandmother; the woman who had inspired him to become a holistic practitioner. The woman whose abuse from family members who were supposed to care for her, had been substantial and unforgiveable. As unforgiveable as the acts committed against ten-year old, and later grown-up, Temple Devaughn.

"I wanted my first time to be special. For it to be in a marriage bed with the man who was part of my happily ever after." A tear streaked down her face, followed by several others. "He—first my uncle, then some stranger—took that away from me."

Jai waited a while longer and when no other words were forthcoming, his ears picked up India's coos echoing from the kitchen where his house manager was holding her at the moment. Maybe now wasn't the best time to have Temple interact with the baby. She needed to be cherished and reassured.

"May I have permission to embrace you?"

Temple's expression went blank, but then she snailed a nod and he moved to sit next to her, gathering her trembling form in his arms. He held her for what seemed an eternity. The coos from the kitchen became more insistent and Jai was aware that India would not hold off for nourishment much longer. Marilyn had her on a consistent schedule that even allowed Jai to be in on the late-night feedings. He'd timed his sleep pattern to India's so he could be with her as much as possible. Sometimes that meant snatching a nap on the sofa in his office, but it was well worth it. Each day, he whispered the same words in her ear. *Remember that I love you. Remember who you are. Remember God's purpose for sending you to the earth scene. I love you, India Maharaj.*

Maybe the baby's softness could have a positive impact on Temple as well. "May I bring my daughter in?"

"*Your* daughter?" Temple shot back, lips immediately set in a thin, disapproving line.

Jai wasn't sure what to make of her statement or her tone. She had been adamant about not wanting the responsibility of motherhood. He believed her. So, in his mind, India Maharaj was his.

He extracted himself from Temple's hold and pushed a button on the intercom near the entrance to the living room. "Sandy, please bring India to me."

Moments later, a robust woman with a sienna complexion shifted the baby from her fleshy arms to his.

"Hey, little darling," he whispered.

India made her acceptance known as he smiled down at her and a gum-filled grin lit up her face. Jai took a moment, then placed the baby in Temple's arms as Sandy swept from the room.

Temple held her tentatively at first, then inched her a bit closer as though the baby was a fragile porcelain vase. Jai draped a shawl over her, one he had purchased for this purpose and because he believed she would appreciate its warmth and beauty. Temple adjusted her blouse while India's fingers tightened around Jai's as though unwilling to let him go. Then she nuzzled Temple's breasts, sensing the nourishment that awaited.

Temple looked up at Jai, a question in her dark-brown eyes. He nodded and gave her an encouraging smile. She positioned the shawl and opened her blouse, then shifted the lace bra and India took to the nipple, drawing down the milk. Only then did Jai slip his hand from India's and slide out to leave them in peace.

"I missed out on the pleasures of carrying this child," she said, causing Jai to pause at the threshold. "Watching my body grow. Feeling her develop." Jai glanced over his shoulder in time to see Temple's finger stroking the soft skin of India's cheek, trailing it to her chin. "My first child. She hasn't even heard my voice in those months. She doesn't know me."

Temple lowered her gaze to the carpet.

"You're here now," Jai said coming to stand a few feet away. "That's all that matters to her."

"I did the right thing by giving her to you," she said as Jai stroked the silky crown of India's hair. "I can't provide for her the right way. I don't even have a place to live."

Jai's hand paused as he focused on Temple. Several thoughts whirled through his mind. Her weariness. The suitcase. Her sudden appearance.

"My condo … he's all up in my place. Owns it, and it now smells like him," she said. "And because I rejected his offer of marriage again, he says I have to leave until I come to my senses. After what my mother did to me when I was growing up, I can't even see how she would hand everything over to him—my condo, my bank accounts—all of it while I was … not in a position to do anything. Entitlement. It's one of the things I've always disliked about him. And now the way he smells." She shuddered and the action sent a chill up Jai's spine. "For some reason, now it makes me so nauseous, it's hard to breathe. It never had before."

"You will stay here," Jai offered, knowing this, too, was the right thing to do. "I have more than enough room."

Temple shrank back, cradling India closer. "I can't do that. I've already caused you enough trouble."

"Not you," he insisted, moving his hand from the baby to place it on Temple's arm. "None of what happened is on you."

She sighed. The words would take time to sink in.

"I'll give you some private time, then we'll work out everything else, all right?"

Temple still hesitated for a moment, before nodding.

Jai released the breath he didn't realize he was holding, made it a few inches toward the entrance before she whispered, "Please stay. I'm having such a hard time processing this, and you've been so easy to talk to …"

He crossed the short distance between them, lowered to his knees and situated himself until he sat on the plush carpet next to her thighs. "I'm here for as long as you need. I truly thank you for coming."

"As if I had a choice." A trace of amusement colored her voice.

"You always have a choice with me," he replied, glancing upward to look at her. "I made a request, if you're uncomfortable doing this a second time, we can just go back to the original arrangement of pumping—"

"No, I'm just busting your chops," she teased, giving him a smile.

"Busting my chops?"

She chuckled. "An old way of saying I'm just giving you a hard time."

"I can take it," he said with an answering laugh.

Temple glanced down at India, who had sighed with contentment and kept on nursing, then she focused on him again. "Has anyone ever told you, you have the most beautiful smile?"

Jai beamed at the compliment. "And I make a pretty mean poker face, too." He frowned up his face in a comical fashion and she burst out laughing. The sound of it warmed his heart.

When it died down, she said, "Your face, your smile was the first thing I saw when I opened my eyes."

Jai braced himself, trying not to let that statement affect him, but for some reason it shook him to his core. Twelve months in a coma and his smile was what welcomed her back into the conscious world? So profound.

"The first thing I heard was the words, 'Don't cut her. Don't you treat her as someone who doesn't matter . . . '"

Jai bristled and sat up straighter. "Wait a minute! You were awake that whole time?"

That question lingered for several moments as Temple stared straight ahead. "Actually, I think I had awareness off and on at times," she admitted, absently stroking India's hair. "I remember the music. I remember the movies, the laughter. I remember the water on my skin and that was the best part. I loved the way that felt, the warmth, the weightlessness." She closed her eyes. "I remember an argument between two men on whether to play Bernie Mac or a Kevin Hart comedy for me. That was funny, because one of them realized that I preferred Bernie and he was right. I remember not wanting to sleep because it took me away from them."

Jai inhaled, not wanting to say anything that interrupted her sharing such important things.

"The nurses at Meridian were amazed that I could stand, walk, move. I don't feel like a woman who has been in a coma for—" She frowned, then asked, "Wait a minute, why are you smiling?"

"You've proven everything I believed. Everything I set out to do. I don't get to have these kinds of conversations with patients."

"You should," she said.

"Yes, I'm beginning to believe you're right." A thoughtful silence dropped between them before he said, "We're just so happy when a person opens their eyes that . . ."

"And then I come along and screw it all up."

"No, never that. Your awakening was a blessing—unexpected, but a blessing nonetheless."

Her gaze met India's again, who stared at her trustingly. "I'm beginning to think that having such a handsome, caring man looking after me might not be so bad after all."

Jai pulled his head back. "Handsome?"

"Fishing for compliments?" She smirked and grazed India's cheek with one finger.

He chuckled, shook his head, then shifted his legs.

"She really takes to you," Temple said. "Every time they tried to bring her in, she seemed to be searching … for you."

"It's my singing," he teased.

"Yes, that's something you're good at," she said, laughing. "Thank you for everything you've done. You're a good man, Jaidev Maharaj. The nurses were going crazy over you. You're going to need to wear a fake wedding ring to keep them off."

"Truthfully, that should've happened from day one," he said, meeting her eyes.

"Why are you single?" she asked, flickering a gaze to his left hand.

"Haven't tried to find the right woman, yet. When it's time, she will come. I won't have to go searching."

"Sounds … magical," she said. "All that time recovering after delivering this baby, I began to remember bits and pieces." She adjusted her clothing, allowing India to nurse from her other breast. "But what I remember most is that I felt all this pain and didn't know what was going on. Even took me back to what happened when I was ten. The pain took me there. And then I was with you. But when I saw you, heard you, I knew you were going to make sure I was …. safe."

"Didn't do such a good job of it while you were our sleeping beauty," Jai grumbled, then kicked himself for offering up that unwanted reminder.

"That's not on you. You can't control what other people do." She peered at him, eyes narrowing to near slits.

Jai stretched out his legs on the carpet, reflecting on the interactions he'd had with the newly appointed Knights. Since they became a part of Chetan, the fellas came to him first with any issues—personal or professional. He was more like a brother-mentor than a boss. He appreciated their trust. "No, even though all the signs point to it—and the media and law enforcement are strongly hinting that way. I believe that DNA will tell the story and they won't be anywhere on that page."

India's hands uncurled and he placed his finger back inside hers. She immediately curled her hands around it. "Their lawyers were pushing for that test to happen in utero, but the men didn't want any more harm to come to you or the baby."

Temple's eyes flashed with compassion. "That was … kind."

"That was patience *and* knowing that the truth would come out," he countered. "That is who they are."

"So, this has been hanging over their heads for months?" As she asked, she realized India still had eyes on her. The bonding instinct.

"Weeks. We had just found out you were pregnant," he said, staring at the portrait across the room. "And they've been through worse."

"Tell me about them," she asked, and the question took him aback. Her expression showed every sign that she was serious.

Hiram had shared a few thoughts about the nurses and doctors and his words came to mind. Jai didn't understand how all four of them could be so easily bought and swayed. And those were the ones with no criminal past.

Jai filtered through how much he should share without it being too biased, but he didn't think he could be when it came to them. Their successes outweighed their pasts, but sometimes that's all anyone could see. But that was also the springboard for where they had started on a better path to their current status. Honesty was the best way to go, so beginning at that point would be best.

"They've been guests of the Illinois penal system."

Her eyes went wide as she lifted India and froze. Then, Temple schooled her expression into the more serious one she'd had the majority of them time she'd been here.

"Now you're the one in shock," he said.

"I mean, that is a little risky in your line of business."

"Not risky," he said with a faint smile. "Hopeful."

This time Temple frowned.

"There is no greater courage, strength, and tenacity, than a man who is embracing a second chance at life," he said as he sat next to Temple and pressed a kiss to India's forehead. "They have been a great part of Chetan's success because they believe, wholeheartedly, in my vision." Jai kissed the back of India's hand. "I looked up the file on each one of them, weighed out the crime and their motives. I read through every court transcript—things that were said, other things that were dismissed, and—"

"And then you decided they were worthy enough to work for you," she said, and the censure in her tone was tangible. "You played God. Just like you did with India."

Jai was slightly insulted by the insinuation and the haughty accusation in her tone. "I played a director who was careful to choose men with a zeal to succeed, who wouldn't let their pasts keep them mired in bullshit."

"Ohhh, so we're a little sensitive about all this," she taunted, shrugging while a small smile played about her lips. "Forget I said anything."

"No, it's not that," he said smoothly. "They've gone above and beyond what anyone expected. They've also been combing through recordings and paperwork trying to find legal evidence of what happened to you. That's more than the police have done."

Sandy appeared at the threshold wearing a Switching in the Kitchen apron he'd brought her on a trip to New Orleans. She tapped the place on her wrist where a watch should have been, but was probably on the kitchen counter right now. The woman was a genius when it came to food. And Jai would soon have to take Shaz up on creating a fitness regimen for him. Otherwise, folks would have to roll him around this camp. Yes, the food was that good, and Sandy tried to toe the line between healthy and downright sinful. Sinful won out every single time.

"Temple, would you care for some lunch?" Jai asked.

"No, I'm fine," she said peering down at India who had fallen asleep.

"My chef, manager, assistant, organizer, and the main woman around here, is making Geechee Shrimp and Grits, fried green tomatoes, peach glazed wings, and—"

He could practically see Temple's mouth water and her stomach answered before she finally tuned her lips up to say, "Well, since you're twisting my arm and all that."

Jai chuckled and kissed India's forehead a second time. When he raised his head, his gaze collided with Temple's.

Try as he might, he couldn't look away.

CHAPTER 16

Jai guided his house manager to a spot outside the parlor where they'd have some privacy but could still keep an eye on what was happening between Temple and India. "Prepare the bedroom several doors down from the nursery. Temple will be staying with us for a while."

Sandy's eyebrows drew in, her gaze flicked to Temple, whose interest was solely focused on the baby. "Leave you two alone for five minutes and she's already moving in?" she quipped, peering around him into the parlor again. "And why not next to the nursery?"

"I don't want it to seem like I'm pushing India on her. Give her some time to adjust. She needs some peace right now."

"Do you think that's wise?" she asked, twirling one of her salt-and-pepper twists around her finger. "Getting involved with a woman who's at the center of an investigation that involves you?"

"Probably not," he replied, guiding her chin so that her gaze left Temple and focused directly on him. "But it's what I'm going to do anyway. I took an oath to first do no harm. Right now, that baby needs her mother—even one resenting how she arrived onto the earth scene—and rightfully so."

"Chief, it's not your fault, either," Sandy protested. "You're not responsible for any of that. Don't let guilt about—"

"It's not guilt at all," he admitted, placing a reassuring hand on her shoulder. "Certain things require that I remain at the center of all this because they are within my purview. That's one of the things that I learned from Khalil and being part of The Castle. Issues that come to your attention, happen for a reason. It is our duty to make things better for others if and when we're able."

Khalil Germaine had indeed lived up to his words. After being shunned by his family because of his pursuit of higher spiritual endeavors, Khalil created an exclusive Members Only Club for affluent patrons in the area. The idea was not only to maintain the wealth of The Castle but also to obtain regular access to individuals with the power, resources, and global connections to change communities worldwide. The money brought in was to be distributed to the less fortunate.

His mentor had heard a rumble here and there during his travels that all was not well, but the regular reports he received contradicted the rumors. However, little inconsistencies in what he was being told in writing and what Daron Kincaid had uncovered on a sweep of the place, caused Khalil to dig further into the matter and he realized he'd been severely misled. He cut the world tour short and came home. Guilt had weighed on him heavily. Not recognizing the lies sooner, allowed a criminal element to taint The Castle's true purpose. The saving grace was that Khalil had put in a failsafe clause in the contract that enabled him to make a sweeping revision of the managing members if warranted, relegating the former members to a non-voting consulting status with B shares instead of the managing members with A shares. The rest of the members would have to go through the rigorous process of reapplying for status.

Since the members in question were only "alleged" criminals, Khalil couldn't invoke the clause in the Member Agreements to immediately rescind their positions to The Castle. He also didn't want to use the section that would require all the programs being run within The Castle to come to an end and the properties and wealth distributed among his beneficiaries. He had to appoint managing members who could systematically unravel the web of deceit.

Khalil was determined to regain order and control without expanding the limited number of spots available. The vacancies and member transfers which had returned to The Castle worked in Khalil's favor. He used empty slots to recruit new Kings, his former scholars, without expanding the limited number of memberships for everyone else. The new recruits, along with a few veterans, could systematically clean house by weeding out and neutralizing the nefarious alliance's ability to run amok.

Jai was humbled when Khalil gave them the background details, told them he respected each one of them and expressed confidence that they could handle the task with integrity, courage, and compassion for those that had been damaged by the process.

He snapped back to the current when Sandy touched his arm. Meeting her gaze, he said, "I want you to be reassured that I'm not discounting your concerns."

Jai tipped his head toward her and continued, "You have an important place in my household. Your feelings definitely matter. And if I can ask one particular favor of you?"

Her chin lifted. "Anything, Chief."

"Be attentive to the mother," he whispered. "She has lost her family, her home, and her sense of self. She could use another anchor right now."

"No worries," Sandy said with a warm smile. "I will look after our guest as well."

"Much obliged, Madam Secretary."

"Hope she likes what I prepare because we need to fatten her up." She peered at him a moment, gaze narrowing to slits. "Are you all right, Chief?"

The nickname "Chief" was part of an ongoing joke between them when he first hired her to keep his home life together so he could focus on Chetan and now any Castle business that required his time. She believed he was of the Native American—First Nation—variety of Indian; and not the ones from across the Atlantic Ocean. While he was reluctant to give anyone carte blanch over his life, one incident in particular showed him that Sandy Forest had his back, front, and sides. She was the only one who answered his advertisement in the paper that didn't try to milk him once they figured out he had money. Sandy had come to his home to do a "deep cleaning" which, unknown to him, would take two days as she was serious about getting to everything.

Two sets of obnoxious neighbors were ticked that she had taken everything from the garage and placed them in the driveway so she could clean out his three-car garage. The neighbors were in the process of selling their homes, something that happened almost immediately after Jai had moved in. They complained loudly that the "unsightly" look was driving down the price of their homes. Never mind the fact that her process was only happening over a few hours. Jai was livid and planned to give his neighbors a good old-fashioned tongue-lashing.

Sandy placed her fleshy hands on his, keeping him from trekking across the street. "No, Chief. Let me handle this. And I won't even need Roscoe."

"Who is Roscoe," he asked, mystified.

"Let's just say he's not the family dog," she answered.

Jai didn't know what she had in mind, but he certainly understood that his new house manager was packing some serious steel. Seemed like most of the "queens' did as well. Vikkas' mate, Milan, and Daron's mate, Cameron were both gunslingers. Jai had to wonder, what was it with Black women and heavy metal. And he didn't mean the musical kind.

After the garage floors had dried, Jai placed everything back inside, and Sandy said, "Can you drive me to Home Depot for a hot minute?"

"Am I going to like what you plan to do?"

"Trust me," she said, smiling to put him at ease.

And he did. His mother practically loved the woman and they talked on a daily basis—as did he, since he wasn't allowed to set foot in the family home. His father, still angered at his choice of profession, could hold a grudge like no other person Jai knew.

She purchased a For Sale sign, and he had to fight to pay for it with his own money.

"Sandy, what are you about to do?" he asked when they stood in the parking lot at the store.

"You'll see," she said with another wide smile.

That For Sale sign went up in front of his home, though he had no intention of selling his place any time soon. She stuck it in the grass and witnessed the moment his neighbors came out and nearly cheered.

"Sandy?" He looked to her for clarification.

Aside from another mischievous grin, all she added was, "Didn't I say to trust me, Chief?"

The next day, Sandy took a black marker and wrote Sold across the sign, and then a ridiculously low amount.

That afternoon when he made it home, Jai aimed one question at his house manager. "Sandy, isn't it illegal to put the price on the sign?"

"Maybe unethical, but not illegal," she answered, peering out on the front lawn. "Trust me."

And he did.

That sign stayed outside for an entire month. Prominently displayed all through the open houses his neighbors held. Even through real estate agents pleading with Jai to take the sign down. And definitely through the neighbors finally getting over whatever it was they had against him and showing up on his doorstep, tuning up their lips to ask him to please, please, please, please, please take the sign down.

"Sandy," he said, laughing one day over an awesome dinner she had prepared after yet another neighbor had come calling.

"Trust me, Chief." She slid a warm slice of sweet potato pie in front of him. "You're going to laugh so hard you can't see straight."

Then the sign started coming up missing and Sandy called the police out several times because Jai's house cameras caught the thieves in action. Several of those neighbors, and even their real estate agents were given misdemeanor thefts against their squeaky-clean records that could impact their business or jobs since it had happened several times. They were even forced to pay a fine, make restitution to Jai, and replace each of the items they stole. Then Sandy would start the process all over again.

Finally, the phone stopped ringing with requests. The neighbors and real estate agents gave up. The sale price of their houses went so far down below the amount Sandy had written on his *Sold* sign.

Jai laughed so hard he was in tears.

When they lowered yet again, he was the one to put the offer on the table to buy six houses on his block, and three others a few blocks over for a steal.

"Always play the long game," Sandy advised, giving him a high five. "You didn't hurt nothing but their pockets. And you showed them you were better at the game than they ever were."

That Christmas, he gifted Sandy with the house directly across from his so she had a place for her daughters and grandchildren. Three of the others, he sold for nearly three times what he'd paid for them. Five others were now rental properties.

"Things will sort themselves out," he answered Sandy, realizing that he had learned so much in that six-month experience. "I don't know what life lessons are coming my way, but right now they're putting me through some serious hell."

"Yes," Sandy agreed. "But you already know how to play the long game."

Indeed, he did.

CHAPTER 17

"Somehow, the DNA samples sent to the crime lab became contaminated," Jai said to the Knights sitting around the make-shift boardroom table at a temporary location situated in the heart of Jeffrey Manor. He'd put the area in place for them to do an investigation of their own. "And the police crime lab has to repeat the process."

Groans and murmurs of dissent echoed from all nine men. Some of them rose from the wooden table.

"Contaminated?" Hiram snapped, tossing the *Sun-Times* on the table. "Somebody's playing games."

Andre pushed back, anger marring his rugged features. "I didn't sign up for nothing like this."

"Right now," Jai said, waving them back into the seats. "Another set of specimens are on the way to a facility of *my* choosing, thanks to your lawyers and my brother, Shaz."

"How much you wanna bet Big Red will be on the tube talking about this," Falcon said.

"When the truth comes out, they need to be just as public about our innocence as they were about our guilt," Hiram said, which brought on a round of agreement.

Falcon's almond-shaped eyes narrowed to slits, he slid a set of files to the middle of the table. "Now you know that's not happening. They like things the way they are."

"Where's DeMarco?" Jai asked.

"His grandmother's has stage four breast cancer," Hiram answered. "They're not expecting her to live much longer. We told him we'll cover for him. He's going to be out for a minute."

"Thanks for letting me know," Jai said, making a mental note to have Kelly keep tabs on him and see if there's anything they could do.

"Hey, I'm going to pick up that Italian Fiesta order," Ryan said, slipping into his Chicago Bulls jacket.

Hiram checked his watch. "You could have had them deliver it here."

"Have you seen those Facebook videos of delivery guys, who do all kinds of stuff to people's food?" Ryan shook his head. "Not happening today."

"Could happen directly in the restaurant, too."

"Doubtful," Michael said, moving to stand next to Ryan. "They don't get pissed off about tips—drivers do."

"Word," Kevin said. "I'm rolling with him and can scoop up my kids on the way. Baby's working overtime and my mom's gonna keep them."

He gathered his jacket and they made their way to the threshold.

"Hey, don't forget the red pepper and those cheese packets," Falcon reminded them.

"Knowing good and hell well you don't need no extra cheese," Hiram taunted, chuckling. "Especially with your little—um—issues."

"See, why you have to bring up old shit?" Falcon grumbled as his golden face turned ashen.

"Because the old shit is affecting new shit. Particularly our noses." Andre playfully waved a hand in front of his face.

The group burst into laughter as Michael and Ryan scowled.

Jai tried to keep a neutral expression, but failed as Ryan gave them the evil eye and reached for the door.

"Ha ha. We have a *sit-down* comedian," Chuck said.

Chris frowned. "You mean, stand-up comedian."

"Nah, it's only stand up if he's actually telling jokes," Jai said. "He's just being a smart-ass."

"Ooooooh, you just got clowned," Falcon said, doubling over with laughter.

The humor faded when Chris said, "All jokes aside, I wasn't going to say anything, but I thought you should know. Folks are giving us some serious grief." His forlorn expression told the story more than his words. "My boys are being bullied in school. They're calling me a dead-lady rapist."

"My wife keeps asking me if I did it and if it's why we haven't done that *thang* for a minute." Falcon scowled and his keen features pulled in, causing his eyes to nearly disappear.

"Whoa." Hiram's thick eyebrows shot upward. "What the hell?"

Everyone's gaze snapped to Falcon, who ran a hand through his locs and sighed. "I mean, she's seven months pregnant. The doctor can put his fingers up there and feel the baby's head and what not. Just think what—"

The room instantly filled with cackles, guffaws, and full-on laughter.

"Bruh, that's not how it works," Hiram said, nearly falling off the chair because he was laughing so hard.

"So, what happens?" Falcon questioned, lips lifting in a sheepish grin. "The baby shifts to make room or something?"

Chris popped him upside his head. "You're a straight-up fool."

"Ouch." Falcon rubbed the affected area, giving Chris a hard glare.

"But on the real, my mother asked me that same question," Andre admitted. "It pisses me off that there's even room for doubt. Just 'cause I slipped up back in the day, doesn't mean that I'd do something like that. Ever."

"My family's been acting kind of strange," Chuck admitted, rubbing his bald head. "Soon as I walk into the house, they make my nieces and any other little girls go into another room. Or they'll just kind of pull 'em close." He gestured as though he was clutching a child. "You know, like I'm the Big Bad Wolf out to take a bite out of Little Red Riding Hood."

"Same thing at my spot." Chuck shook his head.

"Kinda think maybe we should've done what our lawyers wanted and got this over and done." Falcon shrugged. "Then people wouldn't be treating us like we've got some type of disease."

"Nope," Hiram said, and all gazes shifted to him. "We should look at it as a gift. This separates the fakers from the shakers."

Chris slid a chart to the side and studied another. "How do you mean?"

"I know who's in my corner now." Hiram held out his fist for a pound, and Falcon tapped his own to Hiram's much lighter hand. "Those who kicked me while I was down don't have nothing coming when I get up."

"Facts," Andre agreed.

Jai observed each of the men he had hired. In his heart of hearts, he couldn't believe a single one of them had done that vile thing to Temple. They all took this second chance at life seriously and were the main reason Chetan had been so successful. They believed in what he was trying to accomplish and for such a pall to be over their lives was unbearable.

"You never even asked us if we did it," Hiram said, snapping Jai back to the present.

Jai tapped the area above his heart. "I know in here, that none of you could do something like this." He glanced at the piles of paperwork and stacks of surveillance discs in the center of the table. The answer was there and they just had to find it. "You all have come too far to let your dick make a decision to dismantle your entire life, and everyone else's." He gestured to the screen. "There is something we're not seeing. We need to figure out *how* it was done. Who had the opportunity? Check every one of the logs and cross reference them with the camera recordings. Focus on that timeline for the month of February."

"I said it before, but we need to circle back to it. What about the nurses?" Hiram asked, half-swiveling in the executive chair so he faced Jai. "And the doctors?"

"That's a whole other beast," Jai admitted, knowing that Kelly had already asked Daron Kincaid, one of his Castle brothers who was a technical genius and gadget guru, to look into their backgrounds and finances. So far, he hadn't turned up anything that pointed to a payoff. People who were doing dirt always tended to think they were slick, sly and wicked. "I'm having someone check into them."

"Will we get in trouble for going so deep into this?" Falcon asked with a sweeping gesture that encompassed all the items Kelly had managed to compile in such a short period of time. "Police don't like it when civilians cross into their territory."

"They don't care about clearing our names." Hiram glared at his co-worker. "*We* care about that." He held up a photo of Temple's fiancée and her mother. "We also should check out the family. There's something not quite right about them."

Andre slid a folder to Jai. "Maybe we look at their social media pages and see what they're saying about what's happened. People love to talk, especially if they think a million-dollar lawsuit is a sure thing."

Jai put another set of documents aside, then paused the footage on the screen, forcing everyone to pay attention to him.

"That fiancée dude never did sit right with me," Hiram confessed. "Too arrogant. Dismissed us like we were something on the bottom of his shoe."

"Being an asshole isn't a crime." Jai flipped to another page containing employee schedules.

"Yeah, but he seemed intent on keeping us away from Temple for some reason," Falcon said, pointing to the nurse notes he held. "No other family had that kind of thing going on."

Hiram peered at the image of a clean-cut, Wall Street type with green eyes and platinum blond hair that was the result of someone's bottle. "From what's mentioned in this file, the mother gave him Power of Attorney. Right after that, he demanded that the cameras come out of Temple's room."

Jai jerked forward, squinting at Hiram. "And who gave them permission to do that when I expressly …"

"Kelly wouldn't have any choice if that request was put in," Hiram said, attempting to defuse Jai's concerns. "She wouldn't go for that any other way."

"This is the exact reason cameras were installed. To protect us." Jai ran a hand through his hair, scanning the expectant faces of the men who trusted him enough that they had forgone a critical step that was in their own best interest. At the moment, on hearing everything they were going through, regret filled his mind. "My apologies, guys. We could've been done with this if you had let the lawyers have their way."

"Nah man, that would've put Temple and the baby at risk," Hiram said, clasping a reassuring hand on Jai's shoulder as the others gave a verbal agreement. "We can wait for the DNA test to be done. *If it* ever gets done."

"It will, and I thank you for that," Jai said.

"You believed in me from day one," Hiram said and the admiration in his voice warmed Jai's heart. "That's love right there. I speak for everybody here when I say we wouldn't break that trust."

Jai pressed his fist to Hiram's, but noticed that Jared averted his gaze. The man was shorter and always much quieter than the others so sometimes he was hard to read. "And I'm counting on that."

As his gaze went back to Chris, Andre, and Chuck, who spent more of their time viewing recordings, but also tended to remain kind of quiet during the process and discussions; Jai made a mental note to keep a careful watch to figure out if they had an agenda of their own.

"We need to wrap this up in about an hour. I have to get home," Jai said, checking his watch. "Sandy's going to her granddaughter's graduation and I'd like to be there when India has her evening feedings."

"Look at you, aiming for single father of the year," Hiram teased.

Something about that statement didn't sit too right with Jai. Nothing about his arrangement with Temple made him feel as though this wasn't a family unit. Every day he woke up in time to make her breakfast and talk with her before he left for work. Each night he came home to have dinner and spend time with Temple and India. They discussed so many things—current affairs, a little about his life, then ventured into talking about her dreams, goals, and desires, the online courses she was taking so she could return to teaching, but this time a different subject.

Sometimes he gave Sandy the evening off as he prepared Temple's favorite dishes while listening to whatever she felt like sharing that day. Her therapy sessions with Sesvalah were helping a great deal in her coming to terms with the violation, and to process her feelings regarding India. Now, if only the counselor could help Jai sort out his feelings for Temple. What started as admiration had transformed into full-on attraction, and he struggled each day to keep those feelings in check. The situation was already complicated and his attraction to her added more layers to an already complex scenario.

He brought her a small gift every day. A way to say thank you, but also to see the smile that lit up her face when he walked through the door.

Single father? No, they were a family. *His* family.

CHAPTER 18

A few days later, the Kings and the Knights had now been closeted in the space within the Castle that Jai had pressed into service for a few hours. After further clarifying what he expected from them, Jai paced the room, pausing when Hiram spoke.

"There's one thing I need to know." He glanced at the other Knights in turn. "Why us, man?"

Jai frowned, then asked, "What do you mean … why?"

"You could've brought in dudes coming straight from college or something," Hiram explained, with a pointed look at the rest of the Knights situated around the table. None of whom had degrees; only some specialized medical training that Jai had a hands-on part in developing. "You chose ex-cons to work at the Center and now to be Knights and have all the benefits of the Castle. So, I'm asking … why?"

Jai settled on the leather chair at the head of the table. "Real talk?"

"Real talk?" Hiram laughed, nudging Michael in the side. "Look at him, trying to sound all Black and what not."

"Not Black," Jai countered, realizing that their lingo was sort of rubbing off on him. "I'm testing the waters to see how far you'd like me to go."

Hiram quickly pulled out a chair between Dwayne and Dro and settled in.

"I looked at what you've done, but I also took into consideration *why* you did it." He nodded to Kevin whose glasses nearly covered the top half of his face. "Kevin shot the man who was constantly beating on his mother. Everyone in this room can appreciate a man trying to protect his parent." Jai tapped an index finger on the table, filtering through his memory bank. "The downside was the fact that she never reported all the times the man had hurt her—despite several visits to the hospital. If she had, that alone, would've changed the outcome of Kevin's case." His gaze fell to Hiram. "That fight you had with the guy who attacked your girlfriend at the nightclub. I read the transcripts. I believe the man wasn't honest about the fact that he had a weapon or that he passed it off to a friend before the police showed up. The Judge went hard on you because of your martial arts training."

Hiram locked gazes with Jai, ignoring the movement of the other men around him. "You knew all of that?"

"I made sure to research each and every one of you. I started with nearly nine hundred and whittled it down to nine," Jai confessed with a pointed look at all the men watching him. "Some of you have stories that are similar—or even caught charges for weed, which is now legal in several states because the government finally figured out a little weed isn't hurting anyone. Which is why all of a sudden everybody's growing it. Including little old Caucasian ladies."

"Puff, puff, pass," Hiram said with a chuckle. "Even Betty White knows the rotation."

The men laughed at his reference to the feisty actress, who was known for juggling two to three boyfriends at a time.

"Those mistakes you made early in life shouldn't define the rest of your lives." Jai swiveled in the wide leather chair, the way Hiram liked to do. "The one thing I made certain of, was that none of you had any domestic violence or sexual assault type of offenses. That was a big factor. I made a mistake early in life and didn't say something that could've saved my sisters and other girls in the family a world of pain and grief."

That admission was met with silence as both the Kings and Knights held any comments, probably realizing that being this open and transparent was hard for him.

"While it wasn't anything I witnessed personally, it was something I felt," Jai confessed, taking in the sober expressions and solemn atmosphere of the room. "The thing about it is, even though it was based on my feelings and not concrete proof, it would've carried more weight in my family than hearing from the girls who were too afraid to speak up about what was happening to them." Jai folded his arms across his chest, trying to still the sadness within him. His gaze drifted to the wall, then he sighed. "I regret it to this day. Strangely enough, my cousin met a woman, who not only turned the family upside down because she was a little older, and she was Black, but she blew the lid off the entire family secret because she refused to let her children anywhere near my uncle. That's when my cousin, Devesh—"

"Wait a minute. Devesh Maharaj? *The* Devesh Maharaj?" Hiram perked up and so did everyone else, except Vikkas who also bore that surname. "That's your fam?"

Jai grinned. "Yes, my cousin has a gift, but he didn't find that out until he went after Reign. Though he had been trying his hand at acting for years, she recognized that his voice would be the thing to put him on the map. Then she sent him for dance lessons and acting lessons, too. Despite the fact that he already thought he was good in that area. And he was for India, but not for the American audience he was trying to capture. She changed his whole outlook."

"Almost the same vibe as you've been giving off lately."

Jai narrowed a steely gaze on Hiram.

"Never seen you smile so much since Temple and the baby came along."

Shaz smirked, and Reno gave Grant a pointed look and they smiled.

Jai lowered his gaze to the set of folders spread out before him, uncomfortable at the thought that he'd perhaps been too transparent. "There's nothing going on between us."

"Yeah, you keep telling yourself that lie," Falcon said with a taunting grin.

"I admire her strength and her courage. I don't look at her …" Jai's voice trailed off as his thoughts kicked in. He didn't realize he'd been silent for far too long. He looked up to find an array of sly smiles and smirks that spoke volumes.

"The fact that you have to think about it, says something's going on. You just don't want to admit it," Hiram said.

Jai scanned the faces of his brother Kings and each of them seemed to agree with Hiram.

Falcon left the table and rested a hand on Jai's shoulder. "You know it's something when you have someone to come home to and there's a family waiting on you. You put in a hard day at work—and there's a woman who puts a smile on your face, and a little one smiles up at you like you're their whole world. There's no better feeling." His grin widened. "Ask me how I know."

"We see you. The same way you look at your patients, you look at us — the whole human being." Hiram nodded. "That's church, man. And we see you, too."

Jai's thoughts went to Temple again and he wondered what else he could do to make things right in her world. Maybe—

Hiram snapped a finger in front of Jai's face. "Now we're going to need you to look at your whole self and quit trying to block that love thang and listen to what's going on around you, man."

"And we're going to need you to do that with a quickness," Hiram said, hooking an arm under Jai's and bringing him to his feet. "Because we have to get back to work."

"Yes, indeed," Kaleb chimed in from Jai's other side as he ushered him toward the door.

"Wait a minute," Jai protested, planting his feet to halt their movements. "Are you kicking me out of a meeting I called?"

"You know what they say," Dwayne said, giving him a mega-watt grin.

"You don't have to go home," Hiram finished, ushering him across the threshold. "But you got to get the hell up out of here."

CHAPTER 19

"You make a scrumptious meal for us every morning," Temple said to Jai, sliding the silver breakfast tray toward him as he sat up in bed. "I wanted to do something special for you."

"You didn't have to do this," Jai said, scanning the contents of his plate. French toast, crispy strips of turkey bacon, vegetable omelet, fresh fruit, fresh squeezed orange juice, grits with salt and butter. "This is a serious spread. How did you get Sandy to allow you to take over her domain?"

"The same way you do," she replied, laughing. "I ask nicely."

"That never works for me." He gave her a playful scowl. "I'm beginning to think she likes you a whole lot better than me. I have to practically bribe her to let me do my thing."

Temple perched on the side of his bed and inhaled. "Jai, I need to start making some plans. I can't just lay up in your place like the Queen of Sheba and let you spoil me like this."

"Says who?" he countered. "Makeda, The Queen of Sheba, already had her entire life together when Solomon fell in love with her, then lavished all kinds of gifts upon her before she left him with a little human going away present in her womb." Jai gave her a smile. "And every woman deserves to be pampered and spoiled."

"Oh, I love the way you think," she said, making herself more comfortable. "But at some point, I need to do something other than lounge around, eat up all this good food, and take up space in your life."

"You're not taking up space. You belong here," he said. "You and India, this is your place. I kind of don't remember what it was like before you came. All I can recall was a lot less laughter and joy."

Temple grinned. "And a lot less noise too."

"I don't mind that at all." He sliced the French Toast and dipped it into the pure maple syrup.

The moan he let loose had all kinds of thoughts running through her mind. Sinful thoughts. She should not think of Jaidev Maharaj in that manner. Not at all. She was his guest, and she wouldn't dare pounce on him like a desperate panther onto prey. But good Lord, with the way the man was savoring his meal she could only imagine how meticulous he was when it came to ... "I'd like to do some painting while I'm here."

"Well, I guess the living room could use a coat or two," Jai teased around a mouthful of food. "Sandy practically lives in Home Depot."

"Not that kind of painting," she said, laughing and handing him a white napkin.

"I know." He leaned forward and she dabbed the cloth at the corner of his mouth. "I'm just busting your chops."

"Oh, see." She laughed. "You want to play like that?" Temple adjusted so her feet were stretched out, and her back was against the pewter and wood headboard. "I could try my hand at becoming a Cuddle facilitator."

Jai's fork paused midway to his mouth. "A what?"

"A person who gets paid to cuddle people for a specified amount of time."

He blinked twice and shook his head. "With total strangers?"

"They wouldn't be so strange after a while."

"Temple ..." He inhaled and let it out slowly. "There are a lot of newfangled things happening in the world, but for the life of me, I will not understand how you would open yourself up to attaching so many different energies to you that way."

She didn't say anything to refute it.

"It's a legitimate business," she countered. "And I can make my own hours and still see to India's needs."

"I get that," he said. "But right now, your focus should be on your own emotional, mental, and physical needs—not on trying to anticipate what others need." Jai adjusted his body on the California King Palladian bed, reached under the pillow on the far side and extracted his wallet. He extended a credit card her way.

"American Express Black? And it has my name on it?" She shook her head and tried to give it back. "I can't accept this. I've taken enough from you already. I need to have a lawyer unravel my life and untangle me from my mother and my ex."

"You can accept it," he insisted. "And you will. Shaz and Vikkas are already on finding the lawyer who put your father's estate plan together. They've had Dro's people combing through law offices in Virginia. Don't worry about any of that. The loft on the upper level is all yours to do with as you will."

Jai glanced down at the bacon and then to Temple and grinned.

"Oh, so you want me to feed it to you as well?" The thought put all kinds of ideas in her head.

"I mean, since we're talking about spoiling people and everything," he teased.

Temple complied and he snapped at the bacon in her hand, pressing a kiss to her fingertips that caused her to tremble.

She scanned the bedroom that had the barest minimum of furniture. A huge bed covered in purple and gold linen, a rug with a Arabic pattern that matched the purple draperies. No night stand, dressers or anything that cluttered the view and made the space seem massive. The entire house was done this way. Every piece of furniture or artwork mattered. Nothing extra. Understated elegance without overdoing the opulence. A man who did not have to prove himself to anyone.

Temple glanced at the card and then to him. "Why are you so good to me?" she whispered. "You don't even know me."

"I know enough. And why wouldn't I be good to you?"

She sighed, long and hard. "Because that's not how my life has been."

"Maybe it's time for your expectation for your life to change."

"What if pain is all I know?"

Jai put the tray aside, cupped her face in his hands. "Then at some point, you'll need to become open to the idea of pleasure. Life tends to rise to your expectation or go in the opposite direction, if you feel strongly about it."

"Pleasure," she whispered the word as if she'd made a wonderful discovery.

"Yes. In simple things," he added. "Breakfast in bed tops that list. And this is some good stuff. A swim in the ocean. A child's laughter."

"Ziplining in Jamaica?" she prompted, and his eyes widened to the size of saucers.

"All right, I can see that." He nodded slowly. "Although, I've never aspired to be Tarzan, I can see the appeal of swinging through the trees at top speed and—"

"On second thought, I'm not Jane, so scratch that."

Jai burst out laughing. "Afraid of heights?"

"I'm not telling," she shot back, and he laughed even more. "And tonight, I prepare dinner and then I get to pick what we watch. The Kings of Comedy, followed by the Queens of Comedy."

"A double-header. And no Kevin Hart."

"He's not a king," Temple scoffed. "He's a court jester."

Moving his head back and forth, Jai said, "Oh, that's brutal."

"It's truth," she countered. "I think it was … Hiram and Falcon who were debating on whether to play him or Bernie Mac one day in my room at Chetan. Hiram called it right. And speaking of calling it right, finish your breakfast, young man."

Jai slid on a bite of French Toast and presented the fork to her. She opened her mouth, accepting his offering, but kept her gaze squarely on him. "Oh, that is pretty good."

"Simple things. Simple pleasures." Jai placed the fork on the side of his plate, then tucked a wayward strand of hair behind her ear.

She trembled the moment his fingertips made contact with her cheekbones and traced the delicate skin all the way to her chin. Her lips parted of their own accord and Jai tried, truly tried, by pulling back, then suddenly moved in as thought he couldn't resist tasting her lips and teasing to the point where he elicited the type of moan that signaled the beginning of a pleasurable time to be had by all.

Moments later, her breathing hitched as her head tilted back and kissed his way across the smooth curve of her shoulders and trailed back to her mouth and sampled another taste.

"Ohhhhh," Temple sighed and trembled so hard she had to grip the sheets to stay upright.

She slid off the bed; the rise and fall of her chest signaled that she was trying to control her body's response to him.

So many times, he caught her watching him, sizing him up only to realize that he was doing the same. She didn't know what it was about this particular man that aroused feelings inside Temple that she never believed she'd ever experience. Being with him like this was dangerous and the wise thing would be to escape now that she was still in control of her wits.

Temple inched away from bed. "I … I … I need to see about India."

His gaze never left hers as he said, "Yes, I totally understand."

She bolted from the room as if she'd suddenly became an Olympic champion.

CHAPTER 20

Hiram slammed Victor against the living room wall. He had shown up at Marilyn's house without any warning, barged in and went off about their youngest daughter. Wanda had gone to her father, spreading all manner of lies that escalated with her adding that Hiram had filled Marilyn's head with accusations that Victor may have molested his daughter.

"Don't you *ever* come in her house, her turf, her domain, and disrespect her this way."

"Hiram, stop," Marilyn pleaded while clutching one of his arms. "You're going to make things worse."

"By letting him control you? Intimidate you?" Hiram said through his teeth. "That's not how any of this works." He pressed harder, ignoring the choking sounds as Victor slid upward on the wall until his feet lifted several inches off the carpet. "If you ever, ever, ever, ever, ever, lay a hand on her again, I will mop this entire building with your punk ass." Hiram didn't take his eyes off Victor as he finally loosened his hold a little and asked, "Baby, you got my bail money?"

Marilyn winced, and also didn't take her eyes away from her ex as she came back with, "Honey, *you've* got your own bail money. You're rolling in it better than he ever has, any day of the week."

That statement alone made Victor's eyes pop wide and his bearded face darkened with jealousy. He glared at Hiram, who saw the effect those few words had on him and grinned. Marilyn knew exactly how to stick the knife in. The pockets.

Hiram also knew how to gouge an open wound, which prompted him to say, "My mother always said 'if you're going to jail, make sure it's worth the trip. Don't just take one hit and end up with a charge. Beat that whole ass, and while you're soaking up three hots and a cot, you'll be smiling and knowing it was worth the effort.'"

That truth lingered for a moment before Victor squeaked out, "I just wanted to speak to her about what happened with Wanda."

"She doesn't need you to come here, in her space, and threaten her like that." Hiram released Victor and let him fall to the floor. "Be honest and say what this is really about. You weren't a good husband to a great woman. You could at least be a decent father to your girls and stop using Marilyn. She doesn't have to make excuses for you anymore." He stepped in and Victor flinched. "You asked your daughter to seduce a total stranger to hurt your ex wife. You pimped her out that way because she was desperate. And it isn't a stretch to believe that you might have done something to her before that time."

Victor scrambled to his feet, brushed himself off as he glared at Marilyn, then turned his angry gaze on Hiram. He pulled his shoulders back and his beefy body trembled with anger. "So, this is why you couldn't be happy with me? Wanted some of that young dick. We're cradle-robbing now?"

"What?" Marilyn yelled as her skin flushed. "You overgrown Negro. You'd better—"

"Just think of yourself as the appetizer husband," Hiram said, putting his arm around Marilyn's shoulder to rein her in so she wouldn't be the one needing bail money. "But for the record, I'm the main entrée and the dessert, too." He kissed Marilyn and heard Victor's grunt of disapproval.

"You're going to marry this fool?" he said, his voice reaching two octaves higher.

Hiram held up the chain around his neck, allowing the diamond ring to shine in the muted glow of the lamp.

Marilyn gasped, clutched an imaginary set of pearls, and the act was followed by Victor's growl of disbelief.

"Whenever she's ready," Hiram said, tucking the chain back under his shirt. "Just had to get you all the way out of her life—and out of her system. I think you accomplished that today. Same old asshole. Same old tricks. And she's having none of that."

Marilyn reached in, removed the chain from his neck, slid the ring off and held it in the palm of her hand.

Hiram slowly extracted it and placed that diamond directly on her finger.

She flexed her hand with pride, admiring the view.

Eyes narrowed to vicious slits, Victor fumed but wisely kept his mouth shut.

"You had a good woman," Hiram said, holding Marilyn close. "A damn good woman. Now you're pissed that the one you're with isn't half the woman this one was, so you're trying to make her miserable because you are. Not happening on my watch."

Victor drew himself to his full height, which was still inches less than Hiram, and brushed past the couple without uttering another word. He yanked the door handle on his way out, leaving Hiram with a satisfied grin in place. "If I may use a cliché, we just said good riddance to some bad rubbish."

The door didn't close all the way before Marilyn pushed Hiram onto the sofa, hiked up her skirt, snatched off the lace panties, straddled his thighs and kissed him like it was the last time she would be able to do so.

His erection did a happy lift in the right direction. "What the hell was that?"

"Foreplay," she whispered. "That was foreplay."

Hiram looked over her shoulder to find Victor watching from the sliver where the door should have met the jamb. "You can leave now. We don't need an audience."

Victor's eyes widened to the size of Firestone tires and he turned to leave, but froze when Hiram gripped Marilyn's buttocks, holding her firmly in place as he kept his focus on his adversary.

"Unless you want to learn how pleasing a woman is actually done …" Hiram stroked her lower back in small circles. She laid her head on his chest. "And from what I understand, you could use a few lessons and I'm a damn good teacher. Leave the key."

The bewildered expression on Victor's face was almost laughable. He hesitated, jammed his hand into his pants pocket, then tossed the key onto the floor and slammed the door.

"That was so mean," Marilyn said, doubling over with laughter.

"Just a little payback for all the times he mistreated you," Hiram said with a comedic lift of his eyebrows. "Nothing like hitting a man where it hurts—his ego and his pockets. Trust me, the image of you right here in my arms, all happy and e'rethang, is going to cause him to lose a lot of sleep tonight."

"You think so?" Marilyn asked with a sultry smile.

"I *know* so. I saw his expression," Hiram said, stroking her cheek with one finger. "He doesn't know anything about this version of you."

"And thanks to God for time, divorce lawyers, and a new lease on life, he never will." She slid off him and unbuttoned her blouse, posing for Hiram to absorb her awesomeness.

"That's some sexy shit right there," he said, tracing the pattern of her red lace bra.

"You like?"

"No … I love." He gripped her hips and pulled her toward his body. "Bring all of that over here."

She paused and released a slight sigh. "Why is it that something that feels so right, sometimes feels so wrong?"

"I don't want to answer that question right now," he replied, nuzzling her neck.

"We have fifty-nine minutes before we have to meet with Jaidev," he mumbled while kissing her breasts. "I want to make good use of them."

* * *

Jaidev's office had been decorated in rich tones of reds and creams, and was a combination of understated elegance and upscale simplicity. Abstract artwork and awards on the wall; a glass desk, leather executive chair, small round conference table, built-in bookshelves that held an array of holistic medicine, spiritual, and nutrition, books.

Hiram and Marilyn slid into chairs across from Jai exactly an hour and a half after their tryst.

On the table in front of Jai, Marilyn placed the pages of a game plan they'd come up with over the last few days.

Jai glanced at the documents but didn't touch them. "What is this?"

"*This* is how you're going to deal with Donald Amos," Marilyn answered,

With his gaze fixed on her, Jai asked, "Why should I trust you?"

"Maybe you shouldn't, but you trust Hiram and he trusts me to help undo the damage they've wreaked on your business. Unfairly, knowing that by the time the truth comes out, you'll have a hell of a time recovering. And it will affect any future plans you have."

Jai shook his head as he scanned through the pages, absorbing some of the suggestions that were put on the table. "We have to do everything above board."

"A lot of good that will do when every one of you are on the unemployment line," she snapped.

With a serene expression in place, Jai countered, "Playing dirty doesn't solve anything."

"See, here's where you and Hiram differ," she said, leaning forward on the leather chair facing him. "He fought for his life and lived to tell the story. He could've tried to simply walk away, but he wouldn't be here right now having this conversation."

Hiram placed a restraining hand on Marilyn's arm but Jai leaned back, listening.

"From that vantage point, I think he'd rather spend eight years in prison than be planted in an early grave."

Hiram flinched and tightened his hold on Marilyn's hand.

"Jai, you have to get your hands a little bit dirty if you're going to stay afloat," Marilyn suggested. "They're stomping you into the ground because they know you're not going to do what it takes to beat them at their own game."

Jai swiveled in the chair and crossed one slack-covered leg over the other. "A little dirty?"

"Just a little." She positioned her index finger a few inches from her thumb.

"Or I could take that one mil Donald's offering," Hiram said.

Both Jai and Marilyn were shocked by this new piece of information.

"And he'll wipe my record clean so I can get a passport and travel, too. But the most important thing is that it'll mean that the center reopens immediately, my brothers get their jobs back and none of this is hanging over their heads any more. I can launch a tattoo shop on the North side in a few months, then come back to this line of work or something else."

"Who is going to hire you for anything after that?" she queried, her expression foreboding and she paused to gather her composure. "Once that negative image of you is out there, it'll be hard to walk that back," Marilyn warned. "This is not a sacrifice you should be willing to make."

"But if I don't, you'll need to leave the Bureau before you're ready. A few more years before full benefit." Hiram shook his head. "Leaving's not worth it right now. The money he's putting on the table will be a cushion until I get things up and going."

"I don't want you to do anything unethical," Jai warned.

"And that right there is your problem." Marilyn threw her hands up in frustration. "You're playing a straight and narrow game and they are playing something totally different. You can't win the game if you let them take you out of it." She slapped her hand on the documents. "Right now, they're winning. They don't have ethics, they have power."

"You could be fired for this." Jai picked up the plan, scanned it, frowning with each page he turned. "I can't use any of this."

"None of this is proprietary info," she countered. "All of it is available through the Freedom of Information Act. I wouldn't give you anything considered confidential. Hiram told me enough about you for me to understand that. Have your assistant …" She glanced at Hiram. "Kelly?"

Hiram nodded. "Yes, she's the left hand."

"Left hand?"

"Hiram's my right hand," Jai explained with a smile. "Especially now that he's taken the lead when it comes to handling the behind-the-scenes effort to get the new center opened on time."

She looked at Hiram, the admiration evident as she said, "Have Kelly put in a request for the same information I've presented to you today."

Jai narrowed his gaze at Hiram, who nodded.

"So, you have a lot at stake," she said, placing her hand over Jai's, drawing his attention back to her. "You must do what it takes to counter them. You can't do that if you don't know the levels of deception they've employed." Marilyn tapped the tip of her finger on the documents she had given him. "Trust me. I do."

CHAPTER 21

Jai held the door open so Big Red and Marilyn could walk into his office. They had taken the risk of coming without an appointment and Kelly had interrupted an important phone call with Temple to let him know the two women were in the outer office.

Big Red's presence was never a good sign. But seeing Marilyn was disconcerting. Last he heard from the fantastic plan she and Hiram cooked up, she was going to resign from the Bureau and work for him. This invasion came as a surprise after that meeting in this very office two days ago.

Since the Bureau's legal team had managed to strong-arm most of the families, some patients at Chetan would be shifted to state facilities. They had won that part of the battle. He couldn't imagine why she was here.

"So, to what do I owe this impromptu visit," he asked, not bothering to hide his sarcasm. "Not that you aren't welcome any time, but …"

"Am I always the bearer of bad news?" Big Red teased.

The fact that she was trying to keep things light was worse than her unexpected appearance.

"Well, you said it, I didn't."

Big Red settled in a wingback chair across from his desk and Marilyn did the same. She tossed what looked to be a court order in front of him.

"Mr. Maharaj, we need to discuss moving the patients back into your facility."

Jai took a moment to process this new development, barely glancing at the caption on the legal document. "Why?"

"Five patients have died within the first two days of them being moved," she confessed, her lips tight as though imparting that information was painful. And for her, it probably was. Admitting any level of defeat was a blow to her overinflated ego. "Eight more are now in critical condition, and a few others are declining. We have a sinking suspicion that the rest will suffer the same fate. At the rate they're going, all the patients will die within a few months, if not weeks."

Jai didn't have a response for that because the implications were staggering.

"Several families have filed an injunction barring their family members from being transitioned to a state facility."

Ah, the real issue. Lawsuits down the line. Lots of them. Shaz had said that would happen. "And that becomes my problem because …?"

"We'd like to bring in a team to learn how to care for them the way you have, and to care for the rest of the patients who haven't been moved as of yet."

Marilyn brought her hand up, gave a slight cough as she shook her head.

Message received. "Absolutely not."

Big Red flinched, then shared a gaze with Marilyn; her expression was almost panicked—if he could put a name to it—but he could swear Marilyn was hiding a major smile. "But I thought—"

"You thought what?" he countered, intertwining his fingers as he sought out whatever calm he could manage. Five of his patients had died. Five! And correction—*former* patients because of their manipulation of a system that was already broken to begin with. "You thought I was going to save your ass, when you, especially, have been raking me and mine over the coals in the media and in political offices that haven't had a peep to say in all this time. What kind of fool do you take me for? A brand new one?"

Hiram's woman had to play off another cough to keep from laughing.

Hearing the number of fatalities was disheartening, but the confirmation that his methods were sound was the best news he'd had in a while.

"Are you coming down with something," Big Red asked Marilyn who shook her head.

"How exactly did you think your request was going to work for me?" Jai asked, raising both eyebrows. "You trashed me, my process, my center, and the men and other employees who made this place work."

"Mr. Maharaj," she blustered. "All we know is—"

"You don't know jack," Jai snapped and didn't bother to hide his disdain. "Your department was so hell-bent on exploiting the fact that my men don't have degrees. You joined ranks with those who felt that infusing holistic practices into modern medicine is … hocus pocus." He grinned. "Your words exactly. Channel Seven, Six o'clock news. I was watching—closely."

Big Red heaved a weary sigh and Jai was almost certain he caught a small nod from Marilyn and she narrowed her gaze, tilted her head to the right twice in succession. All right, so the game plan had changed a little. Jai adjusted his aim accordingly.

"So, unless you're also willing to make some concessions, as well as go on national television and clear my name, the center's name, the men's name—since, by even your own admission, only *one* of them could have committed the crime, then it's no deal of any type." His phone vibrated and he quickly silenced it. "I need you all to be just as public about cleaning up this mess as you were about slandering everything good about this place."

Silence. Big Red's expression morphed from shock to outright anger, then indifference which was close to her norm. Arrogance. None of this affected her on a moral level, only on a professional one.

"No? Doesn't work for you?" He tapped his fingers on the document she brought in and pushed it back to her. "So, let me get this straight. My patients—correction, my *former* patients are in dire straits because you had their families prematurely rip them from the best care possible in order to personally destroy me. Now, you come crawling back and want me to *secretly* handle your business? Were you expecting me to bend over and oil up so you can screw me all over again?" Jai paused, but that didn't keep him from picking up steam. "Do you know this whole thing could have been over with if my men had forced that DNA test while she was still pregnant? They didn't want to jeopardize her health or the baby."

"Or one of them could have been stalling for time before the truth came out," Big Red suggested.

"And here we go," he shot back. "Always looking for the negative slant to things. You went in and obtained a court order to shut me down. When you knew there was another way."

Big Red glanced at Marilyn, as though wanting her to chime in on the situation. A shutter fell over Marilyn's face. From the barely-hidden glee in her eyes, she'd been busy secretly "cheering" him on as he landed jabs at her superior's expense. Team Maharaj all the way.

"Mr. Maharaj, all that aside," Marilyn began in a calm tone. "The health of these patients should be of concern, regardless of whether—"

"They *were* my concern until she and Donald Amos decided otherwise." His attention shifted back to Big Red. "I am not in the business of cleaning up your mistakes. Technically, I'm not in business at all. I'm in a real serious holding pattern. Which means I can't teach you or anyone else a damn thing."

"Not true." Big Red gestured to the documents she had brought in. "Those put you back in operation immediately."

"But under your jurisdiction, management and control?" He shook his head. "Nope, I'll wait until we are officially cleared."

Marilyn parted her lips to protest, but he held up a hand. "I'm not an unreasonable man," he said, scanning the first three pages of the Motion that temporarily put a halt to some of the actions the Bureau had originally filed. "The patients who are still here, and haven't had any of their regimen interrupted, can remain. The ones you've put elsewhere will need to stay exactly where they are."

"That's not fair," Big Red whined, slamming a hand on his desk.

"Oh, but it is," he countered giving her a look causing her to remove that hand. "You managed to scare those families into believing that the care their loved ones were receiving was not solid. They bought into your lies. The patients that are still here are from families who defied you and put in their own court order for them to stay here."

The silence was antagonistic and Jai reminded himself that nothing had ever been achieved by losing his composure when it mattered. Khalil had often reminded him of the same thing in the days when he'd been a hot head. *Don't give up the advantage when it means winning if you can keep your eyes on your objective.*

"See, what happens when you bring them back here and they meet their untimely demise is that now I'm open to lawsuits based on your actions. I'm not willing to take that hit from families who were all too willing to sacrifice their loved one's care in that way."

"What I'd like you to do is reconsider," Big Red snarled.

He stood as the message flashed on his cell's screen that said he was needed at the Castle right away. "Well, Big Red—that's what the fellas call you. I have more important things to tend to." He swept past them, opened the door to his office, then pointed to the empty corridor. "You know my terms. I expect this order to be revised to say full operation with no Bureau oversight. Until then, what I'd like for you to do is get the hell up out of my office. Pronto."

CHAPTER 22

For the third time in as many days, the Knights had gathered in what had become their regular meeting place.

Hiram tapped the screen, placing an index finger on the digital numbers. "This day, right here. See how long he was in there."

The nine other men in the room focused on the timeline. "See, the cameras were off in her room, but the ones in the hallway tell the story."

"Right," Falcon said, getting to his feet, then gesturing to the erratic movements of the man onscreen. "He's pulling his zipper up there."

"Putting his clothes back together like …" Ryan let his words taper off.

On the screen, Curtis slid up to Kevin and they exchanged a few words. Curtis stiffened and inched back. His body language was off.

Hiram looked at Kevin. "Do you remember what you asked him?"

"I think I asked him, if he was all right," he replied, scratching his curls. "He looked a little strange. Well, stranger than usual, so I …"

A few ticks of time passed before he continued with, "He said he was feeling a little ill and just came from the bathroom down the hall."

"Hold up," Hiram said, running a hand across the design in his fresh-cut fade. "There's no bathroom near that wing so he—"

"Oh, come on now. He wouldn't," Ryan said, his eyes glued to the screen.

Chris pushed back from the table, faced pulled into a scowl.

Almost in unison, everyone said various versions of, "He couldn't."

"Time and opportunity," Hiram mused after they overcame their shock and most had their game faces back on. "He had both. We've clocked hours looking at every damn thing. He was in there longer than any of us. And he was the only one in Temple's space with the door completely closed."

Each room at Chetan was created in the kind of space age design that used both solar panels for sustainable energy, even with power grid failures; aqua chambers to ensure mobility and that the patient's limbs didn't wane or become atrophied from lack of movement or use. State of the art sound system that filtered in an array of music choices and live performances. Everything was designed to keep stimulation focused and constant.

"We're only alone with any female patient to check vitals," Michael chimed in. "Even turning them every hour, requires two people, each and every time. That's protocol. Everything else we're assigned to do happens in other areas of the center. *Open* areas."

"We're all in agreement, then?" Jai said, and a chorus of consent followed. "We can turn this over to your lawyers and they can chart it, add it to the discovery before giving it to the prosecutor's office."

Hiram slid another file in front of Jai. "But the big issue is the nurses and the doctors. *None* of them caught on to the fact that Aunt Flo hadn't made a visit?"

"Aunt Flo?" Jai glanced at the men around the table.

Kevin grimaced and crinkled his nose with amusement. "Come on, figure it out, doc."

Ready to move on to more important issues, Jai shook his head.

Falcon lowered his voice and said, "What some women call that monthly thang."

"Oh." This time Jai was the one who grimaced and wanted to kick himself for not making the connection. "For a man who has three children, I don't know why you're always so vague about womanly parts and womanly actions. You always call it a *thang*."

"Whew, look at the time," Michael said, checking an imaginary watch as the others laughed. "But the issue is none of them caught the fact that her vitals or anything had changed and that her body had transformed."

"Well, only a few of her vitals increased a little over time," Ryan said, passing over another set of documents with detailed nurse's logs. "But that wouldn't tell us she was pregnant. And then a couple of months in Curtis had said he only wanted Laura Shawn, Brenda Barnes, Donna Fowler, and Stille Moore to handle her, so ..."

Jai was disheartened that the two women he'd hired straight out of nursing school and two doctors, Laura Shawn and Brenda Barnes, could have had a hand in covering up what happened to Temple.

Kelly rushed into the room, nearly tripping over the high threshold on her way inside. "DNA results are in."

Every man at the table stood, almost like synchronized swimmers.

"None of the men here was a match to the child," she announced, beaming.

"Tell us something we don't already know," Hiram said, his tone as sour as everyone's expressions.

Kelly moved further into the room, scanning all the materials splayed across the table. "Then who do you think did it?"

Hiram gestured to the frozen image on the screen. "We have some idea that it might have been her fiancé."

Her steps faltered and she gripped the edge of the table to find balance. "Wait ... what?!"

"He calls himself that, but she wasn't ever going to marry him," Jai said, amazed at how defensive he sounded. The man had lied on so many levels, but so had Temple's mother. Something was up between the two of them. He'd have Daron and Dro look further into Temple's background to figure things out.

Kelly scanned the table, taking in the mounds of paperwork. "Then why would the mother make him power of attorney for her health care and property?"

"That's something we definitely need to get into," Chris said, "If he's not just the run of the mill pervert, what was his angle??"

"And the mother's?" she queried.

Jai glanced at the page of one file, where Hiram highlighted other major points. The fact that his right-hand man was spot on put warmth in Jai's heart. These guys were a lot smarter than they gave themselves credit for.

The mother had only re-entered the picture when a missing persons report matched an age progression photo that had been put out by the Virginia police department each year. The Chicago police used it to locate a family member to make major decisions for Temple's health care. A The judge had also given them control over all of Temple's assets, property, and her life. He could only wonder what else they'd done while she was sleeping. He'd get Dro and Daron working on it from a different angle, maybe Shaz if something else needed to be done.

"What I'm wondering is why Jai didn't know that the cameras weren't still in Temple's room," Falcon said, propping is feet on the chair next to his.

Kelly's ivory skin flushed with color. Her lips parted, then closed, then did the same thing again. "I'm the reason all of this happened."

"No," Hiram said glaring at Falcon. "Curtis Burnside is the reason this happened. He manipulated a lot of things to get what he wanted."

"But I…" She shook her head and her eyes misted with tears. "I'm so sorry, I …"

"Kelly," Jai began in a patient tone. "It is not your fault."

"Ouch," Falcon said and glared at Hiram who had evidently kicked him under the table.

"Now I see why his lawyer was pushing so hard for me to accept the settlement offer for that one million." Jai gestured to the screen that still held Curtis Burnside's image. He knew the truth would come out. That money would be gone or he would use it to leave the country to escape prosecution."

Hiram looked over Jai's shoulder, pointing the remote to change it to Sharon Liscell's image. "But what does her mother get out of this?"

"I'm about to have some people get into that," Jai said, following Kelly out the door.

* * *

When the two of them were out of earshot, Hiram closed the door and put his back against the wood. "Listen up, y'all."

The Knight's focus went to him. "That suit that was in Jai's office when I stopped at Chetan to drop some paperwork off is on some bullshit,"

"What about him?" Ryan asked.

"I overheard some things I probably shouldn't have, but that pasty-looking dude that's been all over the news with Big Red, has been blackmailing Jai. He wants something but Jai's not giving in."

All gazes remained locked on Hiram.

"You know what he's about?" Falcon asked, folding his hands across his midriff and settling into the chair.

"He wanted him to sacrifice one of us—when everything first broke in the news, even though there was no proof of anything."

Hiram then went on to explain the conversations he overheard between Donald Amos and Jai, insisting that turning one of them over to the public as a way to make any further investigations go away. He'd been riding Jai for a while, even before Temple came along.

"Man, that's deep," Falcon said, adjusting his body in his chair. "I still can't believe he wants us"—he gestured to the others who were wowed into silence —"to be part of that Castle deal?"

Hiram nodded.

"So, what did Jai say to that dude trying to nail his balls to the wall?"

"He told him to go straight to hell," Hiram said, grinning. "He wasn't sacrificing us to save himself."

Michael banged his fist on the table, making everyone flinch. "Ride or die, man. Jaidev Maharaj is ride or die."

"I see you all quiet over there," Kevin chimed in, leaning forward so he could see around Chuck's big frame. "What you thinking, Hiram?"

"Everybody's got skeletons in their closet. You can't do dirt without some of it getting back on you." Hiram scanned the faces in the room.

"I say we work with the Kings to do some research on old boy and the side-kick that's doing his dirty work. Give Jai some ammo to get those people off his ass."

Each of the Knights in the room nodded.

A slow smile spread across Hiram's face and he rubbed both hands together. "Let's do this."

CHAPTER 23

Three months after Temple moved in, Vikkas and Milan's wedding reception was in full swing. The Kings were all his best men, the Knights and their significant others milled about, connecting with people who were going to be an important part of their lives.

Vikkas had used one of three ballrooms within The Castle, so each of the guests had to be vetted before gaining admission to the property. The room had been decorated in a purple, teal, metallic gold theme. A delectable spread including Indian, Middle Eastern, and Soul Food cuisines catered to every palate. The entertainment was off the chain. But before nuptials were exchanged Dro played a masterful rendition of *Missing You*.

During the reception, Devesh and Reign Maharaj had brought the house down with some of their more popular duets.

Jai had left Temple and India with the queens of the court—Cameron, Milan, Skyler, and Zuri. India, and Devesh's twins were soaking up all the attention. "Little charmers," Jai whispered on his way to the buffet spread to grab a plate for Temple before Shaz polished off everything.

"I have it on good authority that one of these little bastards is Khalil's son."

Jai froze in his path. His attention went to the group nearest to the buffet table, and he locked gazes with the man who had voiced those words. He moved in, nearly towering over the six men who were dressed in formal East Indian attire.

"Exactly which bastard are you speaking of?" Jai asked, arrowing in on the man who once made an attempt to include Jai in a plot that would cause Khalil irreparable harm.

Two of the men politely excused themselves and another found a particular interest in the shine on his shoes. The rest were transfixed, waiting for whatever exchange would ensue.

"Well, I … I …"

"None of them are named 'I'," Jai spat. "Speak up. You were so confident a minute ago when you were trying to tarnish Khalil's name. Either your *good authority* is *no authority* or you're straight up lying." Jai tilted his head, getting a read on the man's panicked expression. "Which is it?"

Suddenly a hush fell over the groups of people closest to them. All eyes and attention shifted to Jai and the men in front of him. One by one, the Kings left the area where they were situated close to the queens and made their way to where Jai stood. The Knights instantly took hold of the women who came with them, left where they were stationed, guided them to be near the queens, then claimed the spaces that the Kings had vacated.

The Kings fanned out in a protective barrier so no one could get close to Jai. Meanwhile, the Knights circled the women and Jai knew that if anything went down, they would handle the business in the best way possible.

"What's going on here?" Vikkas asked, gesturing for Milan to remain where the Knights were holding ground.

"Care to repeat the lies you told them?" Jai asked, his tone strident.

"I…I…I" the man stammered, then clamped down on anything else he had to say. He seemed to wither under the glares of nine men who were not only protective of Khalil, but of each other.

"It is only partly a lie," one of the other men spoke up. "The bastard part is not true. But one of you is also his son. That is something the entire Maharaj family is very much aware of."

Khalil excused himself from the group of men he'd been conversing with, and a few quick strides brought him to the space between Grant and Kaleb.

Vikkas' mother, Varsha, stepped in and stood mere inches from Khalil, anger etched on her face. Her chest heaved as though each breath was hard to take. "Please do not do this here. Not today, when this is all about Vikkas and Milan."

"If not today, when?" Vikkas shot back. "If I have a brother, *now* is as good a time for me to know what truths have been hidden." His gaze went to each of the eight men he considered brothers already. The lack of biological ties notwithstanding. Love instead of blood. "Speak up," he commanded the offender, who remained stoic. "You were so willing to disparage my father behind his back, face him and share your truth." He gestured to the entire room. "Share it with everyone so it will be done."

In the extended silence, Jai did not miss the fact that the elders of the Maharaj family were tense with fear when Jai's mother, Aashna, came to stand directly next to Khalil. Only two people wore expressions that could be considered resigned—Khalil and Aashna, the woman by his side, as though they had waited for years for this very thing to happen.

All the Kings, except one, stood still as though filtering through family histories and secrets and trying to make two plus two equal nine.

"I was just kidding when I said Papa was a rolling stone," Shaz whispered to Jai.

"Evidently, he has one other pebble all up an through here," Dwayne said and the Kings shared a glance.

"You are my father," Jai said, moving toward Khalil. The truth had always been there, but he didn't want to embrace it because it meant admitting that his lineage was wrapped in a web of lies. People always commented how much he and Vikkas looked alike—almost twins. But it was the shock of silver hair at his widow's peak which matched Khalil's that had been the most obvious bit of evidence.

"Are you asking me or telling me?" Khalil said, and a collective sigh of relief went up from the rest of the Kings.

Khalil would have answered with a direct "No" if Jai was off in his assertion.

"Of course," Vikkas said, and a mirthless chuckle left his lips as he faced his brother. "Makes perfect sense. What doesn't make sense is how we ended up in separate households."

"That's what I'm screaming," Jai said, narrowing a gaze on Khalil.

Aashna splayed a hand across Khalil's chest, the move more intimate and passionate than it should have been for a woman who was married to someone else.

Jai's jaw clenched, and he glared at Khalil, chest heaving with indignation. "Why was I the one who was thrown away?"

"Never thrown away," Khalil replied, trying to place a calming hand on Jai's shoulder, but he brushed it off. "Given to a family who would love and care for you. And it was not my choice. Not *our* choice."

The contemporary music continued unabated and some persons still conversed, unaware of the drama unfolding at one end of the room. Several other people milled around aimlessly, trying to gauge the meaning of the interaction between two men who, for all they knew, had limited interaction before this time.

"Then why?" Jai demanded, gesturing to Hiram to keep Temple with him. She had tried twice to move toward the circle.

"Because I chose to use my portion of the family fortune to pursue spiritual endeavors, I was stripped of my beloved, my name, and one of my sons."

Rage found its way into Jai's heart and mind, like no other time he could remember. He tried to bring himself to a peaceful place. Truly tried, but the ramifications of what Khalil's words meant, hit him full force. "The Castle? My life traded? All that for your precious calling? No regard for the fact that I would need you."

The Kings moved in, an action that pushed out everyone else leaving only Khalil, Vikkas, Jai, and Aashna in the center. Then the six of them inched backward, forcing the crowd of people to back up.

Temple approached, but Dro signaled to her to give them some time. She stayed put, but her facial expression registered major concern for Jai.

Jai closed his eyes, tempering the swell of emotions warring within him. This explained so much. His mother's overindulgence, but also her sadness. His … father's … indifference; his anger and certainly the demand of not having anything to do with Khalil. A directive that Jai had totally ignored.

"Then out of guilt you try to make up for it by insisting that my mother put me into your school. For what? So I could be close to you? Is that it? Trying to be a father after the fact?"

Khalil took a long slow breath, his olive skin slightly flushed—something no one had ever seen before. "It was never about guilt. That was never my—"

Taking a step back, Jai spat, "I don't want to hear any—"

"Jai—"

Jai cut Vikkas a look that shut him down. No way would he be silenced in something as serious as this. No way in hell.

He didn't miss the nod from Shaz and the sudden movements by the Kings that corralled all the main parties out of the ballroom and to the outside hallway.

Daron closed the door behind them, leaving the curious onlookers and all family behind. Grant, Reno, Shaz, and Daron stationed themselves near the doors so no one could come out and interrupt. Dwayne, Kaleb, and Dro situated themselves close to Jai's mother.

"No, you are not correct in your assertion," Khalil said, and his eyes misted with unshed tears. "When I choose a path, I stay true. It was always my intent to make sure I was in both of my sons' lives when they were past their formative years. No matter that my family forced me to give up my wife, one of our sons, and the Maharaj name as penance."

"You know what?" Jai shook his head. "From this point on, I don't want anything to do with your precious little Castle. Nothing at all."

"Jaidev Maharaj," Vikkas snapped, and all heads whipped to him. "No matter what you're feeling right now. No matter how hard this hurts, do not deny that the sacrifice he made was for the greater good."

"Easy for you to say," Jai shot back, moving so he was toe to toe with Vikkas. "You had our father growing up."

"Yes, and you had our mother," Vikkas roared. "And I ended up with a mother so hell-bent on making him pay for not being her first choice, that she took it out on me." He stepped in so that they were only a few inches apart. "So that makes us pretty damn even."

Reno let out a low whistle and Shaz nudged him into silence.

"He traded her life and ours, for an intangible thing," Jai whispered and his voice trembled a little as he glared at Khalil. "There is no way to feel any kind of good about that."

"And I'm not saying we should, my brother," Vikkas countered in a lower tone, and the words caused Jai to flinch. *My brother*. That term was relative. "What I'm saying is that knowing him, he did not intend for that arrangement to be permanent. Am I right?"

Khalil nodded, a tear making its way down his cheek followed by yet another, then another. Aashna reached up to wipe them away with the back of a trembling hand. He pressed his hand over hers and closed his eyes. The most open display of affection Jai had ever witnessed from his mother, and evidently the same held true for Vikkas of his father because his eyes widened in shock, then quickly morphed into anger.

* * *

"I will come for you and my son when the time is right," Khalil whispered to Aashna.

They stood on the ground where The Castle was slated to be built. At that moment, the only thing in place was a small bridge that was a pathway over a meadow that ran through the center of the grounds. Soon a stone structure would extend the length of the area far and wide. "You will always be close to my heart," he continued.

"I will take good care of our son," she promised, pressing a hand to his chest. "Your mission is so important to the world."

"Not more important than you," Khalil countered, pulling her into his arms. "Just as important, but our families do not see the good it will do."

He had taken on the name Khalil Germaine, reflecting the elements of a man whose work he truly admired—Khalil Gabran. He too, aspired for the world to embrace peace. Khalil was well aware of how attempts at bridging the gap between factions could go horribly wrong. Gandhi had tried for peace and it had failed on the most basic human levels in India. He created Pakistan for Muslims and all Muslims were supposed to have left India, but did not. Now some of the holiest places in India were in trouble because one group was trying to rule and take over everything. That great error was the reason Gandhi had been shot.

There had been no need to make Pakistan. Everyone would have been happier that way. Because of the division, hatred, wars, property issues, rapes and mistreatment of women ensued. Khalil's focus was on having a spiritual connection with all through humanitarian works and by reaching out to those minds who could be molded into understanding that integrity, peace, and courage would be a way of life. Aashna well understood this since her family had been ravaged by dissension—both religious and financial.

Aashna withdrew from his embrace. "You are meant to accomplish much here on American soil. Know that you will never be far from my heart and mind."

"Thank you for putting me at ease," Khalil whispered, bringing her back into his arms. She was the woman of his heart, and his family had arranged the marriage, unaware of how much they loved each other before then. And some seemed especially angry that their marriage did not have the same anxiousness, and sometimes bitterness as most of the others before theirs.

Their love came through no matter how much they tried to hide it. Even their parents commented on it in a way that made it seem they had wished for them to suffer as they had before settling into a life of obligation and responsibility, mired in family tradition.

Love matches seldom happened in arranged marriages. This was a first for the Maharaj family, and most did not know how to accept the inevitable.

"Their demands are cruel and meant to hurt me, but they care nothing for how much it hurts you. Despite what the family says, you are still my

wife and we are bound for life. Right here, what they are demanding of us," he tapped the gold band around her finger. "Is semantics on their part. I will be successful and I will come for you and my son. Before then and after, you and he will never want for anything." He guided her into a secluded area with lush greenery. "When it is built, this place here in The Castle will become your private sanctuary. You will be able to leave messages for me, and I for you."

Khalil spread out the blanket and under the moonlight, they made love repeatedly knowing their separation was but hours—days away.

The precious time spent together left her with another gift from him.

CHAPTER 24

A series of loud bangs on the door signaled that people on the inside of the wedding reception were demanding to be let out. Not because they wanted to leave the venue. More like they were curious about how everything was playing out.

"The Knights have it secured in there. If there's an emergency, there's another exit," Daron said, shrugging. "They can use that."

The banging began again and Reno shifted his gaze to Khalil, who gave an almost imperceptible nod.

Grant lowered the gold handle and the door only opened partway and Hiram whispered something to him.

"Some dude named Gaurav wants to say something to Khalil."

"Let him through. That's my ... father?" Jai said, and his expression was more confused than ever.

Hiram stepped aside and a red-faced man barreled into the corridor.

"You cannot have my wife," Gaurav growled at Khalil, taking in the fact that said wife was securely in Khalil's arms, with no intention of relinquishing that space and Khalil had no intention of letting go.

"Technically, for all intents and purposes, she is—and—always will be my wife on a spiritual, emotional, and mental level. No wedding band or document ever changed that." Khalil tightened his hold on Aashna. "You could only lay claim to her physical presence."

"And if we are being honest …" Aashna began, her soft voice cutting through the silence.

Vikkas and Jai braced themselves.

"Not on a physical level either," she finished and her expression was pure steel.

"Oh, that was cold," Kaleb said.

Daron nudged him, but Shaz also grimaced at that ugly barb.

Gaurav darkened as he growled, "How low class and basic of you."

"Well, it is the truth," she said with a lift of her chin. "You have not been doing your husbandly duty all these years."

With a vein pulsing in his forehead, Gaurav spat. "Hard to do when you whisper his name during the act."

Aashna drew herself up to her full height. "Well, I needed an … an" She waved her hand, gesturing to come up with the word. "an orgasm from all that effort you did not put in. Literally."

"Mama!" Jai roared, his olive skin turning beet red. "TMI."

"Whew, would you look at the time," Reno said, signaling to the rest of the Kings that it was time to make an exit stage left. Jai's mother didn't just throw shade, she had tossed in an entire forest.

Despite Reno's efforts, everyone stayed put.

On the other side of the door, more banging and commotion caused Dro to crack open the door to get Hiram's take on things. He learned that Vikkas' mother was trying to come out.

"Don't let her out of there," Vikkas warned, massaging his temple. "There's already enough drama going on to last us the rest of this year."

Aashna moved forward until she stood in front of Gaurav. "Your mother treated me so poorly and none of this was my fault," she said, ignoring his angry glower. "We would have had a better chance in this marriage if you had taken your manhood out of her back pocket and grew some actual andas."

"What does that mean?" Grant asked.

"Balls," Vikkas and Jai replied in unison.

Complete silence descended in the room for untold moments. Then Daron said, "Yes, so, about blowing this joint …"

This time, the Kings shifted to make that move.

"No, stay," Jai commanded causing them to halt. "I think we're just getting to the good wood."

"Or lack thereof," Vikkas mumbled, looking directly at Jai and raised an eyebrow.

Everyone froze.

Jai tried to school his features into an angry mask, but failed in that effort. No matter the seriousness of the moment, that was funny as hell.

Chuckles and snickers abounded from the Kings. Until Khalil cut a silencing look their way. They fell silent, but Jai saw that even Khalil was trying to not embarrass the man by laughing outright.

Banging interrupted once again. Grant cracked the door nearest him and found that Khalil's father and an older group of men wanted an audience.

"Let them through," Khalil said, and Grant, Daron, and Dro passed the word on to the Knights, who allowed some of the Maharaj family through the doors, then Sandy, Temple and Milan came out as well until Vikkas put an end to the steady stream by signaling for Hiram to shut the doors again.

When five elders gathered in front of Khalil, standing behind Gaurav, he spoke in an authoritative tone, warning. "If you claim her now, then The Castle and all of your wealth returns to the Maharaj family and part of it to me. That was the agreement. You lose everything, your children, their status as Maharaj heirs, your money. Everything."

Khalil brought Aashna to his side as he glared at his father, Jagat, and the elders who stood with him. "The Castle, and all of its holdings, is now in the hands of nine men who are responsible for its destiny. All of this was done through the American legal system. You cannot touch any of it, because it is no longer mine to give."

A roar of discontent went up among family, the voices so loud no one could hear anything clearly.

"Why are you so upset?" Khalil roared, and the voices trickled to a halt as his heated gaze narrowed on Jagat. "So after you forced me to give up my name, my wife, two of my children, and now that

The Castle has more wealth and fortune than both the Bhandari and Maharaj families combined, you want The Castle as part of the Maharaj coffers. When I sacrificed so much to get it to a place where it could sustain itself for centuries to come, you—who doubted what could be accomplished—want to benefit from all of my hard work. Now that—as my sons would say—is some bullshit."

"Wait, did he say, gave up two of his children?" Jai asked Vikkas, who nodded but didn't look away from his father.

Khalil left Aashna's side and positioned himself in front of the elders. "The only persons who believed in me were Aashna and my mother. I knew I would always come for mine when the time was right. But I had to make sure The Castle was out of your reach. No way would I allow you to even touch what I created. Especially when you hurt her this way. On this day, all of my three children will know the truth. They will know what levels you went to because you begrudged our happiness. Wanted us to pay for being in love when you all did not have that privilege. You could have let us go our own way."

"All of my three children," Vikkas said, and Jai tilted his head toward the Kings who also looked at each other, probably back to doubting their own parentage again. Evidently, the geriatric club could keep secrets like no other.

"The only important things on this earth for me are Aashna, Vikkas, Jaidev, and Mira.

"Hold up," Jai said, shifting his gaze to Vikkas' sister whose shocked expression mirrored his own. "Mira?"

"Khalil, do not do this," Varsha warned, her fists balled at her sides.

"Or what, the family will disown me again? Too late. They will try to force me to choose between my mission and my only love. They did that, and they failed. They'll take yet another child from me after they took my son and daughter."

"Wait," Jai said, standing in front of Khalil. "Daughter? What in the entire hell is going on?"

"You want to tell him, or should I?" Khalil taunted Varsha, who seemed to wither under his hard glare. "Tell them how deep your deception went. Tell them the levels at which this family stooped to punish me for my spiritual journey."

Aashna squared her shoulders. "Both of us went into the hospital to give birth to children at the same time. Only one of us came home with a child. I was told my baby was stillborn."

"Only one of you gave birth," Khalil corrected. "The other was never pregnant."

Gasps echoed off the walls.

CHAPTER 25

Jai and Vikkas shared a glance. Milan came to her husband's side and laced her fingers with his. He pressed a kiss to her forehead then put his focus back on the family drama unfolding in the middle of his wedding reception. Jai's gaze searched for Temple and India and he extended his hand for her to come forth and be with him. He placed an arm about her shoulders and drew her near. Mira stood by herself, trying to absorb everything and the implications. Jai reached out and guided her until she stood between the two men who were her brothers.

Evidently, Khalil was just getting warmed up. No one had seen him this angry, and it was a sight to behold.

"Oh, you thought I would not understand what you tried to do?" Khalil asked Varsha. "You bring me a drink and you are all sweetness and happiness, and that is certainly not your nature. And yes, I can fake like the best of them." He winked and gave her a smile. "I was not passed out when you tried to be a wife that one night in our marriage. But I also know exactly what it takes to create a child. And you did not walk away with the goods, my dear."

Varsha's complexion turned alabaster.

"Nice try, though," he said, then he faced the elders. "The family directed her in that deception, then took our baby girl and gave it to Varsha. Because we feared that if we didn't keep that agreement some harm might come to her, we allowed it to happen."

Tears flowed down Mira's face and she shook her head several times.

Aashna stepped toward Mira, cupped the young woman's face in her hands. "But I was the one to breastfeed you, and care for you at the beginning stages of your life because she could not. And we have remained close all throughout your life, despite Varsha's efforts to keep us separated."

Mira's chest heaved as she glared at Khalil. "I swear, if one more secret spills out today … I'm going to scream."

"That makes two of us," Jai said and looked at Vikkas, who lowered his gaze to the carpet, processing all this new information. He now had a sister, as well as a family who was so averse to everything that Khalil represented that they tore apart a happy family to accomplish it. "To find out you have a brother is one thing. To find out that I also have another mother, is another. To find out how much evil has been part of the foundation of your life is something I still can't wrap my mind around."

"And if fate would be so kind, I will spend the rest of my life enjoying your presence," Khalil said, sweeping a gaze first to Jai, then Vikkas and Mira. "This time, no one can take that away from us. This time, it is *your* choice, and no amount of family pressure will ever make you choose between family and your purpose. I did everything in my power to ensure they will be in charge of their destiny."

Varsha released a bitter laugh, as Gaurav smirked and said, "It will be hard to have everything you want. I will *not* give her a divorce, unless …"

"Yes, that is what it comes to. Money," Khalil spat, then his glare landed on the elders of the Maharaj family.

"And I would win and get paid, too," Gaurav snarled. "Don't think I don't know about those early morning visits to your Castle."

"Uh oh," Reno whispered.

"Yes, what you said," Grant chimed in as Dwayne, Dro, and Grant placed their backs against the doors, bracing for what was to come.

"So, hold up," Vikkas said, and the anger in those three words whipped through the room causing everyone to shift their attention to him. "All this time, you've been talking about ethics, integrity, and honesty, and you've been committing adultery … with her." He gestured to Jai's mother. "I don't see how you could choose a woman who—"

"Vikkas, my brother," Jai snarled, moving in so there was only spitting distance between them. "Don't say anything that I will make you regret."

Khalil quickly maneuvered around the Kings and came to stand between his sons. "Vikkas, it is not considered adultery if you're making love to your wife."

The silence behind that seemed to last to infinity and beyond.

"Your wife," Najan Maharaj said with a laugh that reverberated off the walls. "That's impossible."

Najan had been the family matchmaker for as many years as anyone could remember. Every union benefitted him in some way, and every business endeavor somehow had his signature placed on them. Nothing happened within Maharaj, Bhandari, Gupta, and several other families without his machinations.

After Khalil's admission, all gazes left the sons and were now squarely focused on the father.

"Yes, my wife," Khalil asserted with a smile. "My marriage to Varsha was privately annulled on the grounds that one spouse was physically incapable of having children, and that spouse—and her family—lied about it. American courts really despise that sort of thing." Khalil's smile brightened his face. "Then that divorce you forced onto Aashna and on me was a religious one—and only could affect our standing in our family, but it isn't recognized by the American government or any other official agency."

"So, what are you trying to say?" Najan asked and a few others around him nodded, as they too, wanted to understand what Khalil asserted, in plain terms.

"I could not commit adultery with a woman who is still, legally and completely, my wife. And has been for all of these years."

"Whoa," Dwayne said, wriggling his eyebrows. "Do not rule out the geriatric crew."

Kaleb nodded and one side of this mouth lifted in amusement. "What he said."

"But you went through with a divorce with me earlier this year," Varsha said, her gaze reflecting her confusion.

"Because the family needed to see that and you need that outward closure. We were *never* married in the eyes of American law."

Varsha staggered backwards until she landed on Najan whose hands came up to keep her from falling.

"And that being said," Khalil enunciated his words firmly as he stood in front of the elders. "We do not have any reason to keep up pretenses any longer, just to keep certain aspects of the family intact. Because the most important facets of the family are protected and made whole."

Guarav pointed at Khalil. "You … you … you."

"Yes, yes, and yes," Khalil said, taking Aashna's hand in his.

"What kind of crazy family did I marry into?" Milan said, looking up at Vikkas.

"That's what I'm saying," Vikkas added, meeting his wife's eyes. "I didn't know any of this."

"None of you are welcome in this family. Low caste heathens," Najan said, with disdain dripping from his voice. "We should never have allowed you and your family anywhere near ours. You have always been beneath us, even though you put on airs like you were above everyone."

"So, you're distancing us from the Maharaj family again, yes?" Khalil asked in a calm tone.

"Of course," Guarav spat. "There is no place for you, your … whatever she is." He waved toward Aashna. "Whore is a better word."

Jai stepped forward at the same time as Khalil, but Vikkas gripped Jai's hand and blocked Khalil on his path to dismantle Guarav.

"Need to borrow Roscoe for a moment, Chief?" Sandy asked, stepping up beside Jai.

His head whipped to Sandy. "You brought a .45 to my brother's wedding?"

"Weddings and funerals," she replied, totally unashamed. "That's where folks lose their natural minds. Roscoe helps 'em find it."

"My kind of woman," Cameron whispered as Daron smirked and Dro gave a nod of approval.

"Mine, too," Khalil said, putting his hand out. "Pass it over."

Sandy was only too happy to comply.

"No, don't do that," Vikkas warned, gesturing for Sandy to put it away. "No one is going to jail on my wedding day."

"How about the morgue," Khalil said through his teeth. "That would work for me."

"And your two bastards, and that little whore, too. Can't see how we will marry her off to anyone," Najan said and gestured to Mira as Guarav nodded vigorously. "Take them and go your way."

Khalil swept in and was only a few inches away from putting his fist into Guarav's face before a quiet whoosh made everyone back away. Najan and Guarav suddenly slumped to the ground.

Daron's gaze narrowed on Cameron, who said, "Ooops."

All eyes went to the men struggling to find their bearings.

Dro chuckled and said, "Now *that's* definitely my kind of woman."

Mira's chest heaved in an effort to remain calm, and Jai put his arms around her, so did Vikkas.

She welcomed their embrace.

Moving like a colony of confused ants, several family members moved in to scoop the fallen men from the ground and stand them up. They couldn't remain upright on their own and two family members had to flank their sides so they wouldn't fall down again.

"That's not a fast-acting agent?" Dro asked Cameron. "You didn't try to kill them?"

"No, but over the next give hours they'll wish they were dead," she quipped and Dro held back a chuckle.

Kaleb put out his fist for a pound. Cameron glanced at Daron, who nodded before she happily obliged.

"They will have none of their share of any monies that are coming to them," the tallest of the elders said, bringing everyone's focus back to the secrets that had sprinted from the closet and were now running a Chicago marathon. Somehow, it didn't feel as though said secrets had made it to the finish line.

"That is how you really feel," Khalil said and the smile on his face should have been the tip-off that they were in trouble. Again.

The consent went up from the Maharaj and Bhandari clans. All except Khalil's mother, who inched away to put some distance between herself and his father.

"Do you remember that set of entity and corporate documents you had the new family lawyer you hired draw up a few years ago," Khalil asked, and the man flinched under the scrutiny of everyone in the corridor. "The ones that state that only male heirs of full Maharaj-Bhandari bloodline can inherit, and only full Maharaj-Bhandari females can receive a portion at majority?"

Najan and several elder members of the Maharaj clan stiffened, probably feeling that another blow was coming. And they were not prepared.

"And that it would take proper DNA testing to prove who had exactly how much of that bloodline, right? You know, availing yourself of today's technology."

Najan chanced a look at the rest of the clan, who didn't seem thrilled at hearing that bit of news.

"Just so you are aware," Khalil began in a voice loud enough to carry across the corridor. "As part of my marriage gift to my son, I filed the bloodwork of both Vikkas Germaine, Jaidev Maharaj, Devesh Maharaj, as the only full-blooded male heirs to the Maharaj fortune, holdings and estates, and Mira and Anaya Maharaj as the only female heirs the American and international courts can recognize."

The shocked gasps echoed throughout the area and the elders' expression ranged first from confusion and ended with abject anger. As well they should. Najan, in his efforts to line his own pockets and to be seen as someone important in American culture, had effectively guided the Maharaj affairs into the American legal system, rather than East India where the power would remain with the elders.

"Help me to understand," Jagat said.

"Vikkas and Jaidev, as the oldest heirs, now control every aspect of the Maharaj fortune." Khalil let out a dramatic sigh. "And my—what did you call her? No, I won't repeat that because it is absolutely not true, but Mira also has a controlling interest as pure blood." He smiled. "Now, if anyone wants anything to do with that money, the properties, businesses, corporations, or the estates, they will need to put in a petition to both of them. And my daughter also has to sign off on the final approval. My children now control … everything."

The shocked expressions from everyone in the room was epic. The silence went on so long the buzz of conversation from inside the ballroom carried to the group.

"Jaidev Maharaj," Sandy said with a laugh. "Your father knows exactly how to play the long game."

"Indeed," Jai said with a lingering look at his newfound father. He still didn't know how to feel about it, but feelings wouldn't change anything.

"Well, on that note," Vikkas said, hooking an arm under his brother's and Milan's and moving them toward the door. "The food's getting cold."

"And the champagne's getting warm," Jai added, grasping Temple's hand and taking her with them.

"And we have a marriage to celebrate," Devesh Maharaj chimed in and gestured for everyone to make tracks back into the ballroom.

Guarav finally found his foot, and lunged forward, charging toward Aashna, fists waving in front him as he aimed to hurt the woman Khalil loved.

Only one thing halted him.

"You lay a hand on my beloved," Khalil said as the Kings changed direction and circled him and the Knights put themselves around Aashna. "And I swear on whatever God you believe in, there will not be room on the planet for the both of us."

"Roscoe?" Sandy asked handing over the gun.

Khalil turned up his palm to accept. "Don't mind if I do."

CHAPTER 26

"I need to leave here."

Jai put aside the latest summary from the Knights, then perched on the sofa, trying to wrap his mind around that unexpected statement. He let his gaze travel up her red skirt and to the simple white blouse to avoid assimilating what she'd just said. The distraction she presented didn't help. The light from the window only highlighted her peaches and cream skin and dark wavy hair, making him want to touch her.

"I need a clean slate," Temple whispered, jerking him back to the present. She secured the baby in the car seat before she moved from the living room toward the foyer and the bags that awaited. "For me and India."

She was leaving him? Why? "And raise her on your own?" he asked, unable to understand why now, or at all, since he'd provided not only a place to live, but unrestricted access to the daughter she swore up and down she didn't want.

Things were going well. She was actually bonding with India and Sandy, painting in her free time, getting some much-needed rest, taking some online courses so she'd be able to return to teaching in a different capacity, and had even polished off a few novels. All in six months, they had developed a wonderful life routine that he had taken for granted.

Caring for India and showering her with the love and affection both had lacked in some form growing up. Breakfast together every morning, dinner every evening. Live comedy shows and concerts most weekends. Reading novels to each other at night. Enjoying and exploring different types of music and art. Stolen kisses here and there that ignited a flame that they both feared to stoke.

"With no father?" he asked.

"She's young enough to adapt," Temple shot back but the doubt in her eyes said she wasn't so sure.

Jai took in her determined stance and conceded with a nod. "I understand."

"Do you?" she snapped, her shoulders tense with defiance as though she had expected him to put up more of a fight.

"No, but I know that's what you need to hear for you to walk out of here and find your way." Simply saying the words sent a thousand daggers into his heart. "I'm not in the habit of fighting battles people don't want me to win."

Her eyes watered but no tears escaped those dark-brown orbs that pleaded with him, but for what? For him to beg her to stay?

Jai was all for fighting to keep Temple and India with him, but she had to meet him halfway. Every time it looked as though they were getting closer, she pushed him away. The need for her had become so strong, it sent Jai to Khalil to ask for help in sorting through the possible scenarios that made her reluctant to commit. Jai had been in what he termed minor relationships, but they weren't as fulfilling on a spiritual level. The women loved the idea of him being a healer, but failed to see why he couldn't embrace the more traditional—more financially rewarding—line of work. He had never felt the desire to become part of a machine that was the end of a cycle that kept people unwell and in poverty.

"I'll have Sandy gather up the rest of your things and send it wherever you like," he said in an expressionless voice. "India should have something familiar, since it won't be her surroundings." *Or me.*

Temple hoisted the baby bag on her shoulder and gave him her back to ponder. He sent a quick text to Daron Kincaid before he gathered the items she had stashed in the foyer and took them outside to an unfamiliar SUV that waited in the driveway. The driver didn't bother to get out to help, causing curiosity to mingle with anger. She could have at least allowed him to take her wherever she wanted to go. Maybe she meant more than a clean slate. This felt more like "cutting all ties."

"If it's not too much trouble," he said, coming back into the foyer for the next set of bags. "Could you drop me a line to let me know how you all are doing?"

She froze and closed her eyes as she pressed India closer to her breasts. "I don't … I don't think that's a good thing," she said, glancing over her shoulder. "A clean break is best."

Pain slashed across his heart. This chilling action came from left field and was knocking him for a major loop. He stared at her, unable and unwilling to understand the reason Temple would put them through this unnecessary agony.

"Fine," he said in a terse tone. "Whatever."

Temple's jaw clenched as she first clamped down on whatever it was she planned to say, then her own anger came through. "Why are you so upset? You wanted me to bond with the baby, so I did. You wanted me to want her, now I do."

"I'm not upset," he countered. "Especially not about that. I'm disappointed that you would uproot our lives this way, but not upset." Jai moved in and stood a few inches from Temple, not to intimidate her, but to look into her eyes to see what was going on with her. "Just so you know, she'll always have a place in my heart and in my life, as you will. You're welcome to come back if you need me." Jai placed a hand on the crown of India's head before leaning in to kiss her forehead.

She reached for him, showing her bare gums in a grin, and it took every effort to hold true to his resolve to let them go. He had so many questions but asking them right now would not be the wise thing.

"I know what unconditional love is about, even if you can't wrap your mind around it." Despite his effort, his words emerged with a harsh edge.

Temple brushed off any further offer of help, snatched open the door and was outside attempting to dodge the pellets of rain before he could cover her with the umbrella he had snatched from the foyer closet. She looked as he watched her slide into a car that had the ride-share emblem on the back window.

Jai never knew his heart could hurt so much. The Knights were right. Having someone to come home to, to fill his days with laughter and his heart with joy, was such a beautiful thing. He'd had no idea he needed this in his life. They hadn't even pulled out of the driveway and he was missing them already.

His phone vibrated. Daron was on the other end of the line.

"You want me to track her?"

Yes. Yes. And yes.

"No, she's going out of her way for me not to know where she'll end up," Jai responded and closed his eyes against another unwelcome shaft of pain that washed over him. "I need to respect that."

"Are you sure?" Daron asked.

"She knows how to reach me."

And she knows how to hurt me.

* * *

Temple had the driver wait for a moment. Her heart constricted and she resisted the urge to run back to tell Jaidev she was wrong and had changed her mind. Every day she was falling deeper for a man who had dropped into her life under the most unusual circumstances. There was no need that Jai didn't anticipate, no matter how small. The way he took care of her endangered her independence. If she wasn't careful, she'd become addicted to him.

He couldn't love her. Not someone as broken as she was. The man believed in obligation and responsibility, taking those elements to a whole new level. At no time did it make sense that he would fall in love with her and welcome a ready-made family. She never had that kind of luck.

No, leaving Jaidev Maharaj was the right thing to do. She had witnessed firsthand through her mother how being totally dependent on a man could destroy a woman, and she wasn't going to be that woman.

Temple had to find her own way. No matter that her heart felt as if someone had smashed it to a pulp with a sledgehammer.

CHAPTER 27

"So now the focus is on this new place," Jaidev said to the men after he had taken them on a full tour of The Castle. They now sat in the boardroom with their attention turned to the screen. "This new facility we're going to build in Jeffrey Manor. I've given you all of the recent mishaps. You've already mapped out a better operating and procedural system, but this medical center within The Castle walls is also going to be a place that is under our direction. How can we make it better? When you finish reading this, come up with a plan that will—"

"Mr. Maharaj, what's going on with you today?" Andre, the quietest of the Knights, asked.

The men remained silent, seemingly as interested in the answer as well.

"I don't know what you're talking about." He quickly turned his attention back to the screen. "When the issue with Chetan is all done, this will be our next facility. This is just a dark place in the center's life right now. I have to believe in the light."

"But you don't believe in love," Hiram asserted and Jai wondered where the hell that came from.

"What do you mean?"

"How is Ms. Temple?" Falcon asked.

Jai inhaled, already weary from a sleepless night, wondering if she was all right, if India was missing him as much as he was missing her. So many times, he wanted to send another text to Daron and have him activate the earrings he had placed in India's tiny ears the moment she came home from the hospital. Yes, early, even for that, but he had her safety in mind. He resisted, but the struggle was truly real. "She's gone."

Everyone seemed to speak at once, but the common question was, "Gone?"

"She took the baby last night and left," he said, and those were the hardest words to pass his lips. "Said she needed a fresh start."

"Now that's some …" Hiram shook his head and tossed his pen on the table. "I can't believe you, of all people, fell for that line of bullshit."

"What she said is that she needs space," Jai countered, a little miffed that they were coming at him this way. He felt bad enough that he had no reason why things had gone south, and didn't need them rubbing it in. He tapped his fingers against the tabletop, wishing the meeting was over.

"What she meant is that she wants to be sure you're in it for the right reasons," Hiram said, placing a hand over Jai's, halting his nervous movements.

"You know how y'all came together was kind of different," Michael said. "She might feel you're only there from guilt, and not because you actually care about her."

Hiram laughed, taking in Jai's expression, which given his state of mind had to reflect the confusion within. "I'm surprised you haven't figured that out yet. You might be a genius, but you're a little slow when it comes to that love thang, my brother."

"Man, you'd better listen to what this dude right here is saying," Ryan chimed in, clasping a hand on Hiram's shoulder. "Go get your woman. This flowers, peace, hair grease program ain't going to fly all the time."

They all laughed and Jai felt a smile tilt the corners of his lips as he joined in. "I'll take that."

"My girl held me down all those years," Falcon admitted. "Now I can give her anything she wants, but what she wants is me. She loves *this* me." He pointed an index finger to his chest. "The man who goes off to work and is with people who are living right, got their heads on straight. Keeps me going on the right path. I don't want to do *anything* to mess that up."

Jared leaned back in the chair and flexed a little. "I got a savings account with some extra money in it, and I'm not talking about funny money either. Those things you did to make sure we don't fail—life skills, stuff we didn't learn growing up—who does that? I mean, for people like us. Dudes from the hood."

"My mother struggled," Hiram confessed and all eyes went to him. "She lived paycheck to paycheck and had to borrow from her friends to make ends meet. Credit cards were always maxed out, drowning in debt all the time. Then high blood pressure kicked in, heart disease and not taking care of herself. She couldn't teach me how to live, how to do the things that I know how to do now. Her way is not the way I want to live."

"How any of us should live." Andre looked at each one of them. "I'm on this side of the bars and learned that just because people didn't end up doing a bid like me doesn't mean they live much better."

Kevin nodded at Jai, gratitude in his gaze. "You look at the person's heart; make sure you have happy employees and good vibes all around, man. That's … church."

They chuckled at his use of the word that Hiram had made famous.

"I feel some kind of way on my days off," Chris admitted, pushing the laptop further away. "Like I'm missing something. Nobody's talking like that about their jobs. None of the people in my family …" He shrugged. "They hate their jobs. I can't say that. And I'm grateful for that."

"We got this," Hiram said, waving him toward the door. "Go get your woman."

Jai shook his head. "I need to give her a little more time."

The special earrings that Daron fashioned for the Kings and their family were securely placed in India's ears. At any time, he could find where she was and that brought him a little peace. But riding the line between encroaching on Temple's space simply to satisfy his own personal need to be in control, was exactly the thing she had pointed out. He had chosen a life where he had managed nearly every aspect of it. This experience with India and Temple from beginning until now had caused such an upheaval he didn't know which way to go.

Andre inhaled and let out a long, slow breath as he slid down in the chair. "Women say they don't believe in fairytales or any of that happily ever after stuff, but they like for us to come a little close."

"I hear you, but I'm expecting a visit from Marilyn later this morning to start the process for getting this place up and running again."

"We'll handle it," Chuck said, and the others nodded or voiced a verbal agreement. "You trust us with everything else, trust us to do that as well."

He couldn't come up with another objection, so Jai threw his Knights a grateful look.

"Awww, look at you trying not to break out with that ugly cry," Falcon teased, nudging Jai in the side.

Jai grinned and gathered up his belongings from the table. "Thank you. I said I wasn't going to ask but is everything all right with …"

"A little tough on the home front, since the crime lab is now saying the second set of DNA results the police recovered is missing," Chuck explained, sliding his notes to Jai. He had been the one commissioned to keep Jai up to date on things.

"Missing," Jai roared. "Now *that's* some bull—"

"Church," Hiram agreed. "But the lawyers have put in a motion for the court to accept the DNA results from the lab you hired."

"Don't worry," Falcon said, gesturing to the pages Jai held. "The lawyers are doing their thing, then people will see how wrong they were. They still weren't happy about us not pushing for that DNA. But if we hadn't had this challenge, we wouldn't know how this end of things work.

Hiram tapped the edge of the small-scale model of the new center that was situated next to the replica of one made from the medical center in The Castle. "Man, I like this right here. It feels different." He nodded as though agreeing with some unspoken thoughts rolling through his mind. "Like it's ours somehow."

Ryan stood and stretched. They had been at it for a while. "I'm thinking about maybe taking up some architecture classes because you're going to build some more of these? And not just in the States, right?"

"Indeed."

"Then we'd like to be the ones who do this part," Jared said, tapping an index finger on the edge of the documents in front of him. The others seemed to be in agreement. "You know, the building, the planning, the zoning, the structure, program, systems, electronics and security—stuff like that."

"He's right," Hiram chimed in. "I kind of saw this happening as a bad thing, but something good is coming out of it, too. I don't think I've ever looked into doing something more than what I've had going on."

While Jai realized this crew was beneficial to rebuilding after everything the state had done to tear things down, the men actually had a point. He hadn't even told them that he had another task for them related to The Castle. He wasn't able to do much with the Center on The Castle grounds until everything was resolved with Chetan. What he did know was that the place had access to treatments that weren't available on American soil and medications that would never make it to the American market. Once again, he was finding evidence that cures and targeted treatments were available and the American pharmaceutical industry was well aware, but were not producing them because money was not made in cures, it was made in research and treatment. He was going to do his best to change all that. The Castle's medical center held a wealth of information and options. No wonder the wealthy members didn't suffer too long when diagnosed with certain illnesses, even the deadly ones.

"Do you think I should—*we* should. How can we bring something to the table if we can't help build a table?" Hiram spread his hands out. "What I'm feeling here, is that it's better to be on the top end of the spectrum where I'm making the decisions, than coming to a company with my hands out for a job and decisions are being made for me. You're putting all of us on top. I'm feeling all of that."

He scanned the faces of the men around the table, and Chuck, who sat near a smaller round conference table off to the side, seeing something else in their eyes that he hadn't witnessed since they stepped through the doors of Chetan. Determination.

"Go get your woman," Hiram commanded, snapping Jai out of his thoughts.

Jai hesitated. Maybe a little too long because Hiram added, "And we need you to put a little pep in your step while you're at it."

He relented and made it to the door before Hiram said to everyone else, "I'm going to walk him to the car."

"He doesn't know the way," Michael teased.

"You've got jokes," Jai shot back.

Ryan chuckled. "Just say you want to talk to him about some personal things you don't want us to know."

"That's all you had to say," Jared added.

"I'm going to walk him to the car," Hiram repeated. "If you couldn't read between the lines, then evidently Falcon isn't the only one who's been dropped on his head."

"Oh, man. That's cold," Falcon said, shaking his head.

The group dissolved into laughter and good-natured ribbing.

This was like old times and what Jai envisioned when he'd created a seat at the table for them, despite their murky past.

* * *

"Go get your woman and your child," Hiram said again.

"Hiram, I hear you. I hear all of you. I was giving her the space she asked for."

"For a man who has all those degrees and book smarts, you're a little slow on the uptake. She wants confirmation."

Frowning, Jai said, "I still don't understand."

Hiram let out a long sigh as they continued walking. "Are you with her because you have to be or because you want to be?"

"I—" With one hand, Jai rubbed the back of his neck.

"Her, not the baby," Hiram amended.

Jai slowed his roll, stood near his car and gave it some thought. "Because I want her. I admire so much about her. Her smile, whenever she gives one. Her humor, even when it takes me a minute. That kind of strength. She's no victim, no matter how much it feels that way to her. Every time I think about her, I get this feeling that …"

"Does she know that?" Hiram placed a hand on his shoulder. "Have you told her? Or do you assume she realizes how you feel?"

"This morphed into something I didn't expect," Jai confessed, leaning against the hood. "I wasn't looking for love, or a ready-made family. It found me."

"Go get your woman and your child," Hiram ordered, pointing to his car. "Tell her how you feel. Don't let her think a certain thing—she needs to know for sure. At least put forth the effort, so you can be at ease. And then you won't be moping around here second-guessing yourself."

Jai's shoulders went stiff. "I'm not moping."

Hiram raised an eyebrow.

"Okay, maybe a little," Jai conceded. "Go get her? Even though ..."

"Yes. Bring her home. She's family. We all took part in making sure she was all right."

"When did you get so smart?"

"Always have been. Degree in Business Administration from Florida A&M before all that extra happened." Hiram tipped his head toward the meeting room. "And, I have the added benefit of not being one of those nuts in there whose mother didn't have a tight grip and knew which end was up."

"Falcon's going to kick your ass," Jai teased.

"He'll try. And he'll fail." Hiram shooed him toward the car. "Now quit stalling."

CHAPTER 28

A late-night peal from the doorbell echoed through the house, snatching Jai out of a sound sleep. He glanced at his phone, wondering if something had happened. He had fallen asleep with his clothes on waiting for Daron's text to confirm Temple's location.

"I have it," he called out so Sandy wouldn't leave the comfort of her bed. They were both still on India's schedule. Although she had her own house across the street, she sometimes preferred the peace and quiet that Jai's home afforded. With three daughters, six grands underfoot, her place could become a madhouse at times.

He padded down the hallway, took the spiral stairs two at a time until he made it to the foyer and disengaged the alarm. From the sounds on the other side of his door, he knew who came to visit.

Temple stood at the threshold with India in her arms, wailing up a storm.

"She won't stop crying," Temple said in a hoarse whisper, thrusting the baby into his arms. "She wants you."

"Come in out of the rain," Jai said, cradling India and bringing Temple in with the sweep of his arm about her waist. He peered out to the driveway and didn't notice a car or any other vehicle. "How did you get here?"

"I…" she shivered and her words were swallowed up in a haze of tears.

"Never mind," he said, juggling the baby in one arm and helping Temple to shed her coat with the other. "Let's get you out of these wet clothes."

"Please don't be so kind," Temple whispered and her voice broke on those words. "She's already giving me the side-eye."

The baby's cries had subsided to happy gurgles once she lay in Jai's arms.

"She's not giving you the side-eye," he countered, chuckling. "*I'm* giving you the side-eye. You're making this more difficult than it needs to be." He held India and Temple close, relishing the feel of them in his arms. "You belong here with me. She belongs here, where she will be loved." He laid his forehead against Temple's. "You deserve to be happy and I thought you were. I deserve you and I deserve to be happy. You make me happy."

She pulled her head back to ask, "Even with my craziness?"

"Especially with that," he confirmed. "What's life without a little crazy?"

She pulled away, went to sit on a sofa in the living room. "There has to be something truly wrong with you if your own mother can't love you," Temple whispered, then locked gazes with him as he sat next to her. "How can I trust that your love is real? How can I know that you're not doing this strictly because of that saint-like obligation you seem to hold for others? For the Knights? For the Kings?" She placed a hand on his chest and his heart rate quickened. "How do I know if you really love me for me?"

Jai shifted India so she lay against his shoulder, and he brought Temple in closer. "Because I have never felt like this for anyone, ever. When you walked out that door, my heart … my heart stopped beating and it took everything within me not to run after you. It took every bit of my understanding that love does not hold on to people when they're begging to be set free. Love doesn't bind people that way. But oh Lord, did I find out that love hurts. It hurts." He took her hand and placed it on his chest. "I never had a heartbreak, nor did I know it could be physical. A slash to the heart as though someone has taken a knife and plunged it straight in and left it there." He tightened his hold on her hand. "I didn't start loving until I met you. I didn't start … living until both of you came into my life. I didn't realize that I'd just been existing, doing everything I felt would earn my father's approval. Well, the man I always wanted to be my father—Khalil Germaine. The man who is my father. I learned more from him in the short span of time he was my educator and mentor, than I had from the man I thought was my father."

He traced her brow with one finger, then pleaded with her. "If you're not sure about this love thing, then stay long enough to become sure. Stay long enough to figure it out. But don't hurt me or her in the process." He gestured to the house. "This right here, my home, in my life, is where you both belong." Jai paused to let that sink in. "This much I know is true—no matter how we came together, no matter that it doesn't seem like it should be possible, that's not where we should put our focus. We are here."

"Chief …"

He turned to focus on Sandy who wore a sheepish smile as she inched her way into the room. "Me and the little one are going to take a weekend trip to my place."

"She doesn't like being away from him," Temple said, getting to her feet. "I learned that the hard way."

Sandy whipped out her phone, slid the screen to a recording. The next sound in the room was of Jai struggling to teach Temple to sing India's favorite songs. Even with the failures, an excited gurgle escaped India's lips and it caused Temple to look away.

But Jai didn't miss her smile.

"I wish I could sing," Temple admitted.

"Yes, I wish you could, too," Jai said with a chuckle that made Temple give him a playful punch in the arm.

"See, you've got jokes."

"Let's hold on to the fact that practice will make perfect." Then he gave her that poker face she found so funny. "Or at least something close to it."

Sandy stepped in and lifted India from Jai's arms, then tipped out of the room. "We'll be back on Monday," she tossed over her shoulder.

"Monday?" Temple squeaked, and her eyes went wide with panic. She was off the sofa and in the foyer in the time it took to blink.

Jai followed Temple, then stood in her way. "Giving the adults some time to figure life out."

With wide eyes, she asked, "Do we need that much time?"

"That depends on you," he countered, stroking the underside of her chin. "I know what I want. I don't know how much time it'll take to convince you that what I want is you."

Temple looked at him for a long moment. "You have such a way with words."

His lips twitched and he held back a smart retort, because to mention that words weren't all he had a way with would not have been the right thing to say at this time.

"Jai, what are we going to do?" She searched his eyes for something, he didn't know quite what. Reassurance? Sincerity?

He tipped her chin toward him with one finger. "We are going to figure our lives out, but first you'll need to tell me what it is that is holding you back. I know some of your life's experiences, but there has to be something that makes you so afraid to love me. Give me a few minutes." He went to the foyer's closet and helped Sandy into her overcoat and grabbed India's bag to walk Sandy to her house. He also pulled out an umbrella.

"No, you stay here," Sandy insisted. "My daughter's waiting at my front door. We'll be all right. Won't we, India?" she crooned, and he leaned in to kiss the baby before taking her in his arms again. India cooed, which made him smile.

"One for the road," he said, and Sandy chuckled as he cradled her.

"And don't you start singing," Sandy said. "We'll never get out of here. She'll prefer the live to the recorded."

Temple stood by his side as they watched Sandy make her way across the street, though he would have preferred to carry India himself. The rain had let up, and the path wasn't far, but still. When Sandy's daughter gave a little wave and closed the door behind her mother, Jai secured his own home, guided Temple back to the sofa, and waited as she came up with the words she needed to say.

"I ... I have never felt ... safe," she said sighing. "My uncle didn't respect my right to say no. My mother let my stepfather abuse me ..."

Temple shared what happened in that household when Sharon Liscell allowed all manner of ugliness to happen to Temple. Then she told of the night her brother and sister saved what was left of her life.

CHAPTER 29

The night had been filled with sharing secrets, and the close proximity led to intimacy that made Temple open to Jai in a way that almost took them past a sensual threshold that he swore they wouldn't cross until they were married. After a heated session of kissing and exploring on the sofa, Jai pulled away, pacing in front of the first painting Temple had completed when she came to stay. "Jesus Christ, I'm trying to do the right thing here."

"Don't take God's name in vain," Temple warned.

"I'm not taking it in vain, I'm calling for help. Or should I say, I'm calling for Jesus to take the wheel because you're driving this car off the cliff."

Her lips pursed in disapproval.

"Temple, I want to do right by you," he whispered.

"And I'm telling you this is what's right for me," she said, leaving the sofa and standing before him with her luscious breasts on display. The concavity of her belly begging for his touch, her kiss igniting a fire within him that nearly burned the house down, had him holding on to control by a fraying thread.

Temple huffed and folded her arms across her bosom. "See, you're going to want your brothers to be involved, and this whole big wedding and all that. I don't need any of that. The only thing I want is you." She kissed him softly. "Everything you've done for me is like marriage already."

"Doesn't mean you give yourself to me as some type of reward," he countered as he perched next to her. "Suppose I want to keep my virginity until my wedding night."

Her eyes went as wide as she gasped, "You're a virgin?"

"A used one," he confessed and she gave him the stink-eye. "But that's beside the point."

"No, I'm just saying," she shot back. "You'd better have some skills because I cannot strike out three times."

"Oh, the pressure," he teased, stroking her chin. "Those first two times don't count. Those were not of your choosing. This will be your first time, and we're going to do it right."

"I really, really, have to wait?" She batted her eyelashes playfully, then kissed his lips before trailing a finger down to his chest.

"You are so wrong for that," he groaned.

"I'll have bragging rights for the rest of our lives that I seduced you."

"No ma'am. I am not that easy." Then he realized exactly what she meant and said, "I want to be the one man you can claim did absolutely right by you."

Tears streaked down her face. "That's so honorable, and so misguided."

"Why wouldn't you want to brag about the fact that a man wanted to honor you, honor your body by waiting to take that precious step?"

Temple gave him the side-eye. "I always thought that men these days were pushing for waiting because they were lacking in a ... um ... certain package."

Jaidev inhaled and let out his breath slowly, took her hand and placed it on his erection.

Her eyes widened and shot to his. "Oh my."

"And I know exactly what to do with it," he said, removing her hand and placing it on her lap. "Because that's not all I'm good for. Sex is more than just about this piece of flesh, since the biggest organ is between your ears, not between your thighs."

She let that absorb for a moment. "Pass me your phone."

Jai complied and gave her the passcode.

"Daron, can you raise Dro?" she asked, when the call connected. "I need your help."

"Why are you calling on Jai's phone and not your own," he asked. "You—never mind. Give me a few." When he came back with Dro on the line he asked, "What can I do for you?"

"I'm trying to get married as soon as possible."

Silence met that request and Temple stared at Jai, waiting.

"Well, see, the last I heard you had left my brother and I'm going to be real honest here … I'm not going to break my brother's heart by helping you to get hitched to someone else." Daron inhaled, then added, "If you need anything else, I got you, but I can't do that."

Jai smiled and Temple narrowed her gaze at him as she said, "So if I was marrying Jaidev, you would help me get a license, stand up with him for the wedding, and help pull a reception together … say, for next week?"

"Something like that," Daron answered. "And since whatever dude you're hanging with doesn't have that kind of pull, you're on your own, sister."

Jai plucked the phone from Temple's hand. "Brothers, make it happen for us. Today."

Daron paused a second, then roared with laughter. "That's what I'm talking about!"

"But you still have a problem." Dro spoke for the first time.

"What?"

"The clerk's office closes at five," he answered. "They need to lay eyes on you to issue a license. Not sure we can get around that."

"Hold up," Daron said. "Those are only partial facts. The office is closed, and yes you have to apply in person. But, there's always a way around things. Give me a second."

Temple tuned her lips up for a kiss.

Jai obliged and said, "Play nice."

"Okay, so can you tell me what's the rush," Dro asked. "It's not like we can't get this done tomorrow, you know."

Jai filled him in without whitewashing his words and added that they'd like the reception to happen today and not next week. Dro coughed as though clearing his throat. "Well, I did ask. But that first part was entirely too much information."

A few minutes later, Daron came back on the line. "All right, here's the plan, y'all need to hightail it downtown to the North Clark location. I have a contact who's on her way back to meet us there."

"And there's another problem," Dro said.

"Jesus Christ," Temple exclaimed.

When Jai's head whipped to her, she said, "Sorry."

"You cannot be married on the same day the license is issued."

"Do you ever have any good news?" Jai said, his tone as sour as his facial expression.

"Are you telling me you want to have a fly-by-night arrangement that doesn't include the everyone?"

"Everyone?" Temple asked, getting to her feet. "I just want something small and intimate. Just the two of you as witnesses."

"And you're not going to have the rest of the crew in for something as important as this?" Dro retorted, sounding pissed.

Temple mouthed the words, "I told you."

"Like I said, I'll round up the Kings and Knights," Dro said, and he used that tone which meant he wasn't going to be deterred.

They disconnected the call and Temple fell into a fit of giggles.

"We have to call Sandy." Jai keyed in her number, then gave her the info.

"See, I leave you all alone for two hours, and y'all are trying to get married—wait did you say, tonight?" She laughed so hard she caught the hiccups.

"He's trying to make an honest woman out of me," Temple said.

"And she's been over here trying to make a *dishonest* man out of me," Jai tattled.

"I'm on my way back," Sandy said, without hesitation.

Temple blinked and grimaced. "No, we just wanted—"

"No ma'am," she insisted. "You are not having a wedding without me, this little one, or some damn good food. I'll get things started over there and come back for her when she wakes. Be there in a jiffy."

Sandy disconnected the call before Temple could protest any further.

"Your family is pretty damn—"

"Amazing. Loving. Determined," Jai supplied with a toothy grin.

"Yes, that too," she conceded, and leaned her head against his chest. "I can't believe this is happening."

"I can," he said, pressing a kiss to her lips.

"Do you believe you'll be worth the wait?"

"Woman, that is an absolute promise," he shot back. "Now, go upstairs pull out something amazing, and let's get the first part of this party started."

Temple scrambled to get up and rushed toward the stairs. Then realizing he was watching, she slowed and did a sexy little sashay the rest of the way.

"You are so wrong for that," he said and her tinkling laughter echoed through the house.

Jai waited until she was out of earshot, then placed a call to Dro and said, "Hold on a second," then added Daron to the call. "Fellas, remember that favor I asked for?"

"You mean outside of the other kabillion ones you and your woman have on the table right now?" Daron said without missing a beat.

"See, why are you bringing up old stuff." Jai stood and brushed off his shirt. "I need you to work a miracle for me. It'll be my wedding present to Temple."

"You know that's a tall order, right?" Dro said.

Daron agreed. "We're still waiting for confirmation on some things."

"But I have faith that you two can do the impossible," Jai said, placing his legs into a yoga pose. "The Impossible's timeline just came a little faster, that's all."

"Spoken by the man who doesn't have to do the mental, Internet, and under-the radar gymnastics to pull it off," Dro said in a dry tone.

"But they call you a fixer for a reason, and Daron's the tech guru who can cut through all the bull and make stuff happen."

"Oh, what pressure," Daron retorted, amidst the clicking sound of his fingers dancing across his keyboard.

Dro chuckled. "Yeah, he's laying it on pretty thick."

Jai glanced down at the erection that refused to subside and said, "Pressure? You don't know the half of it."

CHAPTER 30

Twenty-nine minutes to midnight and the Kings, their queens, Mira, Nurse Jennifer, and Sandy's family were all putting the finishing touches on Jai's home as they waited for Daron, Khalil and Aashna to arrive.

Khalil walked in, guiding Aashna toward the center of the living room. Then another familiar face came in behind them. Sesvalah, a woman with honey cream skin and tiny locs that nearly touched her knees, who Jai had hired to provide counseling for Temple while she was at Meridian. Since then, the sessions have been ongoing, and Temple had made a great deal of progress, so it made sense for her to be a part of the happy occasion.

"Good Evening," Sesvalah said to everyone and was greeted in kind. "I'm here to perform the wedding ceremony."

Jai's gaze whipped to Temple. "You invited your counselor to officiate the wedding?"

"She's also a pastor," Temple said, her chin lifted, showing her determination. "Who did you think should do it?"

"Well, my father." He gestured to Khalil whose lips turned up in a smile. "But—"

"No, it is the bride's choice," Khalil said, with a small bow. "I can simply be the father of the groom, today. And that is fine with me."

"And father of the bride since mine isn't here," Temple prompted.

He gave a slight bow. "I would be honored."

"Why don't we *both* do the wedding?" Sesvalah offered. "You can never have too many blessings going into such a wonderful experience."

Jai looked at Temple, who nodded and said, "That sounds like a plan." Then she addressed Khalil. "But I'd still like for you to walk me down the aisle."

"Indeed." He kissed the back of her hand.

"Hey, get your own wife," Jai teased.

"Trust me, I did," Khalil said with a hearty chuckle.

Everyone laughed.

The Knights arrived in black suits and ties that matched the ones the Kings wore, and they brought in the rest of the items that Marilyn, Cameron, Milan, Zuri and the Kings had asked them to bring. Marilyn came through a few minutes later and Hiram greeted her with a kiss that received some good-natured ribbing from the Knights and Kings. Everyone quickly finished with the décor and setting the stage for the wedding so that when the clock struck twelve, it would be *showtime*.

"You know, all of us being here at this hour reminds me of that old Patsy Cline song," Sesvalah said, settling on the living room sofa.

Khalil frowned for a moment, then realization widened his eyes and he crooned, "I go out walkin' after midnight ..."

"Oh, and he sings too," Sesvalah teased, to the sound of laughter from the group.

"Yes, that makes sense," Temple said. "Jaidev sings to India all the time, and I swear she won't hear anything else."

"That's all right, baby," Jaidev crooned, kissing Temple's forehead. "I'll sing to you, too."

"Yeah, but that's not the kind of song mama will be wanting to hear," Reno said in a sly tone, and his mate nudged him.

"Behave," Khalil said and winked at his wife, who gave him a sassy smirk that spoke to the fact that she was now well aware of what kind of song they meant.

Jaidev had come to terms with the fact that his mother and Khalil had rekindled a flame that never quite went away. Their relationship and Khalil's skillful maneuvering to acquire the Maharaj wealth from the very people who had caused such harm, and put it into the hands of those he knew would do right by it, had sent shockwaves through parts of India, Goa and Dubai. The fallout was epic as Khalil's way of tipping the balance of power meant that the nine of them, women included, were now part of the ruling class.

In some ways, Jai, Devesh and his twin sister, Anaya, Vikkas and Mira had managed to avoid taking on any guilt that their family members tried to heap on, and were becoming closer than any of them had thought possible.

The whole confusing marriage-not-quite-divorce-marriage—annulment—marriage and divorce fiasco had to be brought before an American judge, much to the Maharaj Family's dismay. Their whole argument rested on the fact that none of the marriage part of the machinations held weight, which would unravel the main parts of what Khalil had put in place to wrest control of the Maharaj fortune from the elders and legally put it in the control of the members he was certain would do right by the wealth and status.

Unfortunately for them, Khalil was correct in his assertion that he was still legally married to Aashna which did make certain that Vikkas, Jaidev, and Mira were legitimate Maharaj-Bhandari heirs. Unfortunately, in a split-the-baby down the middle move, the judge did require them to have all the proper paperwork in order and that meant a substantial settlement to Guarav if he could somehow prove damages he suffered as a result of the duplicitous marriage. Varsha hadn't bothered, but Khalil had already given her a fair amount of money anyway.

Guarav, in true selfish fashion was holding out for more money, and had taken to stalling on turning in the necessary documents to have time run out. After several visits to the judge's chamber with no conclusion to the proceedings in sight, Khalil put an end to things by telling Gaurav, "She didn't call you out on the infidelity issue you don't think she knew about, because that's not the reason she was ready to cut ties with you. But the judge might see things differently, since you presented yourself as a faithful and dutiful husband. That one little element can turn things in our favor if a certain mistress decides she wants to … how do I say it … spill the tea and walk off with a little dancing cash that will cost me less than it will cost you, if you continue to make us suffer."

Gaurav's face lost every ounce of color.

Khalil placed a hand on his shoulder and gave a warning squeeze. "Trust me, I have what I want—free and clear—and we can last a lot longer with these proceedings than you think."

The final orders from the judge went through with great haste, and thanks to Khalil's last conversation with Guarav and that tip off to the judge, the man didn't get a dime. Khalil remarried Aashna in a private ceremony with only Vikkas and Milan, Jaidev and Temple, and Mira looking on. Then the two of them disappeared for nearly a month on a seven-continent cruise.

Seemed like every time Khalil left the country was when the exciting things within the family tended to happen. Jai's parents had landed late last night and their timing couldn't be better.

CHAPTER 31

Daron burst into the house, put his back against the door, and gestured wildly for Jai to come close. The rest of the Kings looked at each other first, before following on Jai's heels.

"What's going on?" Reno asked, giving his brother a onceover. "You look like hell."

"Tell me something I don't know." He glanced at Jai and lowered his voice. "I'm going to need you to stall for a little bit."

"What?" Dwayne said, sighing. "We were ready to finally start everything. We were waiting on you and Dro."

Dro tipped in and closed the door behind him, then shook his head.

"Yes, I know," Daron shot back but looked to Jai. "But we're going to need you to delay things a little bit."

"Are you going to tell me why?"

"No." Daron squared his shoulders and met the answering glare head-on. "Stall."

"For how long?"

Daron's expression darkened. "For as long as it takes."

"That is not an answer," Shaz said as Kaleb and Reno nodded. Finally, something the two of them could agree on.

"Trust me. Please."

Jai huffed, glanced at Dro who simply shrugged and walked out to the group situated in the living room. They all wore expressions that ranged from curiosity to mild annoyance at being kept in limbo.

"People, we're going to need a minute for the rest of the paperwork to arrive," Dro said with a reassuring look in Daron's direction.

Temple's gaze narrowed to slits. She thrust her bouquet into Hiram's hands and moved forward until she was only inches away from Dro. "Bull. The paperwork is already here." She stood toe to toe with Jai. "Are you having second thoughts, because we don't—"

"No, my love. Never that." Jai sighed, placing his arm about her waist before concentrating on Daron and Dro. "They're asking for a few more—"

The screech of tires pulled everyone's attention.

Daron raised his gaze heavenward, let out a long, slow breath as Dro's lips turned up in a small smile. They practically skipped to the door, something that was so uncharacteristic that all the Kings did a double-take and shared questioning glances with each other.

"Rut roh," Vikkas managed in his best Scooby-Doo imitation, causing Milan to shake her head.

Daron opened the door only enough to put his head out, then waited.

Others—especially his fellow Kings—tried to come close, but Daron gestured for them to stay back. Footsteps sounded against the pathway leading to the front entrance. The closer they came, the more anxious Jai felt.

"What the hell is he up to?" Cameron said through her teeth.

Milan stood next to her and slipped off the apron Sandy had given her when she first arrived to help with the meal. "Hell if I know."

"Ladies and gentleman, *and* Kaleb," Daron teased, grinning when Kaleb slyly flipped him the bird. "May I present to you … the miracle of the day." Voices all chimed in at once and he put up an index finger to silence them. "No, I'm not talking about a woman who's survived the most tragic of circumstances and lived to tell her story. Or the fact that she's given birth to an amazing child." His gaze lovingly landed on India, who was leaning over in Grant's arms, reaching for a strand of Shaz's locs. "Fellas, you do know, I'm her favorite, right?"

"Lies," Grant said, passing the baby to Dwayne before trying to move past Daron. "Enough already."

"Hold your horses, young man." Dro blocked him with an arm, pushing to back Grant up. "I've got this."

"Must be huge," Vikkas said, halting his own steps in that direction. "This is the most I've ever heard him speak at one time."

Daron gave Vikkas the evil eye and ignored the chuckles that accompanied that true statement. "Like I was saying before I was so rudely interrupted." His smile was back in place. "And I'm not speaking of the miracle that our brother, Jaidev Maharaj, has found love with Temple Devaughn and they're getting married at this ungodly hour of the morning."

"Marriage isn't a miracle, that was a given," Jai said, with an affirming nod.

"All right now," Sandy said, and shimmied her shoulders in appreciation.

Temple nudged Jai in the side, then took a few tentative steps forward, moving closer to Daron, who couldn't keep the smile off his face. The most anyone had ever seen the most serious King in the group smile in any manner.

"May I bring to you, Jai's wedding present …" With that, Daron opened the door to its full reach.

Temple froze, gasped so hard it seemed to extract every ounce of air from the room. Then she let loose with a blood-curdling scream that shook the entire building.

Jai barely caught Temple before her legs gave out.

CHAPTER 32

"Are we too early?" a man with a medium build said as he stepped over the threshold. He was followed by a fleshy woman who could almost be his twin, except for a tight cap of curls and the fact that she walked with a slight limp. Their features were strikingly familiar to the woman in Jai's arms.

When Sandy pressed a cold cloth to her forehead, Temple woke from her fainting spell.

"Donny, Ebbie …" Temple whispered, then left Jai, did a walk-sprint to the foyer and fell into their arms creating a three-way circle. They embraced and the tears and sobs were epic.

Jai looked on, but asked Shaz, "Are you crying, my brother?"

"No, no. Allergies and whatnot." Shaz wiped his eyes with the back of his hand and his Jamaican accent was thicker than normal because that was a straight-up fib.

"Allergies," Kaleb taunted, frowning as he scanned Shaz from head to toe. "Dude, the only thing you're allergic to is not eating."

Dwayne let out a low whistle. Reno's hand went up to stifle his laughter. The rest of the Kings and the Knights didn't bother to try. Shaz's appetite was like the eighth and ninth wonders of the world—exactly in that order.

"You outdid yourselves this time," Jai said to Dro and Daron, who were practically beaming as he embraced them. "You came through for me. But were you able to …."

Dro shook his head and said, "We'll keep looking."

Another woman stepped into the foyer, brushing her dark hair away from her face. "Good Morning, I'm Pastor Karen Williams," she said, scanning the faces in the room. "I'm supposed to perform a wedding today?"

"Take a number," Khalil said at the same time Sesvalah said, "Stand in line."

Everyone laughed and the tension in the room eased back into the happiness and expectation of joy that had permeated a few minutes before.

"If you don't mind," Jai said. "Maybe we can give Temple a moment or two with her brother and sister. She hasn't seen them in …"

"Twenty-one years," Donny supplied.

"Long years when we worried so much," Ebbie said. "We wondered if she actually was okay."

* * *

The night she made her escape, Vaunie Liscell was given a small bag that contained money, a change of clothes, and a list of women she would connect with in every small town where she lodged and pick up another escort along the way.

No one would be able to trace her journey, and neither Donny, Ebbie, nor the only adult who helped them were given any information beyond the last embraces they were allowed.

The next day, the police took the blood-stained bedsheets. Everyone in the town gathered in search parties and scoured the streets, fields, farmlands, and then the wooded areas and hills near their home. Ebbie and Donny were there every step of the way, praying that none of the efforts to find Vaunie panned out. The dogs eventually made tracks to the Greyhound station, but the trail ended there and leads went cold.

The search ended, but their mother was certain that her two oldest

*children and that "meddling teacher" had something to do with
Vaunie's untimely disappearance. At the insistence of Carl Webster, who
put pressure on the sheriff's office, Ms. Crenshaw was even arrested in
relation to the disappearance, with the sheriff trying to force information
out of her about Vaunie's whereabouts.*

*Eventually, all charges were dropped due to lack of evidence, and the
rumors and gossip died down. Uncle Dane was so angered by Vaunie's
absence that he made certain Ms. Crenshaw would not have another
teaching post within their town or any of the surrounding cities. She
sold her house and left soon after. No one had heard from her again.*

*Dane Webster, who now had a taste for young flesh, thought he'd
substitute Ebbie for Vaunie on the first night they came for one of the
limited visitations with their mother.*

*He learned a valuable lesson that ended with a two-month hospital
stay and third-degree burns over seventy-five percent of his body. All
stemming from the pot of boiling grits poured on him as he slept quietly
while their mother was "conveniently" out with friends. Donny held
him in place allowing time for the heated mixture to do its job.*

*The "accident" was quietly swept under the rug by authorities who
had no desire to delve further into the reason Ebbie and Donny had
committed such a crime. They were then sent to live with their father
on a permanent basis, though the relationship remained tense and
troublesome, with the police occasionally still questioning them about
their sister's disappearance.*

*When they came of age, they set out to find Shiobaun "Vaunie"
Liscell*

*Unfortunately, Pastor Kae's efforts at keeping their Vaunie—now
Temple Devaughn safe, meant that they never did.*

* * *

Thirty minutes after Donny and Ebbie arrived and the guests had
indulged in a few appetizers to ward off their midnight appetites,
Temple and her siblings left the parlor and said it was all right to start
the wedding.

Dro played the first chords on the piano accompanied by Milan's violin. Khalil's voice echoed through the parlor, living room, foyer and dining room where everyone was situated. *The First Time Ever I Saw Your Face* was a tribute that Temple had requested for him to sing. The words described when she first opened her eyes and Jai was there for her, holding her hand through the pain and a process that bewildered her. His smile had been her guiding light, his eyes had held such sincerity, her soul had felt at ease.

While Khalil, Dro and Milan rendered the piece with such elegance and beauty, Temple held onto Jai, trying not to let the tears overcome. Then she embraced her brother and sister, holding on to them as though she never wanted to let them go. Over her brother's shoulder, she looked at her husband-to-be and whispered, "Yes, that's not all you're good at."

Jai leaned in, pressed a kiss to her lips that caused several smiles to light the faces around the room.

CHAPTER 33

"I can't believe you talked me into this," Temple said, holding on to Jai for dear life. She didn't dare look down. They were at the highest point of the Jamaican jungle, preparing for the first of many zipline experiences they would have throughout the day. At this angle, the only things on her mind were a few cotton-candy clouds that seemed to be just within reach, the baby-blue sky, brilliant sunshine, and a dense green canopy below that might swallow them whole.

Temple stood taller and looked up at Jai. "Remind me to personally put my foot up Shaz's behind."

"Now, now," Jai said, chuckling. "You mentioned wanting an adventure you'd never forget for your honeymoon. Shaz delivered. You cannot fault him for thinking you wanted a real escapade outside of bedroom gymnastics."

"Yes, but did we have to do this the moment we arrived?" Temple protested. "Suppose I don't survive? I'll never know whether you lived up to your own hype."

Jai broke into laughter. "Trust me, God is not going to let us check out of here before we get to the good parts of the honeymoon and after this we probably won't come up for air, so …"

They had started by going up a winding trail, shrouded on both sides by tall bushes. Then, the ten people were fitted with a harness and helmet before executing the smallest zipline that took them from one side of the mountain to the other. The first one allowed everyone to get used to the process. The ziplines they had done since then grew longer each time. At the moment, ten of them were high up, bunched around a tree, feet planted on heavy gray milk-crate-looking apparatuses that were anchored to the wood as a jumping off platform. A courageous look down meant not seeing the ground at all.

With a friendly grin in place, their loc-wearing instructor and guide said, "At the beginning, we told you there would be a little surprise."

"You mean, outside of nearly losing my mind and my breakfast on the previous ones?" Temple snapped and the others laughed. "But don't mind me. I'm just moments away from a heart attack, that's all."

Their second guide with short-cropped hair, wearing similar gear, pursed his lips as if to keep amusement at bay.

Jai kissed her forehead and chuckled. "Don't mind her, we're both virgins."

Temple's lips twisted in displeasure as her gaze narrowed on him. "You said you were a used one."

"I meant, at ziplining," he replied, resting a hand on her nape and the rest of the people hugging the tree all burst into laughter. "Lighten up, wife."

"So the surprise is," locs began, then paused for effect. "This next zipline is a little different."

Groans erupted from everyone.

Their companions shuffled their feet and one tourist yelled, "Yeah mon!"

His smile flashed white in his dark face. "We'll be going down instead of across."

"I am going to kill him," Temple said, closing her eyes. "You are going to be minus one King."

"So it's a drop," Jai asked, casting a glance at the rugged vista below them.

Their tormenter nodded. "Straight down."

"We can do this," Jai said to Temple, stroking her back.

"What do you mean *we*," she countered, swinging her gaze from the drop below to Jai.

The first set of guests completed the drop with very little effort, some yelling at the top of their voices as they went. Temple, however, was still hugging the tree as if it was a family member. "I'm not doing that."

"Come on, love," Jai coaxed her, using his most persuasive tone. "You've done the others and you're practically a pro."

"Yes, finally, but that's going across—this is…" She peered over to the side and then quickly closed her eyes. "Down. I'm not doing this."

"We'll have to take her back if she's not going forward," the guide said. He put two fingers in his mouth and produced a loud whistle. An answering whistle came with a yelled, "One for the return."

"Make that two," Jai said in a resigned whisper. "If she's not going forward, I won't either."

"Nooooo," Temple objected, laying both hands on his chest. "You love this sort of thing. Keep going and tell me how it ends."

"No ma'am. We either go together or not at all." He nodded to the guide and said. "Tell them it's two."

The guide complied.

"Well, the others did make it down okay," she mused, peering over the side again. "I guess …"

"We got you," Mr. locs said raising both hands. "See, I'll go down and be the one to catch you."

"You promise?" she asked, still looking toward the ground.

The guide whistled and informed the others to hold off, slid down and made it to the next landing, then held out his arms. "I've got you."

Temple closed her eyes and said a word of prayer. Then she positioned herself, and the loc-wearing guide slowly lowered her to the descent point. Things started off slow, then the last few feet hit at top speed.

"Whoooooo!" Temple squeezed her eyes shut. Suddenly, a pair of hands cradled her bottom. "Honey, I think you caught the wrong end," she said to the guide, whose smile could have wrapped around the tree.

"Lady, I think I have the *best* end," he quipped.

"Yes, you do," Jai said, scowling down at the grinning guide. "And that part of her is married, too. Hands off my woman, dude."

The crowd laughed as the guide quickly put his hands up and Jai give him the evil eye.

Jai was the next one down and he quickly put his arm around her waist and pulled her close. From where Temple stood, the next zipline was the length of three football fields.

"Are you ready?" Jai asked her.

"I've done seven so far," she answered, still looking out to find where the end of the line happened to be. "I think … I think I can handle it."

"You want me to go first?"

"Yes, I think I'd like you to be there to catch me, so you don't catch a case."

Jai gave her a sheepish smile. "I wasn't going to hurt that man."

A smile of her own played around her lips. "I can't tell."

Jai tackled the next one like a champ, and waited for Temple to follow. He heard the whoops, screams, and laughter long before he could put eyes on her. That smile, seeing the wind blowing through her hair. She was handling this one like a pro. The guide pulled her the rest of the way in and Jai was there to welcome her into his arms.

"How was it?"

Smiling wide, Temple said, "I think I loved it."

Jai tipped one brow? "Want to do it again?"

"Heeeeeeeeell no." She stepped away from him, also putting distance between her and the landing pad. "I have not lost my mind."

Jai couldn't help the laughter that spilled from his lips.

* * *

Jai draped his nose along he jawline taking in her floral scent. Plagued with such a profound and powerful need, he kissed Temple's lips, awakening her from the nap that was sorely needed after their experience in the jungle. He guided Temple to their private pool, immersed her body so that every part of her was wet and wonderful.

Those dark brown eyes locked on hers, consuming her very soul. Jai's tongue traced the outline of her lips, teasing, parting them so that he could explore the moist interior. She ceased all ability to breathe as he held her tongue hostage, freeing it only to inhale and deepen his reach. The heat that overwhelmed her nearly caused Temple to lose consciousness.

His hands, equally as dangerous, held her close, stroking a heated path down the smooth curve of her back, worshipping her buttocks and thighs before parting them so she could welcome him into her world.

"Is it always like this," she asked, lacing her hands in the dark silky locks of his hair, before stroking the silver streak that was a stark contrast to the rest. A ray of light in all that darkness, just as he had been the morning sun to her barren earth.

"It will always be this way ... for us," he whispered before pressing a kiss to her ear, then using that wicked tongue to trace a heated path from her earlobe, her cheeks, the smooth expanse of soft skin across her neck, shoulders and downward until he reached the firm pebble at the center of her breast. There, he teased, tasted, suckled, varying a rhythm that rendered her unable to speak anything but his name. All she could feel was him. All she could taste was him. All she could hear was the sharp intake of his breath every time some part of him connected with her body.

"Jaidev," she whispered, fanning her hand on the surface of the water.

"Yes, my love."

"You promise to always love me like this?"

Jai pulled away to look deep into her eyes. "As long as the Creator keeps life flowing through my body and blood flowing through my veins, I will love you with everything I have to give."

The heated liquid flowed around them as he massaged away all aches, pains, and with it any worries she might have. She melted into him, more ready to consummate their marriage than she thought possible. His kisses were pure rain after a lifetime of drought; a shock to the system after a period of nothingness. Every touch centered her somehow. Every glance ignited that flame that she didn't know could exist. Everything that was Jaidev Maharaj swept away the painful memories and created new ones, loving ones, forever ones.

"Are you ready for me?" he whispered into her hair.

"As I'll ever be," she responded, parting her thighs to give him full access to her core. He dove under the water, placed her thighs on his shoulders, buried himself within her center and feasted as though she was his last supper. She could not help but cry out his name, cry out expressing the myriad of unfamiliar sensations whipping through her.

When the trembling subsided he broke the surface of the water, lowered her thighs until she was wrapped around his waist, anchored as he held onto her body. Then he was with her, inside her, melding them as one, leaving no doubt that she belonged with him, to him, for him—always him.

Temple's breathing caught at the full length of him resting inside her, allowing her to enjoy this new feeling of oneness. Moments passed before he pulled out and the absence of him nearly crushed her spirit. He peered down at her, watching as her hands reached out for him, pulling him back, guiding him into the place she never wanted him to leave. She arched toward him, her hands laced in the silky strands of his hair.

This time, her choice. This time, her love. This time, it was … forever.

CHAPTER 34

"Curtis served me with legal papers," Temple said, placing a sleeping India in his arms. "He wants custody of our daughter."

The fact that the man was out on a substantial bail despite the level of charges against him, and he was now using the legal process to draw things out before the trial, only proved exactly how unbalanced the justice system was.

She could never understand how all evidence and proof was in place at how he raped her—including her deposition where she recounted that she could remember some things, and his scent was the most telling thing of all—and he wasn't already under the bottom of somebody's prison, was unthinkable. Since the Knights had witnessed him on camera straightening his clothes and all that and sent in everything else they had found, and the DNA was absolute proof, how could he still be out here in the world causing Temple all kinds of grief.

"That's not going to happen," Jai said, moving from the sofa to stand at her side. He scanned the paperwork over her shoulder. "We'll consult with a lawyer and sort things out."

"He's stating that I didn't want the baby and was giving you custody, and he never consented to that. Isn't that rich?" Temple frowned, and he guided her back to the sofa to take a seat. "But how would he even know that?"

"I'm going to assume that someone is still feeding him information. I'll have Daron get into it."

Temple cradled India to her breasts. "He's trying to make me pay. First, because I wouldn't have sex with him before marriage. I wanted my first time to be special. He wasn't feeling any of that. He constantly sent me porn videos. Porn, of all things. Trying to get me hot and bothered to make me want him. All it did was turn me off." She locked gazes with Jai. "I tried watching one I didn't like the way the women were treated. Like only parts of the women mattered. We are so much more than the sum total of body parts, but that's all he saw in me. Thought my resistance to him was something to be conquered." Temple sighed, and a world of weariness was in that sound. "All my mother saw was my father in me, then she saw my bank account." She stared across the room at her painting on the wall, one that reflected her hope that she would find her father one day. She had worked on it for days after their marriage and Jai insisted that it be placed in a prominent position in their home. Temple shook her head. "They never saw me. Never the real me."

"They don't matter anymore," Jai whispered, cupping her face in his hands. "Right now, India, me, your art—that's what counts. No one else gets a front seat in your life. You hear me?"

She nodded.

Jai placed a call to Shaz, explained the situation, then followed up with a query.

In response, Shaz said, "I can't answer that question without knowing all of the details and reviewing your case first. Can you call my office and schedule a consultation?"

Temple's anxious expression made Jai's rejoinder necessary.

"Shaz, this is me you're talking to," Jai warned. "If you're treating me like some walk-in off the street, the next time I see you, I'm putting my foot so far up your ass you'll be spitting shit for dinner."

"I'd like to see you try," Shaz shot back. "I'm a fitness instructor who can bench press your ass if I need to."

Jaidev had to rethink his strategy, because he also had martial arts training at Macro and it would be a fair fight, but he wanted Shaz on his side. "Point taken, but we need your knowledge."

"What I'm saying is that I'm having dinner with Camilla right now," Shaz said. "This is date night."

"Oh, well," Jai said in a resigned tone. "Since you put it that way."

"Never mind," he growled. "She's already telling me to handle it. Get in here in an hour."

"That's more like it," Jai said. "I knew that threatening you with bodily harm would get you to see things my way."

"No, it's Camilla threatening to shut off the love works that got results. And bring me some of that cabbage dish Sandy made last night."

"How do you know …" He shared a speaking glance with Temple who grinned. "You know what? Never mind."

* * *

An hour later, Jai pulled out the chair across from Shaz and settled Temple, though her shoulders were still stiff with worry, then claimed the space next to hers.

"I will be up front, I don't specialize in that type of law." Shaz placed the documents on his desk in his home office. "I've offered advice to friends and family before and it didn't turn out so good. Mostly because I didn't have a full understanding of the issues. With Camilla's case, I managed not to foul up because … well, you understand. In cases where I didn't know what I was getting into, the situation turned into something we couldn't foresee, and I ended up referring them to someone else. I did the research, and this is going to be that kind of case. But I can tell you what you're going up against."

Shaz narrowed his gaze on Jai and something unsettled his soul.

"So, what I found from what one of my colleagues sent me, is that when a woman becomes pregnant, sometimes the alleged rapist has the same parental rights as any biological father. That is, unless a state has passed laws that say otherwise. Some women are forced to be in contact with the alleged rapist whether they want to be or not."

"We can cut the *alleged* part," Temple snapped.

"She was in a coma," Jai offered. "She was raped. You know that."

"There is that, but in the eyes of the law," Shaz answered. "Until he's *convicted* of the crime he's being accused of, there will be a lot of *allegeds* thrown around."

"But it doesn't have to be used by you," she said softly, lowering her gaze to the hands folded in her lap.

Shaz's shoulders relaxed as he shifted his locs so they fell behind his back. "No, it doesn't. Point taken." He stood, rounded the desk, and placed a hand over hers. "While you may not want to be in contact with him, you might be forced to, simply because certain States give him rights."

"But I thought the laws here in Illinois meant—"

"Who'd you hear that from?" he asked.

"Vikkas," Jai answered.

"Of course," Shaz scoffed. "Our *international* law brother. But he's not aware of the local laws, and truthfully, until you called, I wasn't either. Though he is right about Illinois. Did you send him the paperwork or just give him the gist of what's going on?"

"We had a chat."

"Hmmmm." Shaz gestured to the documents in Temple's hand. "Pass that to Jai."

She complied, and he scanned the document and looked back at Shaz. "What am I missing here?"

"The same thing as Vikkas because he hadn't put eyes on that part riiiiiight there." Shaz tapped a fingertip to the top edge, bringing special attention to the caption on the Petition for Sole Custody.

"State of Iowa …"

"Iowa," Shaz pointed out. "*Not* Illinois."

"But what does that mean?" Temple asked, plucking the paper from Jai's hand and taking another look. "Curtis doesn't live in Iowa."

"Evidently, he does now," Shaz countered. "He did it for one reason alone."

"Iowa does not have the same laws on the books as Illinois," Jai said, releasing a long, slow breath before he let loose with a string of curses in Hindi.

"Right now, there are thirty-one states with some type of laws on the books where rapists can't seek custody of, or visitation rights, to children they fathered from such a vicious act. Iowa is not one of them. Neither is Minnesota, North Dakota, Wyoming, New Mexico, Mississippi, Alabama and Maryland."

Shaz let his gaze move between Jai and Temple as though making sure they were still with him. "And every state that does have some form of protection for victims also has different conditions to make sure the requirements are met. Twenty states require an absolute conviction to block parental rights. Twenty-six states allow a victim of rape to place the child up for adoption without the rapist's consent."

Temple's grip on Jai's hand tightened. "So that means he can get custody, or joint-custody of India?"

"If we don't get a change of venue, then I'm afraid so."

"He doesn't want that child," Jai growled, and his grip strangled the arm of the chair. "He needs money. Probably trying to figure out a way to make a break for it. I'll call Daron and have him put a track on things, but what I need you to do is set up a meeting with his lawyer and get the ball rolling to find out what amount he really wants."

"I'd advise against that," Shaz warned. "You need to let this play out in the legal arena to—"

"That could take months," Temple protested. Her chin lifted and it became obvious that she was holding back tears. "I don't want him anywhere near our daughter. Point. Blank. Period."

"Set it up," Jai commanded, giving Temple's hand a gentle squeeze. "I don't want her reliving this experience in print or in court."

Shaz dipped his head once. "Consider it done."

CHAPTER 35

Big Red's office was as cold and hard as the woman herself. The décor, the furniture was all bright institutional white, as if to suggest a purity that was not a part of her nature.

"So, damage control is in order," Jai said to Big Red as Marilyn took the seat next to him. "All nine of them need to have their records expunged."

"I can't do that," she said.

"You have connections," Jai argued as he held her gaze. "People alter or lose paperwork all the time. Consider it computer glitches and all that."

"Are you asking me to do something illegal?" Her beady eyes widened. "You, of all people."

Marilyn shifted in the seat next to him and stifled what sounded like a guffaw.

"If you were willing to lay that on the table for Hiram and Falcon when you wanted them to do something that was clearly unethical. Then—"

"Unethical isn't illegal."

"So is having a recording of you admitting that you did something that could land you in jail," he said with a satisfied curl of the lips.

Bid Red winced, and if it was possible, her skin turned a color that matched her moniker.

"And we want that same press coverage it took to smear their names, to be the kind that clears them," Marilyn said, and Big Red put a scathing glare on her former employee who now worked in a high-level capacity for Jai.

Big Red shrugged and said, "I'm not authorized to do that."

"Sure you are. By the same man who had you expedite shutting down Chetan and go on an all-out campaign, a biased one, against nine men who had nothing to do with the crime."

The case had been sensationalized in the media with reports being carried by various stations each day. At first, things seemed to be going against the Center's employees until the evidence they collected was admitted as part of the case. Then everything shifted and the Bureau, Donald Amos, and Big Red were so under fire that everyone around them got burned.

"Mr. Maharaj, I cannot do any of what you're asking."

"You know, maybe the board should take a deeper look into your interactions with Donald Amos." He shrugged. "Phone records and all that."

"Well, he is my boss."

"And that would explain those one, two o'clock in the morning calls to your residence? Every single night when the wife was sleeping, and your wife, too. Followed by sliding out to a no-tell, motel, Holiday Inn."

"Don't forget the Express," Marilyn added.

"Right. Holiday Inn Express, the one in Lansing."

Her skin went beetroot-red as she snarled, "Now who's being unethical?"

"But it's not illegal," he replied, grinning. "For some reason, Donald took a pointed interest in destroying my facility. For personal reasons. You know it and he used you to do his dirty work."

Jai let that statement do a walk around the room. Then she squeaked, "I want to keep my position."

"I'm sure you do," Marilyn said. "Especially since he was able to taint your ethics and it's easy to back track to all the times you did, and also find others this may have happened to." She slid forward in her chair. "You knew good and hell well that what he asked you to do was wrong, yet you plowed ahead with his initiative. Somehow, I think that's going to be frowned upon in someone's neck of the woods."

"This isn't the last time you'll hear from me." Big Red sat straighter in the chair as if she'd been given a shot of adrenaline. "We could've dispensed with all of this if you had simply signed a transfer of your Castle stock and ownership to him. That's all he wanted."

"I have my brothers to answer to," Jai said, getting to his feet. "He doesn't hold any weight when it comes to them. Donald is done. And if you don't make things right, so are you." He tossed the papers toward her. "Wipe their records and get each one of them U.S. Passports."

Big Red slumped in her chair, then stood, gathered her wits and glared at them on their way out the door.

CHAPTER 36

The Knights were still feeling the effects of the unfortunate events. The morale of the facility was a little low, given the fact that when the truth of what some of the staff had done came out, some vicious words had been said, that once spoken, could not be taken back. Accusations against innocent men who now had no trust in the professionals who were supposed to be above board.

Their actions had caused a whole new protocol to be instituted. Checks and balances all the way down the line as a result of the Knight's efforts.

Donald Amos had been brought before a Senate ethics board to answer for his actions. He would never work in a capacity with a government entity that gave him access to such power again. Although, some of his corporate cronies were set to welcome him into the private sector so he would probably land on his feet. Any connection he had with The Castle had been severed. Khalil had seen to that personally.

Marilyn was supposed to be in attendance, but Hiram requested that Jai allow her the time to work with Cameron, Milan, Sandy, Temple, Mira, Aashna and some of the Kings who were helping to prepare for their wedding that would take place in a few days. He was more than capable of handling the parts of the meetings that required her input.

"I called this meeting today because we need to get some things out in the open." Jai's gaze scanned each of the employees situated in Chetan's board room. "Each one of them in here will have a chance to speak their peace. What I'd like for you to do is listen. Not to respond, but to actually hear what they have to say. They deserve that after what went down, yes?"

Murmurs of agreement echoed. Though the nurses and the doctors who were now under professional review because of what they had done were situated in the center of everyone.

"This is my family." Hiram stood at the head of the boardroom table. "Until several months ago, when I met the love of my life, you were all I had. When I went up on that bogus charge, some of my family members turned against me." Hiram threaded his way through the employees who were standing with their backs to the credenza. His designer suit fit him to a "T". All of the Knights had taken to wearing suits to work, meetings and when attending classes. Their transformation into near mirror images of the Kings was astounding. Jai had been right to insist on calling them the Knights. They had taken to their calling even better than the Kings had the first time around. Each of the Knights had spent one on one time with Khalil, and he approved of their efforts. Sometimes beaming like a proud Papa.

"Our facility isn't too much different than other places," Hiram said, gesturing to the window. "It's a building. It has equipment. It has medication. It has patients. It has a vending machine that takes our quarters sometimes …" Everyone laughed as he shifted his gaze to Jai.

"I'm working on it," Jai said, chuckling.

"The difference is you," Hiram continued, and paused to stand near Ryan and Andre. "Every single one of you are the reason Chetan's numbers and success rate is high. Jai—Mr. Maharaj—does have an approach, yes. But it still takes people who believe in what he's doing."

"We want to open more facilities," Falcon said, picking up where he left off. "More places means we'll have more positions and the ability to move up in the organization. More ways for people who have no choice in the currently overwhelmed, overstaffed and underfunded medical system which disregards some people because they don't have money."

Jai switched on the screen which showed the drawings that Hiram had completed for the new center. "Each one of you plays a part in this. I don't just look after the patient's well-being, I look after yours too. That's why we have debt management, a fund for down payments for housing, family trips to reward for exceptional service, and things of that sort that show that you are my family." He scanned the expectant faces of those around the room. "I love the hope and the determination in your eyes when a new patient comes in. The feeling is never the same. Where are they going? When are they going to wake up? All that energy goes a long way into their recovery." Jai put a gaze on the four people, who, along with Curtis, Sharon, Donald and Big Red had almost single-handedly destroyed Chetan. "So, it especially hurts when people break that trust. And when trust is broken within a community of people, there is no way to gain it back."

The Knights circled around the two doctors and nurses as Hiram held out his hand. "We're going to need your badges, please."

Gasps and shock echoed in the room the moment realization dawned.

Three of them complied, but one … the woman who had orchestrated everything with Curtis Burnside, not only because of the money, but he was also sleeping with her.

"You gave them a second chance." She gestured to the Knights. "Why not me? I've learned my lesson, too. And I'm not a criminal, either."

Jai remained silent, preferring to let the Knights handle this one. They deserved it.

"Let me explain to you the level of depravity that your greed allowed." Hiram traded places with Michael so he was only inches away from her. "He paid you to set things up so he could violate a woman who could not say a word in her own defense. A woman who would not, based on his history with her, give consent."

Falcon leaned in. "Then you withheld the fact, when you knew that we had nothing to do with her rape. You said nothing. You let this entire facility and everyone in it almost lose their jobs and careers to hold onto your lie. And how much did they pay you?"

"Was it thirty pieces of silver?" Hiram asked.

"You're not Christ."

"I'm not Satan either," Hiram shot back. "But guess where I'd like to see you burn on Friday."

"You didn't give a damn about us," Christopher said and the vein throbbing at his temple showed how angry he was. "So now we're supposed to care about you?"

"That rape could've resulted in her death," Ryan said. "Detectives turning all of our lives and every single one of us inside out because you lied, and you got other people to go along with that lie. Shows who the real criminals are. And you were going to let one of the men take the fall for it. All for you to please a man who is using you. So, don't try to play on our emotions, sister."

Hiram claimed a seat at the head of the table. "Hope that money keeps you warm at night, because the minute Curtis found out you had to testify against him to save your own neck, he was riding out for the next victim. You don't matter to him, money does."

"You might get another job," Falcon said. "But it won't be in this field, and it certainly won't be like this."

"Second chances," Hiram whispered, shaking his head. "You had that along with the rest of us. So, don't be going around saying that we did you wrong. Own up to your shit."

Jai waved her toward the door. "Security is going to see you out."

"No sir," Falcon said and he nodded to the rest of the Knights. "We'll escort them all out on this walk of shame. They did this on our watch, so we've got this."

CHAPTER 37

Temple, Jai, Curtis, Sharon, and their respective counsels had been in the judge's chambers for nearly an hour. The air-conditioned room was gloomy from the wooden panels and the dark décor.

Pat Breedlaw, the judge who had landed the case on the first day she'd moved from housing court back to family court, had a weary expression that spoke to the fact that maybe she should've stayed in the area of law that had a lot less drama.

Curtis and his lawyer, Travisa McGlothin, had used every device at their disposal to keep things dragging in an effort to force Jai to shell out the cash they wanted to "make this all go away".

Shaz's lawyer friend, Maya Gervais, managed to have the case brought before an Illinois Judge only because the Iowa judge caved after the media became aware of the case. The judiciary regulators had paid close attention to the Iowa attorney's attempt to stall, and not for the purposes of resolution. So, after a little pressure from up top, he granted a change in venue, stating that because the child and mother resided in Illinois, that was where the case should be heard.

"About damn time," Jai muttered to himself when that ruling came down.

Grumbles and threats from the Burnside attorney about greasing the wrong palms, fell on angry ears and the Iowa judge said, "You tried it.

You failed. Back to Illinois with the lot of you."

Both sides presented arguments for and against allowing Curtis—who was well on his way to becoming a popular visitor of the Illinois penal system—to force Temple to bring India for visits to a prison that was a four-hour drive in each direction.

Now her mother's efforts and his at trying to get Temple to marry him so quickly became clear. Neither of them realized that her testimony wasn't needed for the state to move forward with the case. The timing of her pregnancy brought lack of consent to the table, and served up other avenues for the prosecutor to levy for a long-term sentence.

"Even now. Even after what you did to me, and the fact that you're going to see the inside of somebody's jail, you still want me to pay," Temple yelled, and Maya tried to grip her hand to calm her down. "You don't want our child," she said in a calmer tone, grabbing Jai's hand and looking into his eyes.

"Our?" Curtis folded both arms over his chest like a petulant toddler and sent Jai a glare. "It's my child, too. And I have rights."

"Not in Illinois," Judge Breedlaw said in a matter-of-fact tone that brought Curtis' attorney to her feet.

"But he still has to be convicted before his rights are terminated," Attorney McGlothin said with a haughty lift of her chin and a slight smirk on her round face.

The woman was getting paid from Sharon's pockets because she was certain that keeping up this legal action was going to result in a big payday at some point.

Jai was all for giving up the cash to keep his wife from having to go through all the madness.

Temple Maharaj was not having it, and Jai resigned himself to the knowledge that their life would be in turmoil until the judge tired of it, or the criminal case ended and whipped Curtis off to the place that would be his residence for the next twenty-five years and possibly more since public outrage was weighing heavy on the outcome.

"How do you even sleep at night?" Temple snarled at attorney McGlothin, ignoring Jai's attempt to keep her silent. "This man sexually assaulted me while I was in a coma. No way in hell could I have asked for that. And you—a woman—decide to represent him. What kind of vacation is your conscience on right now?"

"Damn," Shaz whispered and Maya Gervais nudged him into silence.

Jai nodded, because he had also wondered the same. "Let's just cut the bullshit," he said, then altered his tone when he added, "Sorry, Judge."

"No offense taken," she said.

"You want money. That's the bottom line, and has been all this time," he said. "How much will it take?"

Curtis shifted his gaze to Temple. "How much is still in that trust fund of yours?"

She shook her head and scoffed. "I was so right about you."

"No." Shaz's harsh word cut through the negotiation.

Attorney McGlothin stood and faced Shaz, who had been included as an advisor on the proceedings from day one. "What?"

"No," Shaz repeated. "I agree with Temple. You don't get to profit from your ugly deed."

Curtis sighed, then a sly smile graced his lips. "Then it looks like we will be tied up in court for a while." His gaze locked on Temple. "You'll never be rid of me." An evil light shone in his eyes and he taunted Jai with, "Don't forget, I hit it first."

"Don't forget she couldn't tell." Jai's stinging rejoinder made Curtis flinch.

Temple gasped, then narrowed her gaze on Curtis. Seconds later, she gave a scornful laugh. "He's right. I'm sure if there was an orgasm involved, it might've brought me back to life." She stood, facing Curtis head on. "Even comatose, a woman can tell when a man's six inches short of giving her any kind of pleasure." She paused, as if racking her brain. "Yes, I do remember that. Three grunts and straight to the finish line. Long on intention, short on delivery. Thank God I married a man who totally makes up for what you'll always lack."

Those words yanked every sound from the room. All heads turned in Temple's direction.

Maya coughed and averted her gaze.

Judge Breedlaw parted her lips to speak, then clamped down.

Shaz nearly slid from his seat.

Jai almost joined him.

Curtis' pale skin turned dark.

Sharon Liscell blinked twice and clutched at her chest as though a heart attack was coming on.

The judge cleared her throat, but didn't say anything to rein Temple in, or keep the court reporter from recording every word. This, Temple having her say, was long overdue.

"You took something from me because you were unwilling to wait until it became a special thing for me," Temple said, brushing off Jai as he tried to make her sit. "Always what you wanted. Your needs came first, which was why I put off marrying you in the first place. I never wanted to marry you." She flickered a gaze to Sharon. "Then you somehow hooked up with my mother. Her hatred of me and your need to take what you wanted made you do something vile. Greed. Straight-up greed. So y'all just planned for me to have this baby, die during the process, use her to invoke that beneficiary clause in the trust, and then just run through that money, huh?" She flicked her wrist in Curtis' direction. "Well, good luck with that. You gets nada. Zilch. Zero. Not a damn thing."

Jai moved in, prepared to intervene when Curtis rose to his feet, but Temple held up her hand to hold off Jai's protest. "It's not about the money. We've got plenty of that. It's the principle of what you did; the principle of what *she* did when I was a little girl. And then what you're still trying to do—screw me over."

Temple then recounted the experiences that night in Virginia and the actions her mother and stepfather had taken that caused her brother and sister to do whatever it took to get her to safety. When she was done, there wasn't a dry eye in the room. Well, except Sharon who had to be told by the judge to be silent several times. And Curtis, who was a narcissist of the highest order.

Taking a deep breath, Temple nodded in Shaz's direction. "I'm with my brother-in-law on this one. They don't deserve to profit off my pain. He's going to jail at some point, and my mother will be in charge of that money. They both can take a ringside seat right next to Satan himself." She looked at Judge Breedlaw and said, "I know you wanted to see where we were at with this, but today will not be that day. It'll settle itself when he's in jail and you finally get tired of this case being dragged and come to the same conclusion—he gets nothing. And I get my daughter without any entanglements from him."

Temple faced Jai, her face still set in stubborn lines, and he was proud of her stance although he wanted to wave a financial magic wand and make it all better. This was in Temple's control, and all he could say was, "I support whatever you feel you need to do."

"Thank you," she whispered into the wall of his chest. "That means the world to me."

Judge Breedlaw said, "Settle down everyone. Mr. and Mrs. Maharaj, please take your seats. I've read arguments, listened to both sides, read up on cases that are similar, and what both counsels don't realize is that I can basically issue a bench ruling and be done."

Curtis and his attorney stood, panicked as she said, "But you can't do that. At least not until—"

The judged arched her brows in outrage. "Can't I?"

"Well, well …" his attorney sputtered, then slumped into her seat and Curtis tried to ask a question but Judge Breedlaw shut him down. "My ruling is going to be simple," she said. "Contrary to the argument you submitted, I don't have to wait for a conviction when the evidence has been supplied by the district attorney for decision-making purposes, but even more telling is his little admission in my office today."

"Admission?" Curtis shot back. "I didn't admit to anything."

"I hit it first," Judge Breedlaw said. "You weren't talking about a smack on her bottom. You ego just helped you admit that you sexually assaulted and feel pretty good about it."

"Your honor, we can appeal if—"

"You can try," she said, her expression darkening. "But, my ruling is … you don't get a dime and Temple Devaughn Maharaj and Jaidev

Maharaj have sole custody of this child."

"But—"

The judge held up her gavel and pointed it at Curtis, who promptly plopped down so hard he almost slid out of the chair and onto the carpet. "I'll have my clerk write the order and I'll sign it."

Sharon Liscell stood and said, "This is an outrage!"

Judge Breedlaw put a stony gaze on Sharon. "You know, thanks to the agreed motion that was put in that I could hear all matters related to Ms. Devaughn and Mr. Burnside, I think I need to right another injustice. Sit down."

Sharon complied and put a frightened glance on Curtis, who looked ready to shit a brick.

"His bail was set at three million and the judge required one million be put up, right?"

Curtis nodded, then looked to his attorney who shrugged.

"One million," Judge Breedlaw mused. "And you were the one to put that money up to bail him out," she said to Sharon.

Sharon grimaced, lifted her chin and said, "Yes, I gave the court everything I had."

"Hmmmm," the judge said and shifted in her chair. "Well, when he fulfills the terms of the bail, that money is supposed to be returned to you, right?"

"Yes, every penny," Sharon whispered, lifting her chin.

"Well, that's not going to happen," Judge Breedlaw said, and Jai reached out to steady Temple's hands. "That money is going to Temple Devaughn."

Sharon was on her feet. "You can't do that!"

"I certainly can."

"I don't want a dime of his money," Temple said through her teeth.

"Technically, it's *your* money," Shaz said and Jai nodded as he took a quick look at his vibrating phone. "They ran through all of yours while you were at Chetan."

"Oh, well," Temple conceded when Maya Gervais also agreed. "When you put it that way. It's been sitting in the court's bank account and should be pretty clean by now." She waved a dismissive hand. "Carry on."

Judge Breedlaw put her focus on Sharon once again. "There is no statute of limitations on getting justice for what you did to her when she was a child, but I can do whatever I can to right that wrong as best I know how. I'm contacting the authorities in Virginia. It might not be much, but this will be fully investigated since this crime has been brought to my attention."

"So now you're going after my husband and my money! You're taking away everything I have," Sharon cried.

"You took away my innocence, so we're even," Temple shot back.

The moment Sharon, Curtis, and his attorney, stood and gathered their things, Temple dissolved into a fit of relieved tears and was met with the comfort of Jai's broad chest, and Shaz's arms about her as well.

Jai checked his phone again and the judge said, "Now, Mr. Maharaj, you remember what I said about phones in my courtroom, I—"

"Your Honor," Jai said, passing his phone to the judge so she could check the screen. "That right there is information that Alejandro Reyes and my employees uncovered and sent to the police."

"What does this mean?" Judge Breedlaw asked and passed the cell back to Jai.

"Curtis Burnside was driving the dark blue car that caused Temple's accident."

Temple's sharp intake of breath eclipsed all other sounds in the room.

"He didn't even have the intelligence to get rid of it. It's been stashed on the lower level of her parking garage all this time that the police were searching for it." Jai graced Curtis with a smile. "The police are now about to add attempted murder to his plate."

Shaz and Jai were out of their seats the moment Curtis ran for the door. They blocked his exit as Judge Breedlaw picked up her desk phone and called for the sheriff to come and detain him.

Temple rushed into Jai's arms, and he locked eyes with the judge over Temple's shoulder, let out a relieved breath and said, "Thank you."

EPILOGUE

One year later, Jaidev guided the salt-and-pepper haired man into the university's classroom.

Grant waited, with India squirming in his arms trying to get to Daron, who plucked her from his hold.

The man froze at the top of the landing when he saw the image on the screen behind Temple Maharaj, whose back was turned to the class. The image was one that had been printed as the cover of *The Miracle Woman*, which was an inspiring memoir and life lessons she had written to tell of her troubled childhood and the triumphs she had experienced over the past year.

"My real name is Siobhan Liscell, but after several tragic events in my life I had to take the name Temple Devaughn." She paced in front of the screen. "I chose the name because the first verse that I found comfort in was from Psalms." She inhaled, reciting from memory. "Do you know that you are God's temple and that God's Spirit dwells in you? If anyone destroys God's temple, God will destroy him. For God's temple is holy and you are that temple."

She paused, allowing the words to echo around the room. Then she gestured to the screen and said, "This particular painting has been my guiding light and the one that has made the artist famous. But it has a personal meaning for me."

Her gaze lingered on the imagery for a moment before she inhaled and faced the class, reading from an unpublished article that Daron had been able to uncover on the web. The piece had been archived somewhere from material that had not been officially published.

"The most beautiful child in the world was a gift to me that was taken away. I painted this because it is my prayer …"

Jai gripped the man's hand to hold him steady.

"When I was a little boy …" she looked up at the first row of students and said, "Yes, all artists start out as babies in the artistic world."

The class chuckled.

"The pastor of my church would walk the aisle at the beginning of Sunday morning service," she continued. "He would recite the following verse from the Psalms …" She flipped the page. "I will lift up mine eyes unto the hills, from whence cometh my help." She gestured to the hilltops in the painting, and then the image of a sky above the earth. "My help cometh from the Lord, which made heaven and earth."

She spoke the next part of the verses and moved onto, "The Lord is thy keeper; the Lord is thy shade upon thy right hand." Her hand whipped across the shadows on the bottom of the painting that represented the shade. "The sun shall not smite thee by day, nor the moon by night."

Her manicured fingers traced the circular image of the sun with the moon's echo right behind it. "The Lord shall preserve thee from all evil: He shall preserve thy soul." She splayed a hand over the image of the little girl that had been had painted towards the top of the painting. "The Lord shall preserve thy going out and thy coming in from this time forth, and even for evermore."

Silence reigned in that room as the students and Jai took that in. Tears streamed down Temple's face as she tried to gather her composure.

"This painting," she said after a few moments, reading from the document, "Was my prayer to God to keep my little girl safe. And if He couldn't keep her safe, at least give her the strength to survive whatever came her way." Her voice broke on those last words. "She was taken from me in the ugliest of ways. Greed. Human greed can do more damage than anyone can imagine. Because people have not learned that there is enough bounty for all of us, and it is given in the measure it is willing to be received." Temple raised her head and looked at the students. "I can only hope that one day …"

The guest left Jai's side and moved forward, one step down, then another.

"I can … only …" Temple's gaze narrowed as she watched the movements of the man inching toward the front of the class. Her gaze widened with realization before her lips trembled with so much emotion, she couldn't speak.

The students turned to follow her gaze and a trickle of questioning conversation ensued and then faded to a tense silence.

He had made it halfway, but was forced to grip the armrest of the nearest chair to brace himself, then paused as though unsure he should go on.

Jai accepted India from Daron and adjusted her in his arms, but she craned her neck to watch what her mother was up to.

Temple's hands balled into fists as though she was trying to steady herself. She inhaled deeply as her eyes misted once again, then blurred to the point no one could see the color of her eyes.

The man took a tentative step forward and that's all he was able to do before Temple barreled toward him and straight into his arms.

One of the students nearby wiped their tears, and whispered, "Glad I'm wearing the good mascara today."

A few other women nodded. Even the guys, who probably weren't comfortable with such a powerful display of long-held affection, misted up as well.

Reno and Shaz left their seats close to the front of the auditorium. Dro and Kaleb rose from the rear seats and flanked Jai on both sides.

Vikkas reached for India and she squealed her delight. Daron gave Jai a head nod. He promptly returned that action.

All of his brothers insisted on being here for Temple and Jai in this moment. Something that Khalil had insisted. *Be there for the highs as well as the lows. Experience your lives together and you will be richer for the experience.*

Dwayne walked down the steps, moving toward the image on the screen, taking in its beauty before turning to the class and saying, "You don't mind if I take over for the rest of today?"

Elvin Drescher had not released Temple, who lay her head against his chest, relishing the moment of connecting with a man who she had longed to see since he'd abruptly disappeared from her life.

"Actually, I think this right here is the lesson for today," she said. Temple turned her face toward Jai and mouthed the words, "Thank you for this. Thank you so, so much." Then she smiled. "Yes, that's not all you're good at."

Jai winked, then released a soft laugh over their private joke.

"Shaz, are you crying?" Dro said, elbowing him in the side.

"I'm telling you, allergies and whatnot," Shaz protested, brushing the last tear from his chin.

Kaleb chuckled, and the rest of the Kings joined him.

ABOUT THE KINGS OF THE CASTLE SERIES

Books 2-9 are standalones, no cliffhangers, and can be read in any order.

Book 1 – Kings of the Castle, the introduction to the series and story of King of Wilmette (Vikkas Germaine)

USA TODAY, *New York Times*, and National Bestselling Authors work together to provide you with a world you'll never want to leave. The Castle. Powerful men unexpectedly brought together by their pasts and current circumstances will become a force to be reckoned with. Their combined efforts to find the people responsible for the attempt on their mentor's life, is the beginning of dangerous challenges that will alter the path of their lives forever. Not to mention, they will also draw the ire and deadly intent of current Castle members who wield major influence across the globe.

Fate made them brothers, but protecting the Castle and the women they love, will make them Kings. www.thekingsofthecastle.com

King of Chatham - Book 2 - Reno
King of Evanston - Book 3 - Shaz
King of Devon - Book 4 - Jai
King of Morgan Park - Book 5 - Daron
King of South Shore - Book 6 - Kaleb
King of Lincoln Park - Book 7 - Grant
King of Hyde Park - Book 8 - Dro
King of Lawndale - Book 9 - Dwayne

Cover design by J. L. Woodson - www.woodsonstudio.com

Naleighna Kai

Naleighna Kai is the USA Today, Essence®, and national bestselling and award-winning author of several controversial women's fiction, contemporary fiction, Christian fiction, Romance, erotica, and science fiction novels that plumb the depth of unique love triangles and women's issues. She is also a contributor to a New York Times bestseller, one of AALBC's 100 Top Authors, a member of CVS Hall of Fame, Mercedes Benz Mentor Award Nominee, and the E. Lynn Harris Author of Distinction.

In addition to successfully cracking the code of landing a deal for herself and others with a major publishing house, she continues to "pay it forward" by organizing the annual Cavalcade of Authors which gives readers intimate access to the most accomplished writing talent today. She also serves as CEO of Macro Marketing & Promotions Group which offers aspiring and established authors assistance with ghostwriting, developmental editing, publishing, marketing, and other services to jump-start or enhance their writing careers. She also founded NK Tribe Called Success for her clients who participate in literary events and media advertising as a group and produce creative projects and anthologies.

Naleighna was born and raised on the Southeast side of Chicago, the setting for most of her novels and where she is currently working on her next books: Mercury Sunrise and Wife-in-Law.

Find her on the web at www.naleighnakai.com,
FB Author Page: https://www.facebook.com/naleighnak/
Twitter: https://twitter.com/NaleighnaKai
Instagram: https://www.instagram.com/naleighnakai/
BookBub: https://www.bookbub.com/authors/naleighna-kai
GoodReads: https://www.goodreads.com/naleighnakai
Pinterest: https://www.pinterest.com/naleighnakai/
Group: www.nktribecalledsuccess.com
www.thecavalcadeofauthors.com

Naleighna Kai novels that may interest you whose characters and storylines are intertwined in *King of Devon*.

Loving Me for Me – Devesh Maharaj's story
Slaves of Heaven – Gabriel Chamberlain introduced the concept for what Khalil used for The Castle.
Rich Woman's Fetish – Sanjay Bhandari's story
My Time in the Sun – Tony and Kari's story, one of the sex trafficking survivors
Southern Comfort – Ali and Joy's story
Was it Good For You Too? Tailan and Delvin's story
She Touched My Soul – Maya Gervais' story [Temple's lawyer]

Loving Me for Me

Will they survive her tragic past, his traditional family, and those who would rather see them dead than in love? Though Devesh's culture and status along with a secret Reign planned to take to her grave has kept them apart for nearly five years; a chance meeting brings them face-to-face once again. This time, Devesh, a wealthy Californian bachelor, is determined to be with Reign despite his family's wishes. The couple has more at stake, forcing them to confront their deepest fears, overcome unforeseen obstacles, and challenge the media as well as enemies who are closer to home.

Devesh finds ingenious ways for them to manage their rocky relationship terrain since Reign heartbreaking life has left her with the kind of trust issues that resurface along with a few "reckless exes." He soon puts everyone on notice that he believes love is 'til death do us part—even if Devesh has to send someone to an early grave to protect her.

Rich Woman's Fetish

Gina Wright escapes a hellacious life by doing the unthinkable—selling the use of her womb to the highest bidder among rich, childless couples from more affluent areas of Chicago. She even accommodates their "special" requests ranging from participating in forbidden fetishes to more complicated liaisons. Gina uses them to amass a fortune, then sets out to fulfill her own dream, one that is shattered in an instant when a freakish accident steals a gift she has always taken for granted.

Years later, Gina learns that one of her surrogate daughters has been forced into the illicit world of drugs and prostitution. When the police and FBI turn a blind eye, Gina risks the anger of her former sponsors and lovers to have their children search for the younger sister they know nothing about. One daughter turns to a criminal mastermind to help locate the teen; another puts her career in jeopardy when she seeks justice in her own deadly way. The search puts a dangerous spin on their already chaotic lives as the women learn more about trust and love and how to depend on each other to do the impossible.

Slaves of Heaven

"I love the Octavia Butler vibe of Slaves of Heaven. The storyline is distinctly Naleighna Kai and uniquely original."
—Crystal Hubbard, National Bestselling Author

The Heaven Project starts with these words, "If we have to kill all of the men to take the women, so be it."

Gabriel Chamberlain's dynamic plan to overcome issues that plague the world by creating a society ruled by a stronger class of women, is met with deadly resistance. His hand-chosen people are forced to begin the perfect life within The Heaven Project in a secluded location. Then a fatal action by one of his wives changes the plan altogether, plunging

The Heaven Project into the very darkness they were striving to escape.

Twenty-five years later, jealousy between Gabriel's sons, David and Robert, leads to a tragic series of events that will unravel the peaceful fabric of Heaven life. Robert purposely seduces one of David's concubines, and the brothers square off in a battle of wills that sets the stage for The Heaven Project's complete downfall. When Robert exacts his revenge by killing all Heaven men who oppose him and capturing the women for his own sordid purposes, David scatters his wife and concubines to the four corners of the United States to keep them safe.

Time passes, and a woman known simply as Mari Sheldon, is living a reclusive life in Chicago. But that changes the day Chase Caswell, a bad boy with a troubled past, walks into her life. The inexplicable attraction between them is enough to bring Mari out of her shell and makes her willing to take a chance on love. Unfortunately, Mari is kidnapped by someone looking to get their hands on a hidden fortune as well as the rest of Mari's sisters who hold the keys to unlock the past and a more promising future. Chase is forced to travel to several continents to uncover his own family secrets and rescue the woman he loves. He finally teams up with a small band of rebels to launch a vicious attack, hoping to free the imprisoned women and children while restoring The Heaven Project to its original purpose.

She Touched My Soul is a gripping, engaging novel of loss, love, and everything in between.

Michael "Magic" Arrington's sudden fame and startling climb up the music charts skyrocketed him into the world of Hollywood glitz and glamour. While all was exciting and wonderful at the beginning, the shady undertakings of the music business caused his life to take a downward spiral, ultimately separating him from his family and his hold on reality. Then he met Maya.

Maya Gervais has completely distanced herself from her past, even going as far as changing her identity to protect her from the one man who wants her dead. She is a civic-minded lawyer who champions for clients who are victims of domestic violence and sexual abuse. So trusting someone enough to fall in love was never a consideration, especially since it could cost her much more than she was willing to give.

After the two have a chance meeting at a concert, a daring escape leads to an exploration of pain and pleasure that sets them both on the path to healing and an into an unlikely romance. However, the path to blissful happiness is never an easy one, as they both have their own demons to confront, including Michael's jealous manager and Maya's reluctance to deal with things she would rather forget.

My Time in the Sun

Kari's perfect life comes to a screeching halt during Sunday morning service when her husband's enemy stands and tells the entire congregation, "Our first lady was a prostitute. A fourteen-year-old prostitute at that. Not exactly the kind of woman we want our little girls to imitate …"

Kari Baltimore barely survived a horrific experience when she was forced to take drastic measures to protect an innocent child. Years later, she's put the past behind her, owns a successful business, and is married to a wonderful man who loves her like no other. All the sordid secrets that she's managed to keep hidden, even from her husband, resurfaces with a vengeance when Terrence Henderson, a man who is hellbent on having the church for his own sordid reasons, shares her past with everyone and causes a rift that is not easily mended.

Tony Baltimore's plans for the saints to "take the church to the streets" has been met with staunch opposition by the board, deacons, and members who believe that staying on the "safe side" of Chicago's police brutality and gang problems suits them just fine. When Terrence uses strong family ties to the church to publicly disgrace Kari as a sure-fire way to take over, a media firestorm ensues, and heated membership split soon follows. Tony makes strategic moves to protect his wife from anyone and everyone coming against her—including members who are so "heavenly" minded that they're no earthy good. When the smoke clears, no one will ever be the same.

Southern Comfort

USA Today Bestselling Author, Naleighna Kai, brings another unconventional story about finding a deeper love in the most unlikely places. The moment Joy's estranged mother shows up on her doorstep and drops off a mysterious child, she's forced to put her first year in college on hold. Two years later, she totally abandons her dream of becoming a civil engineer altogether, when her mother reappears with yet another child from her drug-addicted sister. Twice is enough, and the third time isn't a charm as Joy's outright refusal makes her an outcast from her crime-riddled family. With so much responsibility at a young age, she's never allowed herself to dream of having an intimate relationship. Until a chance meeting ten years later at the most unlikely of places.

Ali serves as the bridge that brings his father back into the family fold, by marrying the woman they choose for him. Now, the last child is off to college and his multi-million dollar businesses are thriving, his wife reunites with the man she abandoned to fulfill her family's wishes, freeing Ali to embark on a journey to find the love he deserves. When he lays eyes on Joy, one word comes to mind—lost. Until that moment, he didn't realize he has a "savior complex", but something about the elusive woman pulls at Ali's heartstrings and makes him take a risk.

Joy and Ali are forced to navigate the murky waters of obligation, karma, and other more deadly challenges to find their way to love.

Was it Good For You Too?

In this national bestseller, Tailan and Delvin complicated their lives by bringing another woman into the relationship to bear his children. Once the surrogate was two months along, she turned the tables by issuing a heartbreaking ultimatum. When threatened with losing the family he'd always wanted, Delvin felt he had no choice but to marry the surrogate and send his high school sweetheart packing, even though he loved her more than life itself.

Now seven years later on a Midwest book tour, fate has given Delvin four days to right old wrongs, and he'll use everything in his power to win Tailan back. Unfortunately, Tailan is harboring a secret that she's kept not only from him but from the entire world. Delvin's determination to have her will give him two choices—either share Tailan with another man or walk away from the strongest love he's ever known.

ABOUT THE KINGS OF THE CASTLE SERIES

Books 2-9 are standalones, no cliffhangers, and can be read in any order.

Book 1 – Kings of the Castle, the introduction to the series and story of King of Wilmette (Vikkas Germaine)

USA TODAY, *New York Times*, and National Bestselling Authors work together to provide you with a world you'll never want to leave. The Castle. Powerful men unexpectedly brought together by their pasts and current circumstances will become a force to be reckoned with. Their combined efforts to find the people responsible for the attempt on their mentor's life, is the beginning of dangerous challenges that will alter the path of their lives forever. Not to mention, they will also draw the ire and deadly intent of current Castle members who wield major influence across the globe.

Fate made them brothers, but protecting the Castle and the women they love, will make them Kings.

www.thekingsofthecastle.com

King of Chatham - Book 2

While Mariano "Reno" DeLuca uses his skills and resources to create safe havens for battered women, a surge in criminal activity within the Chatham area threatens the women's anonymity and security. When Zuri, an exotic Tanzanian Princess, arrives seeking refuge from an arranged marriage and its deadly consequences, Reno is now forced to relocate the women in the shelter, fend off unforeseen enemies of The Castle, and endeavor not to lose his heart to the mysterious woman.

King of Evanston - Book 3

Raised as an immigrant, he knows the heartache of family separation firsthand. His personal goals and business ethics collide when a vulnerable woman stands to lose her baby in an underhanded and profitable scheme crafted by powerful, ruthless businessmen and politicians who have nefarious ties to The Castle. Shaz and the Kings of the Castle collaborate to uproot the dark forces intent on changing the balance of power within The Castle and destroying their mentor. National Bestselling Author, J.L. Campbell presents book 3 in the Kings of the Castle Series, featuring Shaz Bostwick.

King of Devon - Book 4

When a coma patient becomes pregnant, Jaidev Maharaj's medical facility comes under a government microscope and media scrutiny. In the midst of the investigation, he receives a mysterious call from someone in his past that demands that more of him than he's ever been willing to give and is made aware of a dark family secret that will destroy the people he loves most.

King of Morgan Park - Book 5

Two things threaten to destroy several areas of Daron Kincaid's life—the tracking device he developed to locate victims of sex trafficking and an inherited membership in a mysterious outfit called The Castle. The new developments set the stage to dismantle the relationship with a woman who's been trained to make men weak or put them on the other side of the grave. The secrets Daron keeps from Cameron and his inner circle only complicates an already tumultuous situation caused by an FBI sting that brought down his former enemies. Can Daron take on his enemies, manage his secrets and loyalty to the Castle without permanently losing the woman he loves?

King of South Shore - Book 6

Award-winning real estate developer, Kaleb Valentine, is known for turning failing communities into thriving havens in the Metro Detroit area. His plans to rebuild his hometown neighborhood are dereailed with one phone call that puts Kaleb deep in the middle of an intense criminal investigation led by a detective who has a personal vendetta. Now he will have to deal with the ghosts of his past before they kill him.

King of Lincoln Park - Book 7

Grant Khambrel is a sexy, successful architect with big plans to expand his Texas Company. Unfortunately, a dark secret from his past could destroy it all unless he's willing to betray the man responsible for that success, and the woman who becomes the key to his salvation.

King of Hyde Park - Book 8

Alejandro "Dro" Reyes has been a "fixer" for as long as he could remember, which makes owning a crisis management company focused on repairing professional reputations the perfect fit. The same could be said of Lola Samuels, who is only vaguely aware of his "true" talents and seems to be oblivious to the growing attraction between them. His company, Vantage Point, is in high demand and business in the Windy City is booming. Until a mysterious call following an attempt on his mentor's life forces him to drop everything and accept a fated position with The Castle. But there's a hidden agenda and unexpected enemy that Alejandro doesn't see coming who threatens his life, his woman, and his throne.

King of Lawndale - Book 9

Dwayne Harper's passion is giving disadvantaged boys the tools to transform themselves into successful men. Unfortunately, the minute he steps up to take his place among the men he considers brothers, two things stand in his way: a political office that does not want the competition Dwayne's new education system will bring, and a well-connected former member of The Castle who will use everything in his power—even those who Dwayne mentors—to shut him down.

AUTHOR BIOS

Naleighna Kai is the *USA TODAY* Bestselling Author of Every Woman Needs a Wife, Open Door Marriage, Loving Me for Me, Slaves of Heaven and several other controversial novels. She is founder of NK Tribe Called Success, The Cavalcade of Authors, and is a publishing and marketing consultant. www.naleighnakai.com

S. L. Jennings is a military wife, mom of three, coffee addict, Willy Wonka enthusiast, and real-life unicorn. She's also the New York Times and USA Today Bestselling author of Taint, Fear of Falling and the Se7en Sinners Series, along with a few other titles that she's too lazy to type. She's been with her high school sweetheart for almost twenty years, and he still can't get her Subway sandwich order right. But he's cute and brings her vodka, so she keeps him around. They currently reside in Spokane, WA with their three stinky boys and their equally stinky cat. www.sljenningsauthor.com

Martha Kennerson is the bestselling and award-winning author who's love of reading and writing is a significant part of who she is. She uses both to create the kinds of stories that touch the heart. Martha lives with her family in League City, Texas. She believes her current blessings are only matched by the struggle it took to achieve such happiness. To find out more about Martha and her journey, visit her website at www.marthakennerson.com and you can follow her on Facebook and Twitter.

J. L. Campbell is an award-winning Jamaican author who has written over thirty books in several romance subgenres. Campbell, who features Jamaican culture in her stories, is a certified editor, and also writes non-fiction. Visit her on the web at www.joylcampbell.com.

National bestselling author, **Lisa Watson**, is a native of Washington D.C., and writes in the Multicultural & Interracial, Contemporary, Romantic Suspense, and Sweet Romance genres. Her memorable novels for the Harlequin's Kimani line, The Match Broker series was listed as one of 2014's Top 25 Books of the Summer, and Top 50 Best Reads. Lisa lives in Raleigh, North Carolina with her husband of twenty-two years and two teenagers, and is avidly working on book one, Alexa King: The Guardian, in her second new Romantic Suspense series, The Lady Doyen and Book 2 in the Love and Danger Series. www.lisawatson.com

Karen D. Bradley is a national bestselling author and screenplay writer. English and Grammar were never her strongest subjects, but as life would have it, her weakest link would become her saving grace. Writing fiction became one of her favorite forms of therapy. She has penned several contemporary fiction, suspense, and romantic suspense novels. Visit Karen on the web at www.karendbradley.com

Janice M. Allen is a National Bestselling Author who has always been an avid reader of fiction. She even edited the work of other authors for several years. But she gets an incomparable thrill from creating stories that entertain readers and cause them to reflect on real life issues. No Right Way To Do A Wrong Thing is her first novel, followed by her short story Cayenne. www.janicemallen.com

London St. Charles has always had a passion for the pen, paper, and books. She is a Chicago native who uses the Windy City as a backdrop to the romance, suspense, and contemporary fiction stories she writes. London published her debut novel, The Husband We Share in 2017 and is one of nine authors in the anthology, Sugar. She also composes an online newsletter, London Writes, that keeps readers abreast of what's going on in her world. www.londonstcharles.com

MarZe Scott is a lifelong resident of Ypsilanti, Michigan and Graduate of University of Michigan. A lover of all things creative, MarZé enjoys reading, free-hand illustrating, jewelry making and makeup artistry.

Known for her vivid and captivating storytelling, MarZé has been writing short stories and poems since elementary school and developed a taste in high school for writing about provocative topics like the consequences of casual sex. You can find Gemini Rising, MarZé's debut novel, and short story Next Lifetime wherever books are sold. www.marzescott.com

SERIES MENTORS:

LaVerne Thompson is a *USA Today* Bestselling, award winning, multi-published author, an avid reader and a writer of contemporary, fantasy, and sci/fi sensual romances. She loves creating worlds within and without our world. She also writes romantic suspense and new adult romance under the pen name Ursula Sinclair also a USA Today Bestselling Author. www.lavernethompson.com

Kassanna is a strong believer in love at first sight and happily ever afters. Writing has always been her passion but fate sometimes has other roads that must first be taken .Navigating the road less traveled was not only unexpected but in the end extremely rewarding. Her books are mainly contemporary romance but she has delved into the paranormal, fantasy, and plans on expanding into other areas as the ideas come to her. Right now she is enjoying life and seeing her works come into fruition make it that much more pleasurable especially when her books make others smile. Kassanna wouldn't have it any other way. www.flavorfullove.com